Forever Entangled

Forever Bluegrass Series #1

Kathleen Brooks

An original work of Kathleen Brooks. *Forever Entangled* copyright © 2015 by Kathleen Brooks

Cover art by Sunni Chapman at The Salty Olive.

Chapter One

Los Angeles . . .

Ryan Parker had only a split second to realize everything was going to hell. The gun being pressed to his head was the second clue someone had sold him out. The first had been the rhetorical question The Suit's alleged second-in-command had asked.

"Why do you think I know this person called The Suit?"

That had been his clue that someone had snitched on him since Ryan had never mentioned the international terrorist to Abdul. Before Ryan could act, the guard standing behind him had the barrel of a gun pressed to the back of his head. It wasn't the first time, and it probably wouldn't be the last. Ryan was having another bad day. As an undercover agent for the FBI, he wasn't allowed too many bad days. But when your cover gets blown and you walk unknowingly into a trap, it happens. And this guard was about to find out what happened when Ryan was grumpy.

Ryan gave a deadly laugh. "Sure you don't. You're just his second-in-command."

Abdul crossed his arms over his expensive Italian suit. Who knew terrorists were so fashionable these days? Expensive suit, fancy haircut, and Botoxed skin were a far cry from his modest lifestyle in Afghanistan.

"While we come from the same country, that doesn't mean we know each other. The world isn't that small a place. Or is the FBI just arresting everyone from that region? Or is it Homeland Security?"

Ryan just shrugged and sent him a smirk. "I guess you don't know everything. Who said I was an agent? I've been loyal to you these past months."

Abdul shook his $400 coiffed head. "It doesn't matter who you are. You're dispensable."

"Don't you want to know what's about to happen to you and The Suit?"

"I don't need to know." Abdul stood at his full height and still only came up to Ryan's chin. "I'm not the one with a gun to my head."

"For now," Ryan quipped as he sent a wink to the man he was trying to prove was a direct link to the international terrorist the FBI believed to be known as The Suit.

They had changed the face of terrorism. Gone were the mountains of Afghanistan. In their place were the foothills of Malibu. The Suit waged his war with deep pockets and fancy cars. Ryan was determined to find The Suit's real identity.

Ryan had been on the case for seven months. He hadn't talked to his family or friends in all that time. He had applied to an advertisement for fast cash online. Playing a clean-cut, laid-off businessman, Ryan had infiltrated the organization run by Abdul. He had become a recruiter in the affluent parts of Los Angeles for the organization. Sadly, he recruited way more teenagers than he had thought possible. He'd signed up enough kids that he was awarded a Ferrari by Abdul. All their names were now with the FBI, and his recruits were being rounded up at this very moment.

His cover had been blown. Ryan had pressed his watch and sent a signal to his handler as soon as it happened. Per protocol, all the people Ryan had turned over were being quickly picked up and isolated. Further, Ryan's evidence showing Abdul was planning a terrorist attack during a big football game was enough to get warrants and arrests for those he had recruited and all the members of the organization. The trouble was it had become increasingly clear that while Abdul may be second-in-command, he was neither the money nor the brains behind this operation.

The one thing stopping Ryan from leaving the mission was because to this day he hadn't been able to make a connection to The Suit or any leader for that matter. That's why he was making this last-ditch effort to get Abdul to confess before the inevitable bloodbath started. Ryan just hoped it wasn't his blood.

"For now," Abdul chuckled. "You Americans all think you're cowboys in the old days of the Wild West. You have a gun pointed to your head, two other guards waiting to tear you to pieces, and you think I'm going to let you walk out of here alive just because you might have some information for me?"

Ryan shrugged and the gun pressed tighter against the back of his skull. "Fine. If you're going to kill me, at least tell me who your boss is before you do. You know, for curiosity's sake."

"Kill him," Abdul responded as he turned to walk out the door.

"Not in a talkative mood?" Ryan called after him.

Ryan waited until he felt the subtle pulling back of the gun, indicating the man holding it had moved his finger to the trigger. The second he felt that slight release of pressure he dropped to the ground. The man fired into the air Ryan's head had occupied just a split second before and the fight began.

Ryan swept out his leg and kicked the gun holder behind his knees. The man fell to the ground hard, and the gun skidded across the marble floor. Ryan spun around the guard and wrapped his thick forearm around the man's throat from behind before hauling him to his feet.

The other two guards had their guns aimed and were awaiting Abdul's command. "What are you waiting for? Kill them both!"

Ryan used the guard as a human shield as the bullets flew. He had to use all his strength to keep the dead man upright. It felt like hours, but it was only seconds until he heard the *click* of two empty gun clips. Not hesitating, Ryan let the dead guard drop to the floor and leaped for the gun lying on the ground.

His hand closed around the butt of the pistol. From where he knelt, he aimed it at the guards at the same time they clicked their fresh clips into place. Abdul stood behind the two men and looked in shock and anger at Ryan.

"You still think you are going to come out of this alive, cowboy? You have two."

Bang, Bang. Ryan shot the two guards. They dropped to the floor at Abdul's expensively clad feet.

"You were saying?" Ryan stood up and walked toward Abdul with the gun still drawn. "Last chance before I turn you over to the higher-ups. I've heard they have some new techniques they've been dying to try out. You tell me everything now, and I'll see what we can do to keep you alive."

"I'm not going to tell you anything, cowboy. You can't make me talk. I'll be released in no time. I know people. Powerful people. I may be sent back to my country, but I certainly won't be dead." Abdul tried to act cocky as Ryan continued forward with the gun pointed right at his head.

"That's all right. I'll let it be known you're cooperating with authorities."

Abdul sent him a forced smile and shook his head. "You're persistent. I'll give you that." He held out his hands. "But you might as well take me away. I'm not talking. I'll be a martyr for my cause."

"I won't give you the notoriety. You'll be locked in isolation for the rest of your life with no word of this in the media. You'll just vanish. So much for your martyrdom. And when you realize how little you mattered in the grand scheme of life, you'll ask for me and you'll tell me everything."

Abdul didn't have time to respond. The door to the penthouse office crashed open as an FBI SWAT team swarmed the scene. Abdul held up his hands and went down onto his knees in silent surrender. The team handcuffed him and dragged him from the room. Ryan lowered his weapon and cursed as his hands were pulled behind him and the handcuffs were slapped on.

"I got this one, boys. Sweep the entire floor and pack it all up. I want to look over every piece of paper in here," a man in a cheap suit ordered as he grabbed Ryan roughly by the shoulder.

"Tell me you got something from the wiretaps?" Ryan demanded as his handler led him from the penthouse.

"Enough to lock him away, but nothing to lead to his boss. Do you know you're shot?"

Ryan looked down at the blood seeping onto his pant leg and over at his bicep. "Damn it, not again."

Ryan sent a wink to the doctor as she put the finishing stitch in his arm. Her cheeks turned a cute shade of pink, and Ryan knew he'd found his entertainment while he was riding the desk. Being shot sucked.

"Is he good here, Doc?" his handler, Arnie, asked as he stepped into the room. Arnie was in his early forties and had light brown hair liberally streaked with gray that always seemed to look like he had just rolled out of bed. In fact, Arnie's entire appearance always looked like he had just rolled out of bed. He was perpetually wrinkled but his mind was as sharp as a tack.

The doctor smiled at Ryan and let her hand slide down his bicep. "All done. He's finishing off a bag of fluids and some antibiotics. We will keep him overnight to make sure there's no sign of infection. You were lucky the shots weren't more severe. You should be good to go in a couple days. I'll be back to check on you in an hour."

Arnie waited for the doctor to shut the door before he plopped down in the chair next to the bed. "I've posted guards outside."

"Is that really necessary?" Ryan asked.

"Yeah. It is. While your real name isn't known, your cover is blown, and by now The Suit will be out looking for you. I've covered your tracks well. You're dead now."

Ryan smirked. "It'll be hard to work if I'm dead."

"Not you, Jonathan Turner. You died in the penthouse. Your alias got shot in the face by the SWAT team after you resisted arrest. Sorry about that." Arnie let out a tired sigh and ran his hand through his hair again.

"Thanks. I appreciate you covering for me." The situation must be bad if they went to such extremes to hide his identity. "So, what aren't you telling me?"

If it were possible, Arnie's hair seemed to stick out even

further as he ran his hand through it again. "There's a leak. We don't know if it's internal or if someone just got lucky. Yours is the third cover to be blown. You're the only one to walk out alive. So now we just have to wait to see if someone tries to kill you."

"Wait, there were two others undercover before me? Why didn't you tell me that?" Ryan stared at his boss and friend as he repositioned himself in the bed.

"Didn't want to worry you. It would make you act differently. It would cause anyone to do so without even realizing it. I'm leaving this with you." Arnie pulled out a file and tossed it onto the bed. "The rest of the office thought you were on loan to the Boise office. Here's the case you were supposedly working on."

"Idaho?"

Arnie shrugged a rumpled shoulder. "It was punishment for overstepping your bounds. That's the story I've put out. Plus the head of the Boise office, Agent Shaw, is a friend of mine from the Academy. I trust him and so should you. If anyone calls to verify that story, he'll do it and then notify me."

Ryan flipped through the case. Yikes, mail fraud. That would be punishment indeed. "What's this?" he asked as the Idaho case turned into Arnie's personal notes.

"Those are copies of my notes on The Suit. I know there has to be a connection somewhere. I don't know if I've just looked at it too much or what, but I can't find it. I was hoping you could look it over during your time off."

Ryan raised his eyebrow. "And why am I taking time off?"

"In a couple days, I will tell the office you're returning in a week. It would look too strange for you to return right after someone's cover had been blown. Since you're recovering from the gunshot wounds, you might as well do something useful with your time besides seeking comfort from the doctor."

Ryan only grinned at his boss. "I'll see if I can squeeze in some time to look it over."

There was a quiet knock on the door and a nurse stepped into the room. "I'm sorry, sir, but visiting hours are over, and Mr. Owens needs his rest after suffering the trauma of a mugging."

Ryan slowly placed his blanket over the file to hide it from view. After Arnie had uncuffed him upon leaving the penthouse, they'd driven to a bad part of town and Ryan had gotten out of the car. Arnie fired off a couple of shots into an old dumpster and left Ryan with nothing but the clothes on his back and his gunshot wounds. Ryan had beat on doors until someone had agreed to call him an ambulance. For the police, EMT, and hospital records, it would read that a Tommy Owens was mugged on the opposite side of town from the penthouse.

"Thanks for coming, Dad. Tell Mom I love her and not to worry," Ryan said with such sincerity that the nurse took his hand in hers and gave it a squeeze.

"Don't worry, Mr. Owens. I'll take great care of your son tonight."

Ryan tried not to laugh when Arnie rolled his eyes. Ryan was twenty-eight, and it drove his boss crazy that he could look old enough to pass for his father.

"Rest up. Remember, no strenuous activity or you could injure yourself."

Ryan felt the nurse gently press her fingers to the inside of his wrist to take his pulse. She checked his blood pressure and filled out his chart before sending him a wink and a promise to bring him some ice cream. As soon as the door closed, Ryan pulled out the folder. He opened it first to the Boise case and reviewed the file until he had it memorized. A small medical team came in to check on him before he could look at the notes on The Suit.

"How are we doing? You look like you're in pain," the doctor asked as she looked over his file.

Ryan kept his hand on the folder hidden under the sheets and tried to relax his forehead. "I'm better now that you're here."

The doctor smiled at him and nibbled her lower lip as the nurse measured out a shot. "Then you'll love this. This will help with the pain so you can get some sleep. We'll be back to check on you later."

Ryan smiled as everyone left and then pulled out the file. He was eager to jump into the notes, but his darn eyelids kept falling. He pushed the file under the sheet and covered it well. It would have to wait until tomorrow. Somehow, he would crack this case.

Chapter Two

Keeneston, Kentucky . . .

S ienna woke to the sound of her phone ringing. She groaned and reached across her bed for the phone on the nightstand. What had possessed her to give her cell phone number to her patients? Oh yeah, the lucrative contract she had received from the Lexington Thoroughbreds.

Since graduating with her doctorate in psychology four years earlier, she had paid her dues and earned the respect of the coaches at the NFL's newest team, the Lexington Thoroughbreds. She planned to expand her small business to include the local universities as part of her clientele. Right now, she worked four days a week at the Thoroughbreds' offices and counseled players on everything from mentally preparing for games to working their way through divorces. The other days of the week she saw anyone who wanted her services. Some were high school coaches, some were college players preparing for the pros, and she even saw some high school players in order to help them with the stress of being recruited by colleges. But only the players and coaches of the Thoroughbreds had her personal number.

"Dr. Ashton," Sienna mumbled as she put the phone to her ear. It was still dark out so whoever it was had either

KATHLEEN BROOKS

gotten up early or was just getting in for the night.

"Yo, Doc. I got a question for you," the friendly deep voice said from over the phone.

"Jaylen? What time is it?" Sienna asked as she sat up in bed.

"Three in the morning," he happily responded. "Oh, were you asleep?"

"That's typically what people are doing at this time." Somehow this twenty-two-year-old made her feel old at twenty-nine.

"Oh, sorry, Doc. I'll make it quick. Is it true that having sex hurts your game on the field? 'Cuz I have this hottie who is dying for a little Jaylen Cox lovin', if you know what I mean." Jaylen chuckled.

Jaylen was in a fight for the starting running back position and the first regular season game was only two days away. The final lineup would be announced tomorrow during practice.

"While there has been no evidence of it hurting performance, some believe it helps relax you, and in fact gives you a mental boost," Sienna got out before she was cut off.

"We're on, Boo!" Jaylen called, and Sienna heard a girl giggle in the background.

"However, it has been shown that lack of sleep does hurt your game."

Jaylen paused for a moment then held the phone away. "Sorry, Boo. It'll have to wait until tomorrow morning. I gotta get to bed. Doctor's orders."

Sienna smothered her laugh with her hand. Jaylen had to be her favorite patient—even if he did call her in the middle of the night. He did exactly what she told him, was always polite, and always had a smile for her.

"Thanks, Doc. I don't want to do anything to mess with my game. I better get to bed. See you tomorrow."

"Goodnight." Sienna hung up her phone and kicked the covers off her bed. She padded barefoot over the hardwood floor to the kitchen of her small bungalow home on the outskirts of Keeneston. She had bought the old house last year and had just finished putting all of her touches into it. It was five minutes from downtown in one direction and five minutes from her parents' farm in the other direction. After working all day in Lexington, it was nice to come to her little spot in the country. And Keeneston was definitely *country*.

The small town now had two stoplights. The main stoplight was downtown. The town had been built in the 1700s and still possessed that old world charm. The buildings were brick, painted in historic colors from the past. The windows were large and filled with displays from local artists, antiques, and decorations. Main Street was lined with flowers and American flags. Everyone knew your name and horns were only honked to initiate a greeting. Of course, that was both good and bad. Since everyone knew your name, they also knew your parents' names, your grandparents' names, and when you were doing something you weren't supposed to be doing. She and all the Davies cousins had really hated it when they were teenagers. But now that she knew she wanted a family of her own someday, she was sure there was no place better to live than Keeneston.

Sienna opened the cupboard and pulled out some tea. She heated the water, filled her mug, and went to the small back porch that overlooked part of Desert Farm, owned by Their Royal Highnesses, Mohtadi and Danielle Ali Rahman. They were royalty to a small Middle Eastern island called

Rahmi. However, they'd always just be Mo and Dani to her. Especially since Dani was her mother's best friend and Sienna's godmother.

Sienna took a sip of the hot tea and sat on the cushioned chair. She curled her feet under her and used her father's oversized football jersey from when he was a quarterback in the NFL to cover her toes. While September in Kentucky wasn't cold per se, it always seemed like it after the hot, humid days of summer. Her mother, Kenna, had suggested that a man would keep her warm on nights like these. Her father, Will, had told her a dog would do just as well, which is how she found herself with Hooch.

Sienna had broken up with her boyfriend six months ago. Things had gotten serious, but just like with the others, she bolted as soon as marriage came up. Her mother groaned; her father cheered. She had drowned her sorrows at the Blossom Café with one of Zinnia Meadows's concoctions called Chocolate Glop. It was just that, a big glop of warm, melty, gooey, rich chocolate cake with ice cream on top.

After consuming two of them and a glass or three of the Rose Sisters' Special Iced Tea, her best friend, Sydney Davies, drove her home and deposited her in bed. When Sienna had awoken to the feel of water dripping on her face, she'd opened her eyes to find Hooch. He kinda looked like the dog from that old movie, *Turner and Hooch*, except he was a massive black dog with jowls that hung like floppy ears from his mouth, sitting over her on the bed, drooling. His tree trunk-thick tail thumped against her comforter happily as he snorted through his bulldog nose. Sienna had taken one look at the ugliest dog she'd ever seen and had fallen in love.

Sienna once had heard the handle to the porch door

jiggle, and Hooch had ambled out of the house with his perpetual *I'm so sleepy* look on his wrinkly face. After discovering Hooch had just walked into her house *through* the screen door, she'd replaced it with a glass door with a handle knob. Hooch had learned after one day how to use his nose to lift the handle and push the door open. But at least the door closed now so other animals didn't wander in during the night and jump into her bed.

The porch's floorboards shook slightly as Hooch dropped to sit in front of her. He rested his drooling jowls on her lap and closed his eyes. Snores shattered the silence of the night and Sienna just laughed. Who needed a boyfriend when she had Hooch?

The Lexington Thoroughbreds' stadium wasn't actually in Lexington. The massive complex sat on twenty-five acres right outside of Lexington, and luckily it was on the side closest to Keeneston. It didn't matter that Sienna had worked there for two years. She was always amazed when she pulled up to the massive complex that held seventy thousand people. In addition to the stadium seats, locker rooms, vending areas, and so on, there were also six thousand club seats and eighty suites on top of the Thoroughbreds' executive offices and conference rooms.

Sienna pulled into her reserved parking space in the employee lot and walked to the glass doors that led to the offices and training rooms before getting into the private elevators and making her way up to the executive offices. She waved at Janice Hemingway, the fifty-two-year-old secretary who ran the office. No one got past her unless they had an appointment. She chased off football groupies, pissed-off fans, reporters, and unhappy exes who tried to sneak in.

"Morning, sugar," Janice called as she looked over the rim of glasses. Her black hair was pulled into a tight bun at the top of her head. "What happened? You don't look like you slept at all."

Sienna unconsciously patted her light auburn hair and wondered if she had more concealer in her office. "Had a phone call in the middle of the night. It always takes me a while to get back to sleep."

"You need a man in your bed," Janice said, giving Sienna a maternal stare that was nearly identical to the one she received from her own mother.

"I don't need a man. I have Hooch," Sienna called as she headed to her office.

"That ain't a dog. That's a snorting horse. And nothing should drool that much! It just ain't right," Janice called after her.

Sienna passed the trio of owners' offices. Her father and a bourbon Thoroughbred named Earnest Gallagher represented one third of the team's ownership. A silent partner, Mo, owned the other two-thirds. When her father had told his best friend about the possibility of a team moving to the area, Mo had researched it and decided it was a good investment, considering Kentucky had no other major league teams in any sport. Mo decided to invest in the Thoroughbreds so long as he didn't have to serve as the face of the franchise. He didn't want the attention or responsibility of running the team. Instead, he left that up to Sienna's father and the general manager, Brad.

"Yo, Doc!" Jaylen Cox called out as he jogged down the hall. Sienna smiled at him and inserted her key into her office door. "You were right. I went to bed right after I hung up with you, and I feel like a million bucks."

"Do that every night this week, and you'll feel like the twelve million bucks you're being paid," Sienna teased the giant man following her into her office.

Jaylen and all his muscles dove onto the couch. "I had morning sex and feel great. You're right about that making you all relaxed and shit. You should try it."

"Et tu, Brute?"

"I don't know Brute, but if he'll give you some, I say go for it. You're real tense, Doc."

Sienna snorted. Great, now she was even sounding like Hooch. She had heard that owners sometimes could resemble their dogs . . . maybe she did need a man.

"So, what's up? I have an appointment in a couple minutes," she asked to deter further conversation about her lack of a sex life.

"I wanted to say thanks. I got the job! I'm the new starting running back of the Thoroughbreds. My agent will be thrilled. He's coming this afternoon to meet with all of us and to talk to the front office about different stuff."

"You should know what that stuff is, Jaylen," Sienna lectured for the hundredth time. Too many of her patients had no clue what was going on with their own finances. They just let their agent handle everything.

"I know, I know. I'll look over everything he gives me today. I promise." Jaylen stood up with his trademark smile and walked over to her. "But if it weren't for you and your techniques to help me stay calm and focused on the field, I wouldn't have beat out Hummel for the starting spot." Before Sienna could say anything, Jaylen had her wrapped up in a bear hug. "You're the best, Doc."

When he stood her back on the floor, Sienna had a smile to match his. "I'm proud of the work you've done, Jaylen.

Have you talked to Adrian?"

"Yep. Talked to him this morning. He wished me luck and told me to do better than he did as a running back because he was coming after me for the spot all season long."

"How do you feel about that?" Sienna asked as she walked with Jaylen to her door.

"I think it will keep me motivated. But it's not all I'm thinking about. I'm just happy to have my shot to show the world what I can do. Of course, all the ladies will be trying to keep me from my doctor-prescribed sleep," Jaylen winked as he bounced down the hall.

Sienna smiled before taking a seat at her desk. She had a lot of work to get through before her next appointment.

Sienna picked up Malik Coleman's file and said goodbye to Coach Banks, the head coach of the Thoroughbreds. Coleman was her age, but she was sure he felt more like sixty than twenty-nine. He'd had two surgeries and was going to limp along for his last year of his contract with the Thoroughbreds. In their previous session, he'd admitted he was in constant pain from a shoulder injury he'd received in the last game of the postseason.

The soft knock at her door brought Sienna's head up. The tall and lean Malik stood at the door. "Are you ready for me, Doc?"

Sienna smiled at him. The way he gingerly moved made her think of her grandfather, and she had to stop herself from rushing to help him. "Is your shoulder still hurting?" she asked instead, taking a seat across from Malik.

"Like the devil. And now my knee is acting up again. It's so swollen the team doc had to drain it this morning. But tomorrow is the last first game of the season for me. I just need to ride the bench and collect my retirement at the end of the season. I'm meeting with my agent to discuss my retirement funds and everything soon."

"Is that what you've been focusing on?" Sienna asked.

"Sure have. I've been doing the visualization you taught me to help speed my recovery. But when I meditate at night, it's the sight of the ocean I focus on. Thanks for all the tips on relaxation, by the way. I've been able to get around three hours of uninterrupted sleep now."

Sienna gave him a professional smile. Pain had been keeping Malik awake at night for the past year. His doctor gave him sleeping pills, but Malik had a history of drug addiction and didn't want the temptation. Two months before, he had turned to Sienna initially for help with his lack of focus on the field, which resulted in his injury at the end of last season. He finally disclosed his insomnia to her two weeks ago.

"Four hours is our next goal. I've been talking with experts in this field and have learned a guided meditation I hope will put you to sleep for even longer. All this week I want you to call me when you're ready to go to bed. You can put the phone on speaker, and I'll guide you through it. The phone will disconnect when I hang up and hopefully you'll sleep even better."

Malik's eyes rounded in surprise. "You'd do that for me, Doc?"

Sienna smiled kindly at him. "Of course. I'll have you feeling like a new man in no time."

Malik's lips curved into a grin. "And maybe I'll be up for finding a girl to fulfill the morning sex prescription you gave Jaylen."

Sienna felt her face flush. "I didn't . . ."

Malik held up his hand to stop her. "Whatever, Doc, it worked. You should have seen him in the gym this morning. He was killing it."

"I don't even want to know what he's telling the guys," Sienna said and shook her head.

Malik moved to sit up. "If you don't mind, I have to cut it short today. I'm meeting with that new physical therapist you recommended."

"Layne Davies?" Sienna happily asked of her friend from Keeneston.

"That's her. My doctor wasn't thrilled I chose someone other than his old crony, but I really didn't like him last time I saw him. I talked to Miss Davies last week and was really encouraged by her attitude. Plus she comes to me with that new fancy practice of hers."

Sienna stood and walked with Malik to the door. "I hope she can help you. Let me know how it goes when you call me tonight."

Sienna let out a sigh as she returned to her desk. It was already two o'clock, and she hadn't even eaten yet. Her policy was when she was with a patient she kept her door closed. If she didn't have a patient, then her door was open and anyone who needed to see her could walk in. Today was the day the final lineup was posted, and she'd been inundated with players dropping by. Some just wanted to tell her the news. Some wanted help so they could improve on a certain aspect of their game. And some needed to vent at having been moved to second string or the practice squad.

"Knock, knock." Sienna looked from her desk to the handsome man in a suit at her door. He certainly wasn't a player. He was city handsome. Not athletic handsome like her players or country handsome like some of the men in Keeneston who worked on the horse farms. He was gym membership built with dark brown hair in a perfect swish of the bangs and a suit that must have cost a fortune.

"Can I help you?" Sienna asked, watching the man confidently step into her office.

"I'm Seth Hayes, a sports agent," he said smoothly and held out his hand. "I'm here meeting with some of my players and thought I would introduce myself. They've all talked very highly about you."

Sienna stood and shook his hand. He held it a moment longer and smiled. It didn't take a doctorate to know he was hitting on her. As she looked him over, she decided he just might be the answer to her six-month drought. An obviously sexy man who was interested in her and who lived somewhere else sounded good to someone a little . . . how would she phrase it . . . commitment shy.

"It's nice to meet you. Which players do you represent?"

"Malik Coleman, Jaylen Cox, Zack Sanders, and Deon Wofford. I know a couple of them see you. Jaylen can't stop talking about you. It's why I wanted to meet you."

Sienna smiled at Jaylen's name. "He's a great guy. I'm happy for his success. He has a long career ahead of him."

Seth sent her a sexy playful grin. "I sure hope so. I know you probably already ate, but I've been in meetings all day. I was hoping I could talk you into a second lunch."

"Actually, I haven't eaten yet."

Hope shone in Seth's dark green eyes. "Great. You're the local. Why don't you pick, and it'll be my treat?"

"Let me just check my schedule," Sienna said, hopeful that she didn't have any more appointments for the day.

She was starving, and not just for food. "It looks like I have a clear schedule. There's a bourbon bar in Lexington I enjoy. They have great burgers. Let me give you the address and I'll meet you there."

Sienna wrote the address on a piece of paper and handed it to Seth.

"Perfect. I'll meet you there. May I walk you to your car?" he asked.

"That would be nice," Sienna smiled up at Seth. She closed her files and put them in her satchel before locking up the office. Maybe Janice and her mother had been right after all. Having a man around who looked like Seth and was as nice as he was wouldn't hurt a thing.

Chapter Three

"**Y**ou want a . . . a salad?" Zinnia Meadows asked again.

"That's right. With grilled chicken, not fried," Sienna told the curvy chef at the Blossom Café. Tonight was her second date with Seth. They had had lunch yesterday and talked all the way through happy hour and into dinner. When they finally parted, Sienna made a date for the next night. Saturday night was no longer the loneliest night of the week for her.

"Okay, spill. Do you have a man?" Zinnia asked in a conspirator's whisper.

"Man?" Violet Fae Rose-Vasseur, the owner and original chef of the café, asked from her spot by the window. The Blossom Café was an institution in Keeneston, just like the Rose sisters who had started it. The tables were wood and the chairs mix-matched and painted cheerful colors. It was simply known as "the café" to locals. It had the best food around, you knew all the people there, and, most importantly, it was gossip central. Which was why Sienna should have known better than to open her mouth.

Miss Violet and her two sisters, Lily Rae Rose-Wolfe and Daisy Mae Rose-Lastinger zeroed in on Sienna like sharks on the scent of fresh blood. Somehow, these ninety-five-year-old women could hear her whispered conversation on the other side of the restaurant.

"You didn't tell me you were seeing someone," her best friend, Sydney Davies, commented from the table next to hers.

Sienna glanced to the stuffy man sitting across from Sydney and back to her best friend. "Aren't you in a meeting?"

"Yeah, but you seeing someone takes priority over Saks carrying my clothing line."

The man from Saks didn't seem to think so, but Sydney was the hottest designer around right now, and everyone was dying to get her clothing line into their stores.

"It's just a second date," Sienna told the now attentive patrons of the Blossom Café.

"I've got ten on it lasting five dates," Daisy called out before the eruption of betting began.

"Really? I'm only worth ten dollars now? I remember when bets placed against my love life were worth twenty," Sienna said sarcastically to the Rose sisters. Betting was a town-wide hobby run by the three little old ladies sitting innocently at the same table every day. They may all be married now, but they were still the same Rose sisters who fought to get the first bit of gossip, ran the betting books, and made the best food in town.

"We're retired now," Daisy told her.

"We have to live on a budget, and our financial advisor told us we have enough to live on only for another fifteen years," Lily explained.

"Fifteen years worth of money saved up," Sienna said in shock. "How much more are you trying to save?"

"Five more years or so," Violet answered as if it were completely normal for people to live well past one hundred fifteen.

"Well, I'll put twenty on Sienna dating him for more

than five dates," Sydney told the restaurant.

Sienna groaned. "A pity bet, really, Syd?"

Sydney just shrugged her delicate shoulders. "You're my bestie. Which means I'll be over tonight to hear all about him while you get dressed." Sydney winked before getting back to her meeting.

A moment later, Zinnia came out with a grilled chicken Caesar salad and placed it in front of her. "I called Poppy, and she said for me to get the whole scoop."

Four years ago, Poppy and Zinnia Meadows had shown up in Keeneston. No one knew that the Rose Sisters even had cousins, never mind ones who were happy to come help the sisters by taking over the Blossom Café and their bed and breakfast.

Poppy looked after the B&B while Zinnia ran the restaurant. Poppy would often serve as waitress after getting everything organized at the B&B each day. Lily explained she had overheard her mother telling her father one night that she regretted never forgiving her sister. After some help from Nabi, the head of Mo and Dani's security team, she had tracked her aunt to Daphne, Alabama. Then, after some more digging, discovered that Poppy and Zinnia were the only family the Rose sisters had left. They were cousins three or four times removed, but cousins nonetheless. Lily had written to them and offered them jobs if they were up for it. And they were.

After the initial shock of the two sisters' sudden appearance, the town had opened their arms to its newest residents. Within months, it was as if Poppy and Zinnia had lived there their whole lives. They took time to get to know each person who came into the cafe and their whole family history. The fact that the two girls were knockouts didn't hurt either. Although, they always seemed too busy to date.

"Well, tell Poppy there's nothing to scoop yet. When I make it to date five, I'll tell you all about him."

Zinnia stuck her bottom lip out in a pout but hurried back to the kitchen instead of pressing further. Sienna dug into the salad. She had a sexy dress she wanted to wear that night, and she didn't have room for the hot brown she had really wanted for lunch. The hot brown is a Kentucky food tradition. It is an open-faced sandwich stacked with turkey and bacon, smothered with cheese, and finally topped off with plenty of creamy Mornay sauce. It was the best thing on Earth. Unfortunately, it also instantly added five pounds to your hips. Sienna looked down at the salad and frowned. Tomorrow she'd have the hot brown.

Sienna stepped slowly up to her front door, Seth's hand at the small of her back. She didn't want the night to end, but in a couple of minutes Malik would be calling and she took her patient's confidentiality seriously — even with that player's agent and even with the potential shot of ending her sexual drought.

"Thanks for dinner. It was a wonderful night. I'm sorry I have to cut it short." Sienna stood at the door as her fingers played nervously with her key.

"I am too. I'm wining and dining some corporate heads tomorrow during the game in hopes of getting my guys some good endorsements. Then I meet with a couple of them after the game and fly out to Indianapolis to catch the evening game there for more of the same. I'm going to make sure I get back to Lexington soon though," Seth said as he ran his hand down her arm. His gaze had her wondering if Malik could wait an hour to go to bed.

"You certainly travel a lot." Sienna smiled at him.

"The beginning and end of the season are my busiest times. Setting up endorsements for the season and then for the summer. Would you mind if I give you a call while I'm traveling around? It would sure make traveling a lot less lonely," Seth said. He looked kind of embarrassed.

"Of course," Sienna said before leaning forward. She placed a gentle kiss on his lips. It would have gone further, but the earth began to shake.

"Does Kentucky get earthquakes?" Seth asked, pulling her from the porch.

Sienna giggled. "It's not an earthquake. It's just Hooch."

Seth looked at her in confusion. "What's a hooch?"

A bone-chilling howl let loose from inside the house. Horses scattered in the pastures, and the door handle shook ominously. Seth look petrified as Sienna smiled lovingly at the door and went to open it. "This is Hooch."

She opened the door, and Hooch bounded out. Well, bounded may be a slight exaggeration. Hooch meandered his girth out of the door, took a look at Seth, and drooled before letting out a deep bark that echoed through the night.

"He's my baby," Sienna said happily as she rested her hand on a head at least four times larger than her hand.

"That's not a baby; that's a monster. I've never seen a dog so big before," Seth said in horror.

Hooch let out a low growl and flashed the impressive set of teeth he had. "I don't think he likes being insulted. You're a handsome fellow, yes, you are," Sienna cooed. Hooch thumped his tail and wiped his drool on her leg.

"He's actually nothing more than a big baby. He wouldn't hurt a fly. It takes too much energy, doesn't it, big boy?" Sienna baby-talked to Hooch who was close to splintering the porch boards with his tail thumping.

Seth's eyes went even larger. "A gentle giant, huh? Well, I look forward to getting to know you and him better in the future."

Seth stepped forward and wrapped his arms around her. Sienna felt her heart kick up in anticipation of the kiss. He looked into her eyes and gently framed her face with his hand before slowly lowering his lips to hers. It was gentle, it was romantic . . . it was over? Sienna opened her eyes when Seth's lips were torn from hers. She found Seth lying on the porch with Hooch standing over him, a long line of drool dangling dangerously close to Seth's face.

Sienna watched in a mixture of amusement and horror as Seth tried to push Hooch off him, causing the drool to jiggle precariously with the movement.

"Get off, you . . ." Seth gave Hooch another shove to try to dislodge him, but the battle was lost. The drool fell straight into Seth's sputtering mouth.

"Hooch!" Sienna said sharply. "Heel!"

In seconds, Hooch was by her side as Seth rolled onto his stomach and spit off the side of the porch. "Oh God, it got in my mouth!"

"I am so sorry," Sienna cried and rushed toward Seth, smothering a laugh.

"It's okay. I'm just going to wash my mouth out with some bleach. It's all good." Seth waved her off and moved to stand. "That certainly does make for a memorable end to the evening."

Sienna heard her cell phone start to ring. "I'm so sorry, but I have to take this."

"It's okay. I need to get some sleep. Tomorrow is the first day of regular season, and it's going to be a very long day." Seth leaned forward and placed a quick peck on her cheek. "I'll call you."

"I look forward to it." Sienna sent him a wave as she dug into her purse and pulled out her cell phone. "Hello, Malik. How are you doing tonight?" She turned from watching Seth's taillights disappear into the night and focused on Malik.

Sienna sat back against the chair as Jaylen practically bounced around the room. His first time starting for the Thoroughbreds resulted in a game-winning touchdown. His normally happy nature was heightened, and he had even brought her a bouquet of flowers as a thank-you.

"I can't believe how focused I was. Did you see me? It was like I could see the path I needed to run opening up before me. I did everything you taught me and crushed it. Coach Everett was impressed."

Coach Trey Everett was also from Keeneston. He'd played high school football there before going to Vanderbilt and then to the NFL. When he'd moved back to Keeneston, he had helped coach the high school team with Cade Davies and then spent five years at the University of Kentucky coaching before being picked up by the Thoroughbreds as the running back coach.

"I know. Trey told me when I saw him Sunday night at the Blossom Café. You were fabulous, Jaylen."

Jaylen finally collapsed on the couch. "And I've told all the guys about your advice on sleeping and sex. I got a little somethin' somethin' Saturday evening and fell asleep at eleven. They guys laughed at me in the locker room before the game, but they aren't laughing now. They all are going to try it. Although Deon said he might have to bribe his wife for that much sex. He was already on the phone with Seth, asking about the jewelers and if ten carats was big enough."

Sienna tried to keep a professional face but failed as she imagined the entire team begging women to have sex with them so they could relax before each game.

"Oh, and I found this awesome house I want to buy. I asked Seth for all my account information so I can see if I can afford it. As soon as I get that info from the financial advisor a lot of us guys use, I'll be on my way to being the first homeowner in my family," Jaylen said with pride.

"That's very impressive and something to be proud of."

"Seth is hoping to lock up a shoe deal for me if I continue to play as well as I have. Then, I'm hoping I can use some of that money to buy a house for my parents. I'll have to remember to ask my Rook Capital Management advisor about that, too."

Sienna nodded her head. She'd heard some of the players talking about investing with them. The person who ran it was a Wall Street billionaire who had the magic touch. Lots of the agents advised their players to go in with a respectable firm like that instead of giving control of their money to their cousin or best friend like so many did.

"That's very kind of you, Jaylen. Is there anything else you'd like to discuss before practice begins?" Sienna asked.

"I think that covers it, Doc. I can't thank you enough for helping me take my game to the next level." Sienna was picked up from her chair and wrapped up in another bear hug before she could blink.

"You're welcome," she managed to groan as he gave her one last squeeze.

As soon as Jaylen left, Zack Sanders arrived. It was going to be a busy day. All six-foot-four inches and 310 pounds of muscle walked in. His sandy blond hair was wet from the shower, and his face had the beginnings of a beard that Sienna had learned wasn't to be shaved until the season ended. Football players were a superstitious lot, and the entire offensive line believed shaving somehow hurt their chance at winning.

"Hey, Doc," Zack said in his Midwestern accent. "Mind if I sit down? I just got done lifting weights."

"Of course," Sienna motioned for him to sit on the couch. "What did you want to see me about?"

"It's embarrassing," Zack started as a blush crept up his cheeks, "but I need help with something."

"That's what I'm here for. And you know I never say a word, so no matter what you tell me no one will ever know," Sienna said reassuringly.

"It's about women, Doc."

Sienna almost groaned. "Have you been talking to Jaylen?"

"About the sex thing? I already know that. I learned about the mental and physical benefits of sex in college. No, it's more about talking to women." Zack grimaced.

Sienna forgot that Zack had a biology degree from Duke. He was the smartest player on the team and quite possibly in the entire league. "Go on," Sienna encouraged.

"In college, I was always at practice, in the weight room, or studying. I didn't really have time to date and all those women who just tried to bag players seemed so shallow, I didn't waste my time on them. Well, I'm trying to break out of my shell now that I'm out of school and went to a club with the guys after the game last night. I froze, Doc. A real nice lady came and started talking to me, and I froze. I couldn't think of one thing to stay. I stuttered something that didn't even make sense, and after trying to draw me into a conversation, she finally gave up and left." Zack fell back against the pillows and let out a frustrated sigh.

"Don't worry, we'll work this out." Sienna gave him a pat on the knee and got to work.

Chapter Four

Sienna made a cup of tea and headed out the kitchen door for the back patio. When she had gone to school for her doctorate, she had not envisioned helping a giant lineman learn how to talk to women. But that was why she loved her job. She was there to help balance the stress of playing sports with the rest of their lives.

"Good evening, Malik. How did you do last night?" Sienna asked as she answered her phone.

"Great. I feel like at least five million bucks now. I slept for almost five hours." Sienna smiled as Hooch snored at her feet. She looked out over the peaceful countryside and listened to Malik talk with excitement about his improved insomnia.

"Are you ready to begin?" she asked a moment later.

"Let me just put you on speakerphone," Malik told her. "Okay, you're on speaker."

"Now, lie down in a comfortable position," Sienna instructed. She heard the covers move as Malik lay down in bed.

"I want you to take a deep breath . . ."

"Hold on, Doc. I think someone just opened the back door," Malik whispered. She heard the covers being pushed down and the bed move as Malik got out of bed.

"Call the police, Malik," Sienna urged as she

automatically shot to her feet.

"What are you doing here?" Malik demanded. Sienna froze. She didn't even breathe as she heard Malik repeat his question to the intruder. The sound of a fist connecting with flesh burst across the phone line in response to Malik's question.

"Malik!" Sienna screamed. With the sound of a struggle loud in her ear, Sienna screamed his name again. Adrenaline was surging through her body as the sounds of thrashing on the bed were heard a moment before Malik starting making choking sounds.

"I'm calling the police! Let him go! Malik!" Sienna hollered as the night went quiet around her. Hooch growled at the attacker a town away while Sienna listened as the room suddenly went quiet.

"Hello? Malik, are you safe? Are you there? Tell me you're all right," Sienna asked, trying to hold her voice steady. She heard heavy breathing as is if someone were standing over the phone listening to her.

"I'll find you. If you hurt Malik, you won't get away with it," Sienna swore as she heard the breathing growing louder over the phone. Then only silence answered her. She pulled the phone from her ear and looked at the *call ended* displayed on the screen.

With shaking hands, she pulled up the keypad on her cell phone and had to take a couple of deep breaths in order to hit the right numbers.

"9-1-1, what's your emergency?"

"There's been an attack," Sienna stated as clearly as she could and gave the operator Malik's address. "Hurry. I don't know if he's alive."

"Police and emergency responders have been dispatched. Are you still hiding in the house? Is the intruder still there?"

"I don't know," Sienna said as a sob escaped. "I'm not there. I was on the phone with him when it happened."

"What's your name and address, ma'am?"

Sienna told the operator, who then put her on hold to pass information along to the responders. Hooch pressed against her as if he were afraid she might faint at any moment. Sienna managed to pull up a text message. *There's been an emergency. Can you come to my house immediately?*

Almost instantly she received a text back. Help was on its way.

"Ma'am, the police have arrived at the house," the dispatcher said. "The officers have asked that you remain at home. They want to take your statement."

"How's Malik?" Sienna asked cutting off the dispatcher.

"I don't know, ma'am. The officer will fill you in when he arrives."

Sienna nodded her head silently and hung up the phone. She made her way slowly to the front door and unlocked it. She stepped onto the porch and stared out into the darkness as she willed lights to appear. Her whole body vibrated with fear as Hooch pressed his head against her hip and whined in a show of concern.

Less than five minutes later, the sight of headlights tearing down the country road came into view. She heard rubber skidding on pavement as the SUV turned at breakneck speed into her driveway. The door opened a second later as a man clad in jeans, a black T-shirt, and a black cowboy hat bolted from the SUV. His silver eyes matched the streaks in his dark hair, which reflected in the moonlight.

"Are you okay? What's going on?" FBI Special Agent in

Charge Cole Parker demanded as he raced up the stairs. He kept an eye on the house as if determining if there was danger lurking inside.

Cole was married to Paige Davies Parker, one of Sienna's mother's best friends. He had been like an uncle to her growing up. Sienna took one look at Ryan's father and burst into tears. Ryan had had a crush on her since they were six years old, but eight years ago everything changed. She had thought of him as a young kid even though he was only a year younger than her. One night they were playing matchmaker for Nabi, the current head of security for Mo and Dani, the Prince and Princess of the small island country of Rahmi, and his now wife, Grace. During their snooping, she'd discovered that Ryan Parker had become a man after giving her a passionate kiss. Since that night, he wouldn't talk to her, and she couldn't keep a boyfriend because no one ever measured up to him. Ryan was permanently etched in her mind.

"What happened, Sienna?" Cole asked patiently as he wrapped his arms protectively around her.

"I," *gulp* "heard" *gulp* "Malik being attacked." Sienna lost her battle and started sobbing. Not delicate sobs, but body-shaking sobs that robbed her breath.

"Is he in the house? Is the intruder still here?" Cole asked quietly as one hand dropped to the gun on his hip.

Sienna took a deep breath to calm herself. "I heard it all over the phone, and the police won't tell me if he's even alive. They just said an officer is on his way to get my statement."

"Shit. Hon, I'm so sorry. What can I do to help?" Cole asked as she wiped her tears off on his shirt.

"I just want to know if Malik is hurt. Can you call the Lexington police and find out?" Sienna asked, trying to fight back another round of tears.

Cole nodded his head. "Of course. What's Malik's last name and where does he live?"

"Malik Coleman," Sienna answered before giving him the address.

"Oh man, the receiver for the Thoroughbreds? The news outlets will be over this in a heartbeat." Cole let out a long breath. "Okay, while I call, why don't you go inside and make that tea you like. It might take me a bit to get some answers since this will be a high-profile case."

Sienna gave a sniff in response and turned to go inside as Cole reached for his phone. She put a mug of water in the microwave and made her way to the open front door.

"Detective Braxton, I've heard good things about you. I'm Agent Cole Parker, the head of the Lexington FBI field office. I'm calling about the Coleman case. I'm with Sienna Ashton, and she's worried about her friend."

Sienna watched as Cole kicked the dirt with his cowboy boot.

"She's practically family, that's who she is. Now what's going on?"

Sienna went inside to retrieve her mug from the microwave. When she came back outside, Cole was still on the phone. When the screen door closed, he turned around and the look on his face told her everything she needed to know. The mug slid from her fingers and crashed to the porch floor. The tea spilled and ran along the floorboards as the mug rolled down the stairs and came to a stop in the grass.

"He's dead," Sienna stated as shock rocked her body.

"I understand, Detective. I'll wait here until you arrive." Cole hung up the phone and walked straight toward her. "Why didn't you tell me the attacker picked up

Malik's phone?"

"I told you, I heard the whole attack. I can't believe it. Is he really gone?" Sienna asked even though she knew the answer.

"Sienna, I know this is a shock, but I need you to focus right now. I want you to sit down here." Cole led her to the porch swing and sat her in it. "Now start from the very beginning. I want to know every word, sound, feeling you got from the call. Nothing is too small or unimportant."

Sienna felt a shiver run down her back. Cole was in serious cop mode. "Okay. It all started when Malik called me." Sienna recited everything she remembered word for word, sound for agonizing sound.

Cole took off his cowboy hat and ran his hand through his hair. The gesture made Sienna worry. "What is it?"

"Here are the facts I've gotten from your statement. Malik knew the intruder. The intruder picked up the phone and heard your threat," Cole stated in his even cop voice that only served to make her worry more.

"What I'm worried about is the killer knowing who you are. Was your name on the phone? Or was it just your number that we can disconnect immediately and try to bury any evidence of your name being attached to it?" Cole asked as Sienna's mind raced to connect the dots.

"It was my private cell phone. The number shouldn't be publicized anywhere," Sienna told him hopefully. The thought of a killer knowing her identity was enough to make her nauseous.

"Detective Braxton said she was going to come out to talk to you. She'll be here soon. We'll find out more then."

Thirty minutes had never passed so slowly as Sienna battled to control her thoughts. Eventually the sound of a car reached her and lights appeared. The cop car pulled into her driveway and parked next to Cole's SUV. A young woman with dark brown hair, hanging in perfect waves down her back, stepped out of the car. She wore a light blue fitted V-neck shirt tucked into black pants with a badge at her waist. She was so beautiful that Sienna half expected to see her in stilettos, but instead she wore a pair of well-worn cowboy boots.

With one quick look, the detective took in the house, Cole, and Sienna. Sienna's training kicked in as she evaluated the detective. She was confident in herself and her abilities. That was clear from just one glance, but she was also smart. The way she silently observed her surroundings as she walked made Sienna sure she had taken in a million little details and already formed her own opinion of Sienna and Cole.

"I'm Detective Andrea Braxton," she said in a strong Southern accent as she climbed the stairs and held out her hand.

Sienna shook it. "Sienna Ashton."

"Cole Parker," Cole said as he shook her hand next. "Why don't we sit down? Sienna, I'd appreciate it if you repeated what you told me to the detective before we ask any questions."

Sienna nodded and held open the front door. Hooch ambled into the room, and she heard Detective Braxton's composure slip as she let out a quick gasp.

"Don't worry, that's just Hooch. He knows I'm upset and wants to be near me," Sienna told her as the big dog leapt onto the couch and stretched out over her lap. His tail gave a sedated thump and Cole caught the lamp that almost fell from the table next to the couch.

"He's not a dog. He's a water buffalo," Detective

Braxton murmured as she pulled out a tape recorder and a notepad. "Do you mind if I record this?"

Sienna shook her head. "Not at all."

"Why don't you start by telling me how you know Malik Coleman?" the detective asked.

"I'm the psychologist for the Lexington Thoroughbreds. That's all I can tell you unless you have a court order. I'm sorry," Sienna said as she nervously ran her fingers over Hooch's head.

"I understand. Let's move to your phone call with Mr. Coleman. What time did your conversation start?"

"Eleven ten."

"Can you tell me what you talked about?"

"No. But only a minute into the conversation Malik told me to hold on, that someone had opened his back door." Sienna closed her eyes and felt her grip tighten on Hooch as she recounted the conversation. "Can you now tell me what happened to Malik?"

Detective Braxton put her notepad down and frowned. "I'm sorry to tell you this but . . ."

Sienna's hand flew to her mouth. Deep down she knew what was coming, but knowing it didn't prepare her for being told.

"He was strangled. We dusted the phone for prints, but the attacker must have had gloves. Only Malik's fingerprints were on it. I haven't been able to unlock the phone yet," Detective Braxton told her as she reached into her purse and pulled out the phone in a plastic evidence bag. "Dr. Ashton, I need you to call Malik's phone."

"Why?" Sienna asked as she stared horrified at the phone. She heard the heavy breathing and whipped around to make sure it wasn't real.

"I need to see what the killer saw," she explained.

Sienna tapped Hooch on the butt and waited as he hefted himself off her. She reached for her phone on the coffee table and pressed Malik's name. The phone rang and Cole and Detective Braxton both leaned forward. At the same time they cursed and looked at each other.

"What is it?"

Cole looked up. "It says, *Dr. Sienna Ashton*. The killer knows who you are."

Chapter Five

A ringing phone at three in the morning was never good news. Ryan was awake instantly and already reaching for the phone before the second ring. He saw *Dad* show up on the caller identification and worried something bad had happened to his mom, brother, or sister. Jackson was his twenty-five-year-old brother and was training to become a member of the FBI Hostage Rescue Team. His twenty-year-old sister, Greer, was in college. If some jackass hurt his sister, he was going to pay.

"What is it, Dad?" Ryan didn't bother to say hello.

"Sienna's in trouble."

"What kind of trouble?" Ryan asked. Sienna had been his ideal woman for a long time. He had loved her since they were kids. But that was the trouble. Sienna only saw him as a child, and he'd gotten sick of it. Suddenly, eight years ago she became interested. Women . . . she had only become interested because he wasn't. Ryan had pushed aside the nagging thought that maybe, just maybe, it could be more than that.

Ryan heard his father sigh. If it was three in the morning in California, it was six in the morning in Keeneston. "She heard a murder over the phone. The killer picked up the phone and heard her tell him she wouldn't rest until he was caught. The phone had her full name on it.

He knows who she is."

Ryan cursed and then cursed again for good measure. "What do you need me to do?"

"I need you to come home," his father told him in his "I'm a higher-ranked FBI agent than you, and this is an order" voice.

"I can't just leave—"

"Yes, you can," his father cut in. "I've already talked to Arnie."

"And if I don't?" Ryan didn't appreciate being the last to know his assignments and liked it even less that his father wasn't asking.

"I'll tell your mother you were shot again."

"Damn, Dad. That's below the belt."

"Sienna needs someone to watch out for her. The detective and I feel she needs someone out of uniform to do it. The person who killed Malik—"

"Malik? Malik Coleman?" Ryan asked in surprise.

"Yes. He knew the person who killed him. He and Sienna work with all the same people. If it's someone in the organization . . ."

Ryan didn't need his father to continue. If it was someone inside the Thoroughbreds, Sienna had no hope of being safe. "All right. I'll be on the next flight out. I'll see you this evening. Is she at her parents' house?"

"Um," her father stuttered, "not exactly."

"What do you mean, not exactly?" Ryan pushed.

"She made us swear not to tell her parents. She said they would freak out and give away that she's being watched. She, um, didn't say not to tell you, though."

"Does she know I'm coming to watch her?"

"Yeah, about that," his father hedged, sounding rather guilty. "I haven't found time to tell her yet. She's still talking with the detective."

"Coward."

"I'm not the man who ran across the country to hide from love," his father simply stated.

"I'm not hiding from love," Ryan protested.

His dad made a grunt of disbelief. "I'll see you later today. And thanks, son." His father paused for a second. "It'll be good to see you again. It's been too long. I understand how undercover assignments work. Your mom, on the other hand, may be a little peeved she hasn't gotten to talk to you in so long. Now, come home."

The line went dead and Ryan pulled his laptop onto the bed, made a reservation for the five-thirty flight to Lexington, and rented an SUV for the week. He shoved the sheets from his naked body and strode to the bathroom for a quick shower and to pack. As the water washed over his body, he shook his head. Love? What was his father thinking? He didn't love Sienna Ashton. Infatuation maybe. But one night in the sack would cure of him that. After all, she was sexy, and he was just a man. What better way to guard her and prove to her once and for all he was a red-blooded male?

"Are you sure you want to do this?" Detective Braxton asked as Sienna pressed the elevator button.

"I'm positive. This is my job. These players trust me. I should be the one to tell them Malik was murdered," Sienna said as they headed to the team meeting room inside the Thoroughbreds' stadium.

Detective Braxton and her team were on hand to interview Malik's teammates and coaches after they had broken the news. Sienna and the group walked into the auditorium-style meeting room, resembling a college lecture hall more than a conference room. She made her way to the front table and got the team's attention.

"Thank you for meeting me so early," Sienna said as calmly as she could. She took a breath and tried to remember what Detective Braxton had wanted her to say. The team continued to talk and Sienna fought the urge to scream at them. Their friend was dead and one of them could be the murderer.

"Yo! Listen up, the doc has something to say," Jaylen hollered before sending her a wink of support. Jaylen's voice had boomed across the room, and people turned to stare at her.

Sienna clasped her hands in front of her and looked into the sea of men. "I'm sorry to tell you that last night a burglar broke into Malik's house." Sienna had to blink her eyes to clear the tears. "It appears he caught the intruder unaware. He fought the intruder, but he didn't make it. Malik is dead."

No one said a thing. They were too surprised. Tears started to stream down Jaylen's cheek, and Zack buried his head in his hands.

"This is Detective Braxton and her team for the case. They're going to be meeting with you all to talk about Malik, in order to find who did this. They want to start with the offense. If you all could go to the other conference room, they will call you when they're ready for you. For the defense and coaches, I will be in conference room C holding a group support meeting for those of you who want to remember Malik and share stories. I'm also here if you feel you need individual grief counseling. Please, if you have any information that you feel could help us, see one of the officers or myself immediately."

Jaylen stood before his teammates. "Before we go, let us offer a moment of silence for our brother, the best damn receiver we'll ever have had the pleasure of playing with. We'll miss you, Malik."

The team all bowed their head and a minute later the coaches started organizing meetings with the police. Sienna was overrun with people wanting to share stories of Malik, wondering how to deal with the loss, and talking about how to celebrate his life. For now, her own grief was put aside. She had a job to do.

Ryan tossed his bag into the back of the black Ford Explorer and took a deep breath. Home. He smelled the freshly cut grass at Keeneland racetrack across the street from the airport and enjoyed the distinct lack of smog in the air.

He started the car and headed through the outskirts of Lexington. It still was a shock to see the Thoroughbreds' stadium in the middle of what had been an old worn-down industrial area. The employee parking lot was full and Ryan decided to take a chance that Sienna was still there. He turned into the stadium, flashed his badge to the security officer, and drove toward the employee lot.

Sienna had never been more exhausted than she was right at that moment. She didn't sleep the previous night and when she'd tried to take a nap, she heard the sound of Malik's life being choked from him and the sound of the murderer breathing deeply as he hung up the phone.

"Thanks for helping us out today," Detective Braxton said and gave Sienna's shoulder a pat.

"Did you learn anything?" Sienna asked as they made their way toward the parking lot.

"I've got a list of people I still need to talk to—his agent, a cousin, a sister, and some friends who aren't on the team. But no solid leads yet. Don't worry, Dr. Ashton, we'll find him."

Sienna pushed open the door to the parking lot and froze. Ryan Parker was leaning against Detective Braxton's car with his arms crossed over his muscled chest and his hip resting on the hood.

"Who's he?" Detective Braxton asked quietly as she took him in. "Cop?"

"FBI. That's Ryan Parker, Cole's son."

Detective Braxton shook her head. "I joined the wrong law enforcement group," she whispered. "I guess that answers my question on if you need a ride back to Keeneston. Or maybe you could drive my cruiser and I'll go with him?"

Sienna chuckled for the first time that day. "You can have him."

Detective Braxton looked between Sienna and Ryan. "It's a shame, but I think his interest is already taken by someone else."

"Don't count on it," Sienna whispered back before stopping in front of Ryan.

Ryan waited for Sienna to make her way to him. The attractive woman walking with her screamed *cop*, and it was probably her car he was leaning against. But it was Sienna who drew his attention. She had always been impeccably dressed with flawless makeup and perfect hair. But not today. She was in business slacks and a blouse, but her hair was pulled back into a quick ponytail, she wore no makeup to hide the beginning of dark circles under her eyes, and Ryan thought she'd never been more beautiful.

It took all his determination not to leap forward and wrap her in his arms. The instinct to protect her and take care of her hit him hard. The cop whispered something to Sienna, and Sienna's eyes shot to his before whispering something back. Ryan sent her a cocky grin and saw Sienna's eyes travel his length.

"Ryan, what are you doing here?" Sienna asked as the two women stopped in front of him.

"I'm on temporary assignment to the Lexington office. I think Dad wants me around to help him wrap things up for his retirement at the end of the month. They're just trying to find someone to fill the vacancy, and then he's done."

"Oh. I forgot he was retiring. But what are you doing *here*?" Sienna pointed to the ground at her feet.

"I was driving into Keeneston and saw this place and the cars and thought you might be here. Now, don't be rude. Introduce me to your friend," Ryan smiled and looked at Detective Braxton.

"Ryan, this is Detective Andrea Braxton. Detective, Agent Ryan Parker." Sienna introduced the two reluctantly.

"Nice to meet you," the cute detective said and shook his hand. "Since you don't seem surprised to see Sienna with me, I guess that means you talked to your father."

Cute and smart. Detective Braxton was just Ryan's type of woman. It was too bad his eyes kept wandering to the woman who had spurned him his whole life.

"Your dad called you? This wasn't a scheduled transfer?" Sienna asked with underlying anger. That's his girl. She always did have a bit of that redheaded temperament.

Ryan tried to stay focused on her question, but when

Sienna got angry she did the sexiest nose wrinkle, and her green eyes reminded him of a tropical jungle fraught with danger. "What does that matter?"

"It matters because I told him not to tell anyone. He told you about the phone call, didn't he?" Sienna asked as she dropped her voice and looked around.

"Making sure Daddy doesn't hear?" Ryan asked, knowing he was pushing her buttons. But he couldn't help himself. He wanted to see her riled up. He wanted to see her get so mad she'd push him away because right now he wanted to pull her toward him.

"Exactly. You know my parents would flip out, and that is not what I need right now," Sienna hissed.

Ryan just smiled. "Then you better hurry and get into my SUV because I just saw your dad pass by the third-story stairwell window. He'll be down here in seconds."

"Crap. Call me with updates, Detective." Sienna turned to the SUV next to the cop car and dove into the front seat. "Hurry up!"

Ryan chuckled and pushed himself off the car. "Detective," he said with a nod of his head.

"Here's my card. I have a feeling I know why you're here. Call me if anything unusual happens. Right now there's no reason to think the killer would need to come after her, but it certainly wouldn't surprise me either."

Damn. Cute and smart, just like he thought. Ryan took the card and really wished his body would respond to the woman standing in front of him, but he couldn't wait to get into his own car. The flash of Will Ashton's profile as he rounded the final landing in the stairwell caught his attention. He sent Andrea a wink and jogged around the front of the SUV.

"Hurry up," Sienna practically yelled from where she

was bent over in the front seat.

"Want me all to yourself so soon?" Ryan grinned as he tore out of the parking lot.

"Grow up," Sienna shot back as she sat up.

He came all this way to protect her and she still thought he was a child. He was fuming by the time he made it to the security gate. He slammed on the brakes, causing Sienna's eyes to go round. In one quick motion he unbuckled her seatbelt and dragged her across the console and into his lap. His lips were hard and demanding as they came down onto hers. His tongue pushed against her mouth until she opened for him on a moan. Domination was the only thing on his mind as he plundered her mouth. But soon she was plundering back and when her fingers speared his hair and pulled him closer, it was his turn to moan.

The sound of someone knocking at his window had him releasing her. He had thought their kiss eight years ago was life-changing. It had nothing on this one. He had planned a sharp retort, but instead he was thinking of several other things he could do with his tongue and none of them involved words.

Ryan rolled down his window for the smiling security guard. "Yes?"

"You can go through now." He laughed as she pointed to the raised gate.

"Oh, yeah. Thanks." Ryan put the car into gear and headed for Keeneston.

Ohmygosh, ohmygosh, was all Sienna could think as they drove toward her home in silence. She kept her eyes on the rolling hills outside her window because she knew if she looked at Ryan, her eyes would travel down his hard abdomen to something else that had been very hard, and then she would leap on him and have car sex. And car sex was definitely not a sexy kind of sex. And then she would have had sex with a man she'd grown up with and . . . Damn it! She looked. She licked her lips as images of hot sex roared to life in her mind.

"Sienna," Ryan warned, "want to see what happens if you lick your lips one more time while staring at me like that? Now, where's your new house? Dad said it was off the main road."

Sienna snapped her eyes forward, blushed, and saw they had almost missed her turn. "Turn right here. Then it's about a quarter mile down on your left."

A minute later Ryan pulled into her driveway. Sienna reached down to unbuckle, but something had sent a shiver down her back. She looked up and automatically grabbed Ryan's arm.

"What is it?" he asked as he parked the SUV in front of her house.

Sienna just pointed to the porch as fear gripped her.

"Geez. What is that thing? It's not a horse. It's like a genetically messed up donkey."

"Hooch," Sienna stammered. "He's outside."

"I'd sure hope so. I don't think he'd fit inside your house," Ryan joked as he looked at the massive dog.

"No," Sienna said, tightening her grasp on his arm. Her fingernails started to bite into his skin. "He was locked inside when I left. Someone was here. Someone has been in my house."

Chapter Six

"Stay here," Ryan ordered, his body instantly alert. He pried Sienna's hand off his arm and reached under his seat to pull out his service weapon.

"Is that thing you insist is a dog going to eat me?" Ryan asked as he looked over the house for signs of movement.

"No. Hooch wouldn't hurt anyone. He's just a big goober. Oh, please tell me he isn't hurt!" Sienna moved to open the door, but Ryan stopped her.

He took a deep breath and shook his head. "I'll get the dog. You stay here."

Ryan opened the door and Hooch stared off into space. Goober was right. Damn, as he got closer, the dog got uglier. He had thought Chuck, his childhood dog, was ugly, but Hooch put him to shame. All drooling jowls and shoved-in nose. His paws were the size of dinner plates, and it looked as if the dog weighed more than he did.

"Hooch, come here, boy," Ryan whispered as he kept his eyes on the front door and windows for any signs of someone inside.

Hooch thumped his tail, and the sound echoed in the stillness of the evening. The window behind Hooch shook and Ryan gave up on any element of surprise if the intruder was still inside.

"Come, Hooch. Mommy's in the car." Hooch's head

perked up and he came to a wobbly stance. Ryan lowered his gun and rushed up the stairs. The damn dog was so dazed he could hardly stand. With a resounding crash, Hooch sat back down onto the porch. "You took a shot to the head, didn't you?"

Ryan dropped to his knees and grabbed the dog's face in his hands. Sticky drool ran down each arm as Ryan looked into the beast's eyes. Glassy. Anger ripped through him. Someone had broken into Sienna's house and clobbered her dog over the head. The giant knot he found a second later confirmed it.

"Okay, you stay here. I'll check things out and then maybe Grandma and Grandpa Ashton can look after you and your mommy." Hooch's tail thumped again and a potted plant fell from a small table nearby.

Ryan shook his head and smiled at the dog. How had he gone from terrorists to protecting a dog and his sexy owner? Ryan stood up and Hooch fought to get to his feet. He groaned and leaned against Ryan. Ryan had to brace himself for the weight as the dog leaned against him. As Ryan took a step, the dog followed using Ryan as a crutch.

"I guess you're coming with me," Ryan said, looking at the determined dog. They each took slow steps toward the house. When Ryan reached the slightly opened front door, Hooch let out a low rumble.

Ryan lifted his gun and pulled out his flashlight. Clicking it on, he used his shoulder to open the door the rest of the way. He used the beam of his flashlight to scan the house before stepping farther in. He glanced down at the door and saw scratch marks around the lock. This had been where the intruder entered. The house wasn't destroyed. The television was still there along with a laptop.

"You stopped him before he could take anything, didn't you?" Ryan cooed. Hooch pushed away from Ryan, staggered to the laptop, and growled.

Stepping around the small coffee table, Ryan leaned down and pressed the spacebar. The computer screen lit up and pictures of Sienna filled the screen. He minimized them and froze. Her contact list was open alongside her calendar. Whoever had broken in knew exactly where Sienna was going to be and with whom. It would do no good to hide Sienna at a friend's house or a family member's house now. The only way she would be safe was if he was with her.

Ryan pushed his feelings aside and cleared the rest of the house. There was a guest room, master bedroom, living room, dining room, and kitchen with an eat-in nook. Ryan slid his gun into his waistband at the small of his back and took a deep breath.

Hooch leaned against him, and Ryan ran his hand absently down the dog's back. "It's up to you and me, Hooch. Think we can keep your mom safe?" Hooch wagged his tail and a plate from the kitchen table fell off and broke on the hardwood floor.

Ryan walked slowly with Hooch leaning against him to the front door. Sienna had her face plastered to the car window. "Stay here, boy. I'll go get her."

Hooch collapsed into a groaning heap on the porch and Ryan headed to the car with grim determination, forbidding himself to let his heart become involved. Sienna Ashton was just another witness to protect. That was all.

Sienna had always thought she was a badass. She didn't want to brag but when she was thirteen, Annie Davies had picked her up from school every day for a month and taught her self-defense. Annie had been an undercover

DEA agent before falling in love with Cade Davies, who retired from Special Forces to teach biology and coach the football team at Keeneston High School. When Annie and Cade got married, she took a job as a deputy sheriff in Keeneston.

Some people had complained she only got the job because of family connections, but from what Sienna had heard, that changed after just one night. There had been a fight at a football game that Annie and her best friend, Bridget, had been patrolling. After people saw them subduing a bunch of hired thugs, no one questioned her ever again.

But when Sienna had seen the door to her house open, all the confidence from that training fell to the wayside. She had been frozen and disappointed in herself. To make matters worse, when she saw Ryan go down on his knees to check on her dog, her nervous heart made a different kind of beat. Sienna had tried to ignore it as an adrenaline surge, but she was smarter than that. And even when she tried to ignore it, her heart wouldn't allow it. The second Ryan disappeared into her house with his gun drawn, Sienna's heart demanded to admit the one thing she had pushed away for almost a decade. She was in love with Ryan Parker.

"*Be okay, be okay, be okay,*" Sienna repeated over and over in her head, her eyes glued to the front door. It was bad enough her dog had clearly been knocked for a loop. She didn't want anything to happen to Ryan. If she focused on how mad she was that someone would hurt her dog, maybe she could keep her mind from delving further into her feelings for the boy who had grown up with her.

But that was the problem, wasn't it? He had never been like a little brother. He had been her first kiss at six, her first date at thirteen, and it had been Ryan who rescued her when her date to the junior prom dumped her at the last minute. It had always been Ryan. Even when she thought it would be uncool to date someone a grade younger, he had been watching out for her. He had walked her home after a party when her date got drunk. He had told her before she left for college he would always be only a phone call away if she ever needed him. And when she had the epiphany that he was all grown up, she told herself it had been because of his body. And what a body it was. But since then, she couldn't stay in a relationship with anyone else. And now she knew why with a certainty that left her just as dazed as his kisses. She loved him.

Sienna let out a breath when she saw him amble out the front door. She pushed open the door and ran toward him. She flung her arms around his waist and buried her head against his chest. It was so strong and warm, and the sound of his beating heart soothed her. "You're safe."

Ryan tentatively wrapped his arms around her. "I don't mean to sound like a guy, but did I miss something?"

"You came," Sienna said as tears started to fill her eyes, "and you took care of my dog."

"I'm still not certain that's a dog. But what are you talking about?"

"The day I left for college you promised me that if I ever needed you . . ." Sienna sniffed.

"That I would always only be a call away," Ryan finished softly for her as he ran his hand over her hair and held her against him.

Sienna nodded against his chest. She was going to say more, but the sound of a car pulling into her driveway stopped her. Ryan stiffened, and before she could blink she was pushed behind him. He had his hand on his gun tucked against the small of his back.

Sienna had to stand on her toes to see over Ryan's shoulder, but when she did she relaxed. "It's just Seth," she whispered.

If possible, Ryan became even more tense. "Seth who?"

"Seth Hayes, Malik's agent."

"Sienna? Are you okay?" Seth called out, taking the porch stairs two at a time.

Ryan reluctantly let Sienna step around him. He hated the look Seth had given him and the way Sienna smiled up at this character. He was all flash, no substance. It had only taken a split second for Ryan to see it, yet Sienna seemed oblivious.

"You heard about Malik?" Sienna asked as she went into Seth's open arms.

Hatred, jealousy, and a thousand different emotions swept through Ryan, and Seth shot him a sly smile, silently laying claim to the woman in his arms.

"I did. I flew here instantly to help with the arrangements for his funeral. His sister is distraught."

"That's nice of you," Sienna said, pulling away. "Seth Hayes, my friend Ryan Parker. Ryan, Seth was Malik's agent. Seth, Ryan and I grew up together. Where are my manners? Come inside. I'll put on some tea."

Ryan and Seth watched as Sienna absently went inside to start some tea. She flicked on the lights as she went, and Ryan was afforded his first real good look at Seth Hayes.

"Stuck in Friendsville," Seth chuckled with a smirk. "Just a little too late. Sienna and I started dating this week." Seth smacked Ryan's shoulder and started to step inside.

Ryan took a deep breath and followed. It would do no good to get into a pissing contest with her new guy.

Besides, he was right. There was nothing between them besides some heated kisses and what might have been.

"Damn dog!" Seth shouted from inside. Ryan hurried into the kitchen and found Hooch standing between Sienna and Seth with his fangs barred. Ryan tried not to laugh that the dog was so dinged up he was actually staring at the table three feet to the left of Seth, but the point was made nonetheless.

Ryan grinned and shot Seth a smirk as he walked past Hooch and gave him a quick ear scratch before walking over to a surprised Sienna and putting his arm around her.

"I don't know what's gotten into him. He did this the first time he met you, too. He's normally a big teddy bear," Sienna said in embarrassment. Pride filled Ryan when she didn't pull away from him and at the fact her mutant dog liked him better than this flashy sports agent.

Seth narrowed his eyes at Ryan. "It's okay. It'll take time for him to get used to someone new in your life. Now that I'm back in town, how about dinner tonight? You can stay at my hotel. I'm sure you don't want to be alone after such a hard day. Let me take care of you."

Sienna felt the growling before she heard it. She just couldn't tell if it was coming from the dog leaning against her or the man with his arm around her. She was torn, looking between Ryan and Seth, who seemed to be looking more at each other than at her. Oh, so that was how it was. Sienna almost rolled her eyes at the men and the dog in a staring match in her kitchen. She wasn't the reason Seth asked her out. He just saw another alpha male and wanted to show his dominance. But if Ryan were only here to protect her, then why would he care if she were with Seth? In the past, he would have been relieved to be rid of her.

Ryan tightened his grip on her waist and suddenly the day was too much. "That's very sweet of you, Seth, and I appreciate it. But I have hardly slept. I just want to curl up in bed . . . alone, and sleep. I'll see you both tomorrow."

"You can't," Ryan started to whisper, but Sienna held up her hand.

"I'm tired, I'm hungry, and I'm in no mood to argue. Goodnight, you two." Sienna shooed them out of her kitchen and through the front door. With a sweet smile, she shut the door in their surprised faces and threw the deadbolt.

"It's been months with no interest, and suddenly I have two men sniffing around me. Don't they know that you're the only man in my life?" Sienna scratched Hooch and headed for her bathroom. A long soak in the tub, something from her freezer, and then curling up in bed was her plan.

"I'm not leaving until you leave," Seth folded his arms over his chest and stared at Ryan.

"One date and you suddenly think you have claim to a woman I've known for her whole life? I don't think so. I'm not going anywhere." Ryan had never wanted to hit someone as much as he wanted to hit this man standing in front of him. He'd never been the jealous sort, but when it came to Sienna, all bets were off. He just had to make sure not to tell his dad. He didn't want to hear that nonsense about love again. He was just here to protect her, and he couldn't do that with this sleazeball around.

"It just took one date with me for her to want to see me again. You've been trying your whole life and have gotten nowhere. That's pretty pathetic."

Ryan clenched his jaw. Seth had hit a nerve big time. Then, with a deadly smile, he said, "You have it the other way around. The last eight years she's been chasing me. Now, it's time for you to go."

Seth's face turned a darker shade, and Ryan saw the anger in his eyes. He moved down the stairs of the porch and stopped at his car. "If you think I'm leaving before you, then you're crazy. Sienna is mine."

Ryan gave a little snort of amusement. "If you think Sienna Ashton belongs to any man, then you don't know her at all. How about we leave at the same time?"

If Ryan could just get him and his over-the-top Bentley convertible out of here, he could circle back and watch the house for the night. With a nod of his head, Seth opened his car door and Ryan went to his SUV. He pulled out of the driveway and headed for Keeneston, but not before stopping and making sure Seth drove off toward Lexington. As he waited in the dark with his lights off, he called the only person in Keeneston he knew he could trust to keep his mouth shut and not give him any crap about being in love. If his younger brother, Jackson, had been in town, he would have called him. But his cousin Dylan Davies was the next best thing.

"Dylan, it's Ryan. I need a favor."

Chapter Seven

Dylan Davies was Ryan's twenty-three-year-old cousin. He'd always been the black sheep of the huge Davies family. More like his Uncle Cy than his own father, Pierce. Cy had been a spy but when he wanted to, he could turn on the charm. Dylan was built like Cy, tall and muscular. His face was dark and brooding like Miles, the oldest of his Davies uncles. Dylan's size was an anomaly, considering his father was average height and build, and his mother, Tammy, was a little pixie of a woman with a sweet smile and fun spiky hair that brought her up to five-feet-two inches . . . if she really got a good spike going.

The rap on the door made Ryan smile. He hadn't seen or heard Dylan approach his car. His cousin had just completed Special Forces training. Dylan wouldn't tell anyone which division of the Special Forces, and that alone spoke volumes.

"Hey, cuz, new tattoo?" Ryan asked, taking in the black band encircling Dylan's thick bicep.

"Yep."

"How was training?"

"Good. You caught me right in time. I'm heading out tomorrow," Dylan said with his trademark serious face. Ryan shook his head. It was like trying to talk to Uncle Miles.

"Where are you going?"

Dylan just raised an eyebrow over his hazel eyes. The same hazel eyes most of the Davies grandkids had.

"So that's how it is?" Ryan asked.

"That's the way it's gotta be. Now why did you call me to Sienna's house? I'm not really the one to call for a pep talk if you finally grew the balls to ask her out."

Ryan thought about punching his cousin, but that would be a very bad decision. "Why does everyone think I'm the one after her? Has it dawned on any of you that she's the one who is begging me to go out with her?"

Dylan just snorted.

"Some cousin you are." Ryan shoved Dylan, and Dylan's lips quirked, but he didn't move. "Short story, Sienna overheard a murder on the phone."

"Malik Coleman?"

"That's right. And the killer picked up the phone and knows she heard. Dad called me out to keep an eye on her. Someone broke into her house tonight and copied her calendar and contacts. Plus there's this sports agent sniffing around her, and I want to make sure he or anyone else doesn't come back tonight while I run to the café to get us dinner."

"Damn. I'm sorry I can't stick around to help longer."

Ryan smiled at his younger cousin. "You're helping right now. I'll be back shortly."

"You can count on me. She'll be safely tucked inside when you get back. Oh, and bring me one of Zinnia's double bacon cheeseburgers," Dylan said before hopping out of the SUV and melting into the night.

Ryan shook his head. His cousin was scary. Thank goodness Dylan was on his side.

Ryan smiled as he stepped into the Blossom Café. It was almost closing time but the place was still packed. People waved to him and shouted out their greetings. It was good to be home. There was no other place like this in world.

"Hey, hon." Zinnia winked as she handed a tray of food to her sister, Poppy, to deliver. "I didn't know you were back in town."

"He's been back for three hours," John Wolfe called out from the special booth reserved just for the Rose sisters and their husbands.

"Then you should have told us," Poppy chided before coming to give him a hug. "It's nice to have you back. How long are you staying this time?"

"Don't know yet. I'm here to help Dad get ready for retirement."

John snorted and his wife, Lily Rae, rolled her eyes.

"Well, we're sure glad to have you back. Be careful, the Belles have reverted to their less-than-admirable ways under their new leadership. Neely Grace is fuming. But she's now a Keeneston Lady, so it's hard for her to do much."

"Thanks for the warning." Ryan cast a quick glance around the café and found danger at three o'clock. The Keeneston Belles was a group made up of Keeneston's most eligible women. They were the cheerleaders, the prom queens, and then sadly, some of the hottest women in town. The trouble was, hidden under their philanthropic deeds, was a more sinister plan to marry the most eligible bachelors of the town. They wanted power and money. Once they got it, they were able to join the elite Keeneston Ladies. Not all of them were bad. Neely Grace Rooney was an attorney in town, and she had gotten them back onto the straight and narrow. Apparently this new crop had wandered off the path. The way all of them at the table were devouring him with their eyes, he had just made the Most Wanted list.

"Hurry up and get over here!" Violet Fae hissed. Ryan looked to the table where the Rose sisters sat and dove for cover as the first Belle started her approach.

"There, there, you're safe now," Miss Violet whispered as she held him to her billowy bosom. Ryan struggled to breathe as she held tight, warding off the Belles.

"Really, Violet? I thought you gave that up when you married Anton!" her sister Daisy Mae chided.

"I have no idea what you're talking about," Miss Violet said innocently as she let Ryan up for air.

"I know we're not as young as we used to be, but if you need any help with Sienna's little *situation*, you just give us a call." John winked as Miss Lily nodded her white-haired head.

"We're always up for some action," Miss Violet said with what could only be akin to an evil smile and pulled a spatula from her apron while her husband Anton's smile faded.

"Not the type of action I thought you were talking about," he grumbled.

"We've been ready for years. Quite frankly, things have gotten a little dull around here," Miss Daisy told Ryan as she slipped a wooden spoon from her sleeve.

"I haven't operated on someone in decades. I'm getting antsy. If you get shot, I'm your guy," Charlie, Daisy's husband, told him. He had been a surgeon but when Ryan looked at Charlie's hands they had a slight shake to them. Ryan cringed at the thought. The collective age of the table had to be nearing five hundred fifty years or more. They'd break a hip if they saw any action . . . of any kind.

Ryan just nodded and the table showed off their dentures as they smiled back at him.

Poppy stopped by the table and shot a glance over her shoulder. "Good call. What can I bring you, hon?"

"Two double cheeseburgers, two orders of fries, a fried Buffalo chicken wrap, and a chocolate glop to go. Oh, and toss in another two burgers. Nothing on those two. To go, please."

"Sure thing." Poppy sent him a wink and headed to give her sister the ticket.

"That's nice of you to get dinner for Sienna, Dylan, and Hooch. They'll appreciate it. Be prepared to share some of your fries with that monstrosity she calls a dog," John said as he shook his head. "Not even I can find out what it really is."

"How on earth did you know?" Ryan should have expected this, considering John's innate ability to discover the town's gossip, but this was too much. The prevailing theories were that John had the town wiretapped or aliens told him.

John just smiled. "If your parents, Ahmed, Nabi, and all those Davies boys couldn't figure it out, then you won't either."

"He hasn't even told me, and I'm his wife." Lily sent him a glare before leaning forward and dropping her voice. "Now, tell us everything about our girl. How much trouble is she really in?"

Sienna rested her head against the back of the tub and let herself cry. The day had been overwhelming. She had thought she had cried it all out on Cole's shirt, but it all came back once she was alone. The way it felt to be alone and hearing Malik's life being taken from him. The feeling of knowing someone had been in her house made her drag Hooch along with her into the bathroom.

She reached over and picked up the wineglass from the small table next to the tub and took a sip. She would dig out a frozen dinner and fall asleep holding Hooch while dreaming of Ryan and hating herself for it. She was in love with a man who only wanted her to prove a point and that made her cry even harder.

Ryan pulled up in front of Sienna's house and was relieved to see that Seth's sports car was nowhere to be seen. He looked around for Dylan but didn't see him. Ryan reached into the passenger seat for the bag of food and almost jumped when he looked up to find Dylan standing at his door. Damn, he needed to learn how his cousin did that.

Ryan opened his door and handed one of the bags to Dylan. "I got you fries, too."

"Thanks. She's in the bathroom crying and drinking wine."

"How do you know that?" Ryan asked. Had Dylan gone inside?

"She left the bathroom window open." Dylan grinned and before Ryan could think twice, he planted his fist in his cousin's face. Dylan's head snapped back and a trickle of blood ran from the side of his lip.

Dylan's grinned widened. "So, that's how it is."

"No, it's not like that."

Dylan chuckled and popped a fry into his mouth. "You keep telling yourself that."

Ryan shook his hand out and reached back into his car. Why was everyone saying that to him? "Hey, sorry about the punch."

When he stood up, Dylan was gone and a key sat on the hood of his car. "You're such a drama queen," Ryan shouted. He heard a chuckle from the shadows and smiled. "Stay safe, cuz."

Ryan shut his car door and headed for the house. From deep within, the house shook. Hooch knew he was there. The thought of the dog being happy to see him made him smile as he took the spare key Dylan had found for him and unlocked the door. He followed the thumping sound and froze. Sienna was lying back in the tub with her eyes closed and one hand absently scratching Hooch's head as the other lay draped across her stomach under the clear bathwater, but when her hand moved upward Ryan cursed as he turned rock-hard at the same time Hooch's tail knocked the wine glass from the table and Sienna's eyes shot open.

Sienna was having a nice little dream. The warm water had lulled her into a light sleep as she trailed her hand over her breast to rest on her stomach. The wine had helped her relax and her thoughts had turned to the way her body had heated at Ryan's kiss earlier. The thought of him seeing her like this, of him wanting to be in the tub with her had her heated. She imagined legs entangled with legs as she leaned against his strong chest, and he wrapped his arms around her. His hands cupped her breasts . . . The sound of Hooch's tail shattering the wine glass hit at the same time as a whispered curse as Sienna had been awakened from her dream.

Her initial thought was to scream, which she did until a hand covered her mouth. She blinked back into reality, and Ryan's face came into focus.

"You're screaming enough to bring half of Keeneston

running," he said with breathlessness to his voice. And that's when she wanted to scream again. Three things hit Sienna hard. One, she was naked and had been enjoying a dream about the man currently standing in front of her while he watched. Two, the idea of him watching her turned her on even more. And three, these revelations weren't the only thing hard. When Ryan had pulled back his hand and stood up, she was at a very good level to investigate point number three. And investigate she did.

"Sienna, you keep staring and I'll go ahead and show you," Ryan said with both pain and hope laced in his voice.

Sienna couldn't tear her eyes from him. If he looked this good in those worn jeans that hugged his thighs just right, she could imagine what he looked like out of them.

"Um," Sienna muttered to buy her time to decide if she really wanted to find out. Well, of course she did, but did she want what would come after finding out? "I mean, a little peek wouldn't hurt."

Ryan sat the bag on the table and pulled off his shirt. She took a look at his chest sprinkled with brown hair and those one, two, three, four, five, six, seven, eight . . . sweet heavens, eight perfect ridges, she decided she had made a very good decision.

In his excitement to get to the food, Hooch gave Ryan a nudge that sent him sprawling backward. Ryan landed hard on his bottom as Hooch lumbered toward the brown bag.

Ryan shook his head as he tried not to laugh. "Ow! Um, that kind of killed the mood. I brought us dinner. You said you were hungry."

The lustful spell was broken, and Sienna sighed as she grabbed her robe from the hanger and slipped it on. "Thank you. I'll meet you in the kitchen."

"Right, um, yeah," Ryan muttered before shoving Hooch away from the bag.

Sienna quietly mourned when he slipped his shirt back on over his head and grabbed the bag of food. In under a second, he and Hooch were gone, and she stood alone in the bathroom.

"What was I thinking?" Sienna asked her reflection and then grinned at herself. "Oh, I know exactly what I was thinking."

With a goofy smile on her face, she brushed out her wet hair and dried off. She stepped into her boxers and tank top before heading for the living room.

Ryan sat on the couch with a beer in his hand, Hooch next to him. A glass of wine was on the coffee table next to her favorite wrap and favorite dessert. As if sensing her, Ryan turned around and smiled nervously. "Okay, Hooch, the lady has arrived."

Hooch gave a low bark and leaned forward to gobble up two burgers at once from his dog dish.

"I was teaching him how to be a gentleman. But, here, you gotta see this." Ryan smiled as he pulled out his cell phone.

Warmth flooded Sienna's heart as she watched Ryan absently pat her dog as he pulled up something on his phone. Not only had he remembered her favorite dinner, dessert, and wine, he'd also gotten her dog dinner.

Sienna now wished she had taken advantage of the bathroom incident, consequences be damned. A man who did this had to have some feelings for her. She just hoped if she decided to put her heart on the line she'd survive if he left her standing alone again.

"Look at this. It's got to be a record or something." Ryan handed her his phone and Sienna broke out laughing at the picture of Hooch staring at the burgers with a lone strand of drool hanging a good two feet from his jowl. And if she thought her heart was his before, it was definitely all in now.

Chapter Eight

Sienna woke with something wet dripping on her face. She didn't want it to be morning, so she nuzzled her head against the warm pillow. The pillow groaned and the dripping continued.

Sienna opened her eyes and blinked. Her head was in Ryan's lap. His arm was wrapped around her shoulder and his other hand was resting on her head. Hooch stood over her, prancing in place, which sent drops of drool falling from his jowls.

"I think he needs to go out. But I didn't want to wake you up," Ryan said quietly. He ran his hand over her head in a soothing way that made her long to close her eyes and snuggle closer.

"Were you up all night?" Sienna reluctantly sat up.

"Not all. I got enough sleep. What's on our schedule for the day? Breakfast at the café?" Ryan asked as he stretched.

"You want to take me? To the café? You know everyone in town will be betting on our marriage date by noon, right?" Sienna asked in surprise.

Ryan cringed. "So maybe not the café, but I did spend the night with you. I should get a good morning kiss, at least." Ryan snaked his arm out, and Sienna let out a surprised gasp as he pulled her down into his lap and placed his lips on hers. This time it was different. It was softer, more romantic. He took his time savoring her and by the time he let her up, Sienna was happily dazed.

Ryan sent her a slow smile that had her wanting to strip naked and leap on him. She was contemplating the idea when he slapped her on the ass. "Come on, Sleeping Beauty. Let's get breakfast. I just got a text from Dad that said Detective Braxton wants to meet with you."

Ryan grabbed the box of garbage bags and a roll of duct tape and headed outside with Hooch while Sienna got dressed. Even though nothing happened the night before, he felt more alive than ever. When he woke from a night of sex with whichever woman he was seeing at that time, it never left him feeling as good as waking with Sienna snuggled up to him with his arms wrapped around her.

It was just because it was different, he told himself. It wasn't what he was used to. Ryan smiled. But he could definitely get used to it. He opened the tailgate and pulled out bag after bag and taped them together as Hooch roamed his kingdom.

"Come on, Hooch," Ryan called as the front door opened. Sienna stepped out in a sundress, carrying a suit jacket over her arm.

"What are you doing?" she asked, closing the door.

"We're all ready for you," Ryan grunted, as he helped Hooch into the plastic covered back of his SUV.

"You're taking Hooch with us?" Sienna asked in wonder while Ryan closed the door on Hooch's happy, slobbering doggy face.

"Of course. I don't want anything to happen to the big . . . thing."

Ryan moved to the bottom step but was almost unprepared for the woman who hurtled herself into his arms. She had jumped halfway down the steps, and he had caught her. He dropped the duct tape and stumbled back but didn't bother asking why she had done that when she wrapped her legs around his waist, ran her fingers through his short dark hair, and stuck her tongue into his mouth. Instead, he grabbed her ass with one hand and wrapped his other around her back, keeping her tight against him as their tongues spoke to each other.

"Someone's coming," Ryan whispered against her lips. His shaft was pressing against a very warm spot, and both of them were flushed and breathing heavily.

The way Sienna jumped off and hid behind him, Ryan thought it was someone dangerous. He had his gun drawn by the time he turned around and aimed it at his father's smug face.

"What the hell, Dad?" Ryan asked as he put his gun away.

Cole's smile grew. "I just wanted to check on Sienna on the way to work."

Ryan felt Sienna poke her head over his shoulder. "Thank you, Mr. Parker. We were just heading to meet with Detective Braxton."

"Yeah, that's what it looked like you were doing." Cole chuckled. Ryan thought about giving his father the middle finger, but he had a feeling his dad would still whoop him for disrespect even if he was retiring soon. "Well, call me if you need anything. I think I'm going to get some breakfast at the café. See you kids later."

Sienna let her head drop against Ryan's back as Cole drove off. In five minutes, the whole town would know what happened. He didn't suddenly decide to go to the café instead of work. Nope, Cole had an inside scoop on the newest bet being placed in Keeneston.

"I can't believe we got busted making out like horny teenagers by your dad," she groaned against Ryan's shirt. How did he smell so good?

"At least he came when he did. Five minutes later and we'd have been naked."

Sienna didn't know if that was a threat or a promise. Hooch woofed from the back of the SUV, and Sienna forced herself to take a step back. She was a smart, educated woman. She worked with sexy famous men all day long, and she'd never lost control like she did with Ryan. She needed to take charge of her body and her mind.

"We better meet with the detective." Sienna took a deep breath and got into the car. She could do this. It was just a matter of mind over body. If there was anything she was a master of, it was the mind.

"What are you doing?" Ryan asked skeptically when he started the car.

"Getting my mind focused."

"What?" Ryan snickered.

"I'm doing an exercise I teach my players to be focused and ready for a game," Sienna told him as she took another deep breath.

"I was that good, huh?"

Sienna's response was cut off by Hooch's happy woofing when Ryan started driving toward Lexington.

Ryan and Sienna sat quietly in the meeting room at the police station as they waited for Detective Braxton. He was focusing on the number of cracks in the tile floor so he wouldn't focus on the feeling of Sienna's legs wrapped around his waist. He needed to get in the game. Maybe Sienna could teach them him those focus techniques she was doing in the car. Because whatever that was, it seemed to work. She sat next to him, holding Hooch's leash and making sure not even their shoulders brushed.

"Dear Lord, you brought the buffalo with you!" Detective Braxton froze in place as Hooch stared. A pool of slobber had formed on the tile where his head had been resting.

"Agent Parker, Dr. Ashton, thank you for coming in," Detective Braxton recovered. "I know the team's season is gearing up, and I was hoping you could let me know if anyone is acting differently. A little too nosey or a little distant."

Sienna nodded her head. "I'll do whatever I can as long as it doesn't violate my doctor-patient confidentiality."

"And how have you been doing? Has anyone approached you or made you uneasy?" Detective Braxton asked as she shot Hooch a sideways glance.

"That's my fault." Ryan felt as if he was a rookie. "There was a break-in while she was at the stadium yesterday. I meant to call you."

Ryan saw Braxton's jaw tighten while she fought to rip into him for such a mistake. "Start at the beginning," she ordered.

Ryan told her about Hooch, the computer, and Sienna's information being accessed.

"Nothing else was taken?"

Sienna shook her head.

"And nothing else happened last night?" the detective asked. Ryan looked to Sienna and saw her blush. So did Braxton, and by the eye roll she gave Ryan, he now knew she understood why he forgot to call it in.

"Nothing that would help you. Have you found anything?" Ryan asked.

"The neighbor saw a man in black clothes with his face covered in a black ski mask enter the house. She called 9-1-1 as well. She didn't see a car and couldn't even guess at the intruder's height. The preliminary forensics has come back, and we have fibers, but no prints or DNA. But now we know we have our next target."

"Me? We don't know he's after me. Maybe he was just checking to see if I heard anything."

A knock at the door stopped Braxton from answering. "The sister is here," a uniform said.

Braxton looked grim as she nodded. "Malik's sister is here, and I need to talk to her. Keep an eye on her," she ordered Ryan. "And next time, call me when someone breaks in. Let's just hope it doesn't get worse."

Sienna stood from the uncomfortable chair and shook the detective's hand. Was she really the next target? She'd been scared about the break-in, but it hadn't seemed malicious. Nothing was destroyed and there was no threat, but she wasn't law enforcement. Maybe they knew something she didn't.

"I need to check in at the office. It shouldn't take long. The team's activities have been cancelled today. Tomorrow there is a full practice, and then they are going as a team to Malik's visitation."

Ryan opened the car door for her and took Hooch's leash. "No problem. I wouldn't mind snooping around some."

"And you think they'll tell you something they wouldn't tell me?" Sienna scoffed. "These guys tell me everything. You're just a stranger to them."

"We'll see." Ryan sent her a wink, and Sienna rolled her eyes.

The trip to the stadium didn't take long, and before she knew it she was standing at the elevator with Hooch on one side and Ryan on the other. The doors opened and Janice looked up from her desk.

"I see you took my advice." She glanced quickly at Ryan and sent Sienna a wink. "Here are your messages."

Sienna refused to look at Ryan. Janice's face darkened as she blushed and when she became short of breath, Sienna knew Ryan had given her that smile again.

"Crap. My dad wants to see me. Is he in his office?" Sienna asked the flustered secretary. "Earth to Janice."

"What?"

"My dad, where is he?" Sienna asked again.

Janice just pointed down the hall, and Sienna slapped her hand against Ryan's chest. "Stop flustering our secretary. Bring that smile down a couple watts."

"Sorry," Ryan told her, but he didn't sound sorry at all. "So, let's go see your dad. It's been a while since I've seen him."

Sienna shook her head. "Oh, no. I am not prepared to explain your presence to my dad."

"Sweetheart, by now the whole town knows I was at your house this morning." Sienna tried to ignore the way her body reacted when he called her sweetheart, but it was hard.

"Well, are you ready to answer those questions to my *dad*? You know, the one with the tendency to meet my dates at the door with a whole football team of men ready to squash them if they hurt me?"

Sienna smirked when Ryan lost a little of his color, but then he smiled and she tried not to get lost in his hazel eyes.

Today they were a little greener than brown. "So, we're dating, huh?"

"Um . . . um," Sienna sputtered.

Ryan leaned forward and pressed his lips to her ear. "And just think, I left you speechless, and I haven't even touched you yet. Wait until I get you naked." Ryan stood up and winked. "I'll meet you in your office."

Sienna continued to try to form words as Ryan sauntered down the hall.

"Sienna, was that Ryan Parker?"

Sienna turned and saw her father striding down the hall in his uniform of jeans, worn cowboy boots, and a polo shirt with Ashton Farm embroidered on the pocket.

"Yes. He's in town helping Mr. Parker get ready for retirement and asked if he could come meet the team."

Her father, Will, had been an NFL quarterback before taking over the family farm and now focused on racing and training thoroughbreds. Her brother, Carter, had inherited their father's square jaw and brown hair, along with his height. Sienna had inherited her mother's green eyes and curves. She also got her height, or lack thereof, from her mother. Which was probably the reason behind her love of high heels. Although, she'd been told that was inherited from her mother as well.

"That's nice to let him come with you. So, you two resolved whatever it was . . ." Will made some kind of motion with his hands.

"Ew, stop asking about my love life." Sienna's nose wrinkled and then she felt like running in the other direction when her father's eyes narrowed.

"Love life? So that's what happened between you two? I'll kill him. I knew that boy was trouble since the time he kissed you when you were six."

"No, Dad, that's not what happened. What happened is none of your business. Tell me again why I agreed to work for you." Sienna let out a long breath and suddenly felt very tired.

"Sienna, I'm glad I caught you here." Her father's eyes narrowed at the sound of Seth's voice interrupting them.

"Good morning, Seth. Dad, this is Seth Hayes; he's an agent for some of our players. Seth, this is my father, Will Ashton, one of the Thoroughbreds' owners." Sienna watched as her father turned hard and shook Seth's hand until Seth cringed. Only then did her dad smile.

"It's nice to see you again, sir. We've met a couple times with my players," Seth tried to say with a smile as he shook out his hand.

Her father didn't bother to respond but instead pulled out his ringing phone. "It's Cole. I need to talk to him."

"No, Dad!" Sienna tried to call out after him, but he had already disappeared behind his office door.

"Most dads like me. I can't believe he didn't remember me," Seth complained.

"My dad's not like most dads," Sienna said, knowing that was the understatement of the year. She also knew she had all of five minutes before her dad tracked down Ryan and killed him.

"Look, Seth, I'm sorry, I don't have time to talk right now."

"That's all right. I have a meeting with Jaylen. I just wanted to see if you wanted me to pick you up for Malik's visitation tomorrow. I don't think you should go alone. I know you were close to him."

"That's very nice of you, but . . ."

"She already has a date for tomorrow."

Sienna whipped around and saw Ryan walking toward

them. She didn't want to, but she felt a little thrill when he put his arm around her and smiled down at her.

"I think we need to talk. Privately." Seth looked pointedly at her and she nodded. First, she just needed to figure out what was going on with Ryan. She didn't want him waltzing back into her life and taking it over only to leave her broken-hearted. She had to find out what was between them one way or the other before she could know what to say to Seth.

"I do, too. When are you leaving town?"

"I'm flying in and out of town all week. I'll be here tomorrow for the private visitation, and then I'm gone the following day when the public one is at the stadium. But I'll be back for the funeral service. His sister is going to sprinkle his ashes here and at the beach."

Sienna pursed her lips and tried not to cry. "I know he wanted to retire there. He would like that very much."

She felt Ryan give her a little squeeze but before she could end the conversation, her father's door opened. "Ryan! Get in here!"

"Somebody's in trouble," Sienna sang as Ryan grimaced.

"Don't worry, Parker, I'll take care of her while you're gone," Seth gloated.

The second the door closed Sienna turned on Seth. "I'm not some bone for the two of you to fight over. You wanted to talk, fine. We had a great time when we went out. There was a possibility of something more there, but with the way you two are acting, I'm not interested. Now, if you want to grow up, then give me a call and we'll see . . . maybe."

Sienna stepped around Seth and walked with her head held high down the hall.

"Yo, Doc, how ya doing?"

"Peachy," Sienna snapped before catching herself. "I'm sorry. A couple of guys . . . never mind. How are you?"

"Doc, the love doctor is in. What can Dr. Jaylen do to get the motion back in the ocean?"

Sienna cracked up. "You just did it. Thanks. So, you have a meeting with Seth?"

Jaylen turned serious. "Time to go over the accounts. I've been reading up on interest rates and different kinds of mortgages like you suggested. I got this down."

"Excellent. Now go get that house." Sienna slapped him on the back and Jaylen winked before heading to the conference room across the hall from her father's office.

Sienna unlocked her door and looked nervously back at her father's closed door before stepping into her office with Hooch. It was time to see what Ryan was made of. The question was how badly did she want him to pass inspection? Who was she kidding? She knew exactly what she wanted. She wanted Ryan to see her as a woman to love, not a trophy for a pissing contest with another man. She wanted her father to approve because no matter how old she was, she always wanted her father's approval. And she wanted Ryan Parker.

Chapter Nine

R yan shook Will Ashton's hand and didn't even blink
when her father crushed his bones together. Instead, he
gave a slow smile and squeezed back. The two of them
stood squeezing their hands in a silent war.

"I talked to your father," Will said and then squeezed
Ryan's hand harder.

"You did? And how is Dad this morning?" Ryan asked,
still squeezing.

"You should know. He said he saw you and Sienna this
morning." *Squeeze.*

"Yes, we've spent the morning together." *Squeeze.*

"And the night?" *Squeeze.*

Ryan had to prevent himself from wincing. "Is none of
your business."

"When it pertains to my daughter, it is always my
business. Cut the crap, Ryan. You know the whole town
knows you had a thing for Sienna, but she never
reciprocated. Then something happened and the situation
suddenly reversed. You never asked her out again. Instead
you left for the FBI. Now you're back the day after a friend
of hers is murdered."

Ryan shrugged. "I'm just helping my dad."

Squeeze. "It seems you're spending too much time with
my daughter to help your dad. Why are you here?"

"We're friends. I'm just saying hi." *Squeeze.*

"When your father saw you this morning, that's not all you were doing or he wouldn't have placed a bet at the Blossom Café that involves the two of you being something more than friends." *Squeeze.*

"And if we were?" Ryan asked as he squeezed with all he had. He couldn't believe he even asked that, but he liked Will, and if he was going to be with Sienna, then he wanted his blessing.

Will dropped his hold on Ryan's hand, and Ryan put his behind his back and stretched it out. It hurt so badly.

"Sit down, we need to talk. I know there's something going on, and you're going to tell me all of it."

Sienna sat back in her chair and let out a long breath after returning her last call. Her respite hadn't lasted long though; her cell phone began to ring.

"Ryan is in town and you didn't call me?" Sydney practically yelled into the phone.

"I'm not talking to you about your cousin. That would be weird."

"No, weird would be talking to Sophie about it since they're practically twin cousins. They have some bond with being born at the same time on the same day, Christmas at that, but whatever. It doesn't affect me, so dish."

"He's in my dad's office right now. My dad called him in, and I haven't heard from them in thirty minutes."

Sydney cursed. "Your dad's going to jail for murder."

"I know, I thought it would be Ryan after he heard Seth asking me out."

"Whoa!" Sydney cried out. "Back this train up. Seth?

Ryan? No, this is too much. Dinner. Tonight. At the café. I want to hear all about this."

"Okay," Sienna laughed. "I'll see you at six. Examining my love life could take all night."

Sienna hung up in a much better mood. This was her life. Not her father's. And she needed to rescue the man she loved from certain death.

Sienna opened her door and stalked down the hallway. The sound of raised voices worried her until she realized they came from the conference room. Jaylen stood up and tossed a handful of papers at Seth and stormed from the room.

"Jaylen, what's the matter?" Sienna called out as the running back barreled down the hall.

"He's upset he can't afford the house he wants," Seth said, coming to stand beside her. "That's the trouble with some of these players. They think they have all the money in the world, so why not drop fifty thousand on a night out with the guys or rent a yacht for a couple weeks? What's a couple million? Then they see the reports and realize they've spent their nest egg."

Sienna felt horrible. She knew how badly Jaylen wanted that house.

"Maybe you could help me with him?" Seth asked. "Between the two of us, we can get him back on the straight and narrow financially and mentally. Let's talk about it over dinner tonight."

"I'm sorry, I already have dinner plans. And Seth, I know we had just started dating, but I need to stop seeing you personally. As you know, Ryan and I have a history, and I'd like to see where it goes. I just need time," Sienna said with her hand on his arm. She felt him tense, but he didn't have time to say anything as they turned at the sound of her father's door opening. The sight that greeted her stopped her from saying anything further. Her father had his arm around Ryan's shoulder, and they were both laughing.

"Damn good to see you again, son," her father said as he shook Ryan's hand. "Take care of my daughter."

"You have my word," Ryan said and returned the handshake.

"What the hell?" Seth exploded.

Ryan felt Will tense beside him. Their talk was something akin to walking through a field full of landmines while blindfolded. Ryan prided himself on being a strong man, physically and mentally, but nothing had prepared himself for Will's stare. In the end, he broke and explained exactly what he was doing here. He expected Will to lose it, but that was when the older man leaned forward, gave Ryan a pat, and said, "There's no one else I would trust to look after my little girl."

At that moment, Ryan had never felt more pride. And at this moment, he'd never felt such amusement.

"Excuse me, young man?" Will said with a deadly tone.

Seth looked flustered and Sienna looked so cute as she stared with confusion at him and her father standing side by side that Ryan sent her a wink just to mess with both further.

"I thought you hated him. I was just surprised, that's all." Seth turned to Sienna quickly. "I'll see you soon for dinner to discuss Jaylen."

"Let's set up a meeting at the office," Sienna said with a weak smile.

Seth didn't respond. Instead he went to pet Hooch, and the dog growled. Ryan and Will smiled at each other as

Sienna's eyes quickly narrowed.

"What's going on with you two?" she asked as soon as Seth was gone.

Will leaned forward and gave his daughter a kiss on her cheek. "He's just the first man you've dated that I approve of."

"You approve? Of Ryan?"

"I couldn't have picked better myself. In fact, I believe your mother and Paige had this planned twenty-eight years ago."

"But, we're not . . ." Sienna started before Ryan grabbed her hand.

"But we need to go. Things to do and all that. We'll see you soon." Ryan shook Will's hand and grabbed Hooch's leash, nudging Sienna down the hall.

"I don't know what to say," she murmured beside him.

Ryan shot her a wink. "Twice in one day and I still haven't gotten you naked yet."

Ryan sat on the back porch of Sienna's house and tossed treats to Hooch. Sienna had just left to meet Sydney for dinner, and if there was one place he didn't need to worry about her being safe, it was the Blossom Café. The sound of the ATV reached him before he saw it crest the small hill. The figure in all black rode it comfortably to the back fence and stopped. He adjusted the straps of his backpack and, in an easy hop, cleared the five-foot fence.

"Hi, Nash. How are you?" Ryan asked as the figure crossed the backyard. Nash Dagher was the apprentice for the security team protecting the Rahmi royal family in Kentucky. He was a year older than Ryan but had spent the past four years doing the same things Ryan had—trying to get himself killed.

"Good. Just got back from Afghanistan. The rolling hills of Kentucky never looked so beautiful after three weeks in those mountains," Nash told him as he took off his backpack and took a seat.

"I've got something I turned over to Ahmed's U.S. government contacts, though." Nash's black hair was shaved short. His normally tanned skin was darker, showing the amount of time he'd spent outdoors this past month. For a kid who had come to Keeneston from the small Middle Eastern island country of Rahmi weighing slightly more than a wet dishrag, Nash's transformation was nothing short of astounding.

Ahmed, the previous head of security and all-around international badass, had trained Nabi, the current head. Now Nash was here. Since Nabi and his wife, Grace, had started a family seven years ago, Nash had been taking over more and more responsibilities. But with his intense physical training regiment and the Rose sisters' diet of good Southern food, Nash had put on eighty pounds of muscle in addition to growing several inches.

"What did you find?" Ryan asked, tossing Nash a drink.

"There's lots of chatter of a big terrorist statement that's going to be made on US soil. The natives called him *Rais*. Literally translated to someone who leads. He's doing things differently over there. He's not ruling out of fear, but almost through dangling riches in front of the poorest of the poor and promising power to the wealthy who have been disrespected."

Ryan put it together in a second. "We have him on our radar, but we call him The Suit. We can't pinpoint his location or even his real identity. Could you?"

"No, and trust me, I tried."

Ryan nodded his head. If what he'd heard about Ahmed in his younger days were true, and Ahmed had taught Nash, then he knew Nash had gone dark to get this information.

"Now," Nash said with a smile, "since I've already placed my bet with Miss Daisy about how long it will take until you and Sienna are engaged—I had within one week—and you've invited me to her place, are you here to tell me your good news?"

"Not exactly. The real reason I'm here . . ."

"Yeah, I know. John isn't the only one with resources." Nash winked.

"Picked up her address on the scanner?"

"You bet your ass we did. Nabi about lost his mind. Faith was sick and Grace was at a horse show so Nabi made me sneak over to find out what happened."

"How is his daughter?" Ryan asked, taking a slug of beer.

"She's fine now. Turned out to be an ear infection. So, what can I do to help?"

"What you don't know is someone paid Sienna a little visit yesterday and had a look at her computer. I need some surveillance equipment. The good stuff that is completely invisible."

"No problem. Where do you want it?"

Ryan pointed to a cluster of trees. "There, the back door, the front porch, by the mailbox, in the kitchen, living room, and outside the bedroom window."

"Piece of cake. I have the outdoor equipment with me now," Nash told him as he opened his backpack.

"Thanks a lot, Nash. So, what's going on with you and

my cousin Sophie?" Ryan took another sip of beer. It was so much more fun being on this side of the questioning.

Nash shrugged a shoulder. "I thought something at one point. It seemed like there was mutual interest, but then, nothing. I've hardly seen her since she graduated college."

"As if you haven't run her name through your little supercomputer to know exactly what she's up to."

"Haven't had time. Nothing ever happened between us, so it's not like I have any claim to her. She chose to leave, and she chose not to tell me, or anyone, where she went. Besides, my time is now being occupied," Nash quipped as he lifted the bottle to his lips.

"You're dating someone? Who?"

"I didn't say I was dating. I said my time was occupied. Now, we have some work to do if we want to get these cameras up before Sienna gets back from the café."

Sienna opened the door to the café and was met with complete silence. Every person stopped talking and looked at her left hand. As if they were one being, they all turned to Miss Daisy's table and started calling out dates. So this is what it felt like to be the subject of a bet.

"Sienna!" Syd called out. "You wouldn't get engaged without telling me first, right?"

"Of course I'd tell you."

"Good, next Sunday's game at the Thoroughbreds' stadium sounds romantic, doesn't it?"

Sienna took a seat across the table from her friend and shook her head. "One, I'm not proposing to anyone. Two, Ryan and I aren't even dating."

"Liar, liar, pants on fire. Cole called my dad and told him that Ryan met with Will today and got his blessing."

"Marshall knows now, too?" Sienna groaned. Sydney's

dad, the sheriff, would tell every other Davies in the town, and that meant every single person in this room now knew her father approved of her dating Ryan.

"Really, we aren't dating," Sienna protested.

"That's not what Uncle Cole said."

Sienna raised her hand in the air to get Poppy's attention. Zinnia was busy in the kitchen and her sister was helping serve tonight.

"Poppy, I need some Rose Sisters' Special Iced Tea. Just bring the pitcher."

That quieted the café again, and they all looked to Sydney, who in turn gave them the thumbs-up sign.

"You're no longer my best friend," Sienna grumbled.

"Sure I am. Now spill."

"I told you, we're not dating."

Sydney gave her best friend the "I don't believe you" look.

"We may not be officially dating," Sienna whispered, caving to the look. "But he's kissed me."

"Was it hot?"

"It was *melt my panties, tear my clothes off* kind of hot. Until his father showed up while my legs were wrapped around Ryan's waist, his hand on my ass, and our tongues doing way more than talking."

"*O-M-G!*"

"Shhh," Sienna scolded, but it was too late. The entire café had heard Sydney's squeal and bets were being placed left and right now.

"Here you go, hon," Poppy said, setting down the pitcher of tea between them.

Sydney poured the two glasses and handed one to Sienna. "To hot men and even hotter kisses."

"Cheers to that," Sienna said, taking a big sip. The key

to drinking this bourbon-laced drink was to get the first three sips down, and then everything else was smooth as silk.

"Are you finally going to admit you've liked Ryan for years?" Sydney asked as she took another sip.

"Maybe."

"Liars have to take another drink," Sydney taunted.

Sienna laughed and took a sip. She loved her best friend. And Sydney knew Ryan had intrigued her since their role reversal years ago.

"Are you finally going to ask all the things you've wondered about for the past eight years?" Sydney asked, reading her mind.

"I sure hope so," Sienna said. The two dissolved into giggles. "What about you? You never mention guys anymore."

"Much to Great-Grandma Wyatt's dismay. I've been so busy I've had to live vicariously through you. And let me tell you, until tonight that wasn't doing much for me."

"How is Mrs. Wyatt doing?" Sienna asked seriously. Mrs. Wyatt's husband passed away years ago and since then, Mrs. Wyatt had dressed in her big hats, flowing dresses, and bright red lipstick every day. She said it was what Beauford would have wanted. But last year she tripped in the stables and broke a hip. Since then, she'd never recovered all the way.

"She's hanging in there. I worry about her. Mom is over there quite a bit and she's hired a nurse to stay with Great-Grandma so she'll never be alone. Enough about sad things, though. Tonight I need to live vicariously through you. Does Ryan make your heart go pitter-patter?"

Sienna tossed her napkin across the table and hit her friend square in the face.

"Seriously, Sienna. Is he the one? You've been dating and discarding men for years, and I think it's because none of them were Ryan. I think you think that, too."

Sienna's eyes narrowed as she poured another glass of tea. "That's a lot of thinking."

Sydney tossed the napkin back across the table as two bowls of bread pudding in bourbon butter sauce were set down in front of them.

Sienna leaned forward and lowered her voice so no one could hear. "You know I love him, even if this is the first time I've said it out loud. I don't know when it happened, but I do."

"I know when it happened. When you two were spying on Nabi and Grace eight years ago."

Sienna shook her head. "It started before then. He has this habit of rescuing me without making me feel like I was rescued. And then there was always the support he gave me on my education. He never thought anything was too big of a challenge. I think it started then." Sienna took a sip of her tea and whispered, "But that night when he kissed me all those years ago didn't hurt."

The two friends dissolved into a fit of the giggles.

"Ladies, I sure hope neither of you is driving home. By the way you two are giggling, I'm going to assume that's an empty pitcher of Rose Sisters' Special Iced Tea."

Sienna looked up and saw two state troopers. "Who's your friend, Matt?" Then she squinted. "Oh! It's just you."

"Yeah, I'm giving you two ladies a ride home."

"I don't think you're the kind of ride she's looking for tonight," Sydney snorted.

"Okay," Matt chuckled as he reached out to help both women stand, "if you keep that up, I won't let you play with the siren."

"I want to play with the siren," Sydney said with wide eyes, stumbling forward.

"It's been a while since Sydney had her siren played with," Sienna drunkenly whispered at the top of her voice.

Matt's grin grew even wider as her best friend smacked her arm. "Shhh, or I'm going to tell everyone you and Ryan have the hots for each other," Sydney said in the same non-whisper.

"Oh, honey, we already know that." Miss Lily grinned from her table.

"We've known that for twenty years," Miss Daisy said without blinking an eye.

Sydney pulled Matt and Sienna to a stop. "But did you know they've been k-i-s-n . . . no, that's not right. K-i-s-s-g- . . . well, kissing since he got back?"

"That we didn't know," Miss Violet smiled as she slipped a ten-dollar bill from her bra and handed it to her sister. "Engaged by next week."

Sienna stumbled across Matt and smacked her friend on the arm. "Why are you my best friend again?"

"Because I'm going to let you play with the siren," Sydney laughed as Matt helped them into his cruiser.

Chapter Ten

Ryan watched Nash hop the fence back onto Mo and Dani's property. They had all of the cameras installed and turned on. Ryan opened his tablet and saw the open feeds. He turned it off and set it down on the small table on the back porch. He picked up his beer, took a sip, and looked out over the rolling hills bathed in moonlight.

As he scratched Hooch's head, he realized that the whole time he was in L.A., he had missed Kentucky. But since being home, he hadn't missed L.A.

"Maybe it's time I moved back home after all," Ryan told Hooch. In response, the dog growled. "Okay, so maybe you don't want me to come back."

The screen door gave a slight creak and Hooch growled again. Ryan didn't have time to look at the person trying to sneak up on him. Instead, he dove off the chair right as the sound of a taser crackled through the air.

Ryan rolled up onto his legs and reached for his gun. He silently cursed, remembering he left it in the living room. The man dressed all in black stepped forward again, but Hooch's large body lying on the porch stopped his forward progress.

"Mr. Parker, your company has been requested," the man said in accented English. He'd heard similar phrases and accents when he was in L.A. But, what would Abdul and his crew be doing in Kentucky? Abdul was in solitary confinement at a secret FBI facility. This didn't make sense.

"I'm sorry, I don't accept invitations without knowing the host." Ryan's mind was running at full speed, trying to find a connection. Did this have anything to do with Sienna or was this about his undercover operation in L.A.?

"I've been instructed not to take no for an answer. If you don't agree, then I'll just come back for your girlfriend," the man told him as they started to circle Hooch.

"I'll be happy to go with you. Let me just call some of my buddies and we'll make a party of it." Ryan kept his eyes on the man across from the dog as they slowly continued to circle around Hooch. It would only be a matter of seconds before the man in black made his move, so Ryan decided to make it first.

"Very humorous, Mr. Parker, but . . ." Ryan didn't give him a chance to finish. He dove over the dog and tackled the masked man at chest level. The momentum carried them into the porch rail. Ryan heard the taser drop a second before the railing broke and they fell from the porch.

With a bone rattling hit, the two landed on top of the railing, now covering the dewy grass some feet from the porch. Ryan thought he had the upper hand, but when he leapt up, the masked man did as well. Hooch howled from the porch and thumped his tail as he watched the two men size each other up.

Enough waiting . . . Ryan kicked out and connected with the man's knee. The stranger grunted, but Ryan had been too far away for the impact to do any serious damage. The man jumped forward and, just like that, the circling was over.

The assailant connected a punch on Ryan's face. He felt

the blood dripping down around his eye, but that didn't stop him from landing an elbow to the man's midsection. Air whooshed from his body, and he instinctively bent at the waist. Ryan pressed his advantage and followed up with an elbow to his opponent's upper back. As the man went down, he hooked his arms around Ryan's knees. Ryan teetered before falling backward.

Hooch barked and Ryan doubled his efforts. "Are you the one who hurt my dog last time you were here?" Ryan asked. They both scrambled away from each other.

"That was my superior. And he wants to see you. You're coming with me, Mr. Parker, or I'll simply kill you and take you that way."

"I'd like to see you try. You haven't had too much success yet, and I still have my secret weapon." Ryan grinned.

The sound of a siren broke through the night and steadily grew louder. The masked man looked quickly toward the road and Ryan leapt. They went down in heap of fists, elbows, and palm heel strikes. As the siren grew closer, the fighting became more frenzied. They rolled and Ryan lost his upper advantage. With a swift uppercut to his chin, Ryan was seeing lights — red and blue lights, to be specific.

"Ryan!" he heard two women scream.

"Police, freeze!" he heard a voice call out. The man who had tried to punch his lights out didn't listen. They never did. And the weight on his chest was relieved as he rolled off Ryan and took off toward the horse farm. Good, let Nash catch him.

Matt's face appeared a second later. "Are you okay?"

"Fine. Help me up." Ryan held out his hand to the state trooper and groaned in pain as he stood up.

"How are you feeling?" Matt asked.

"It sounds as if it's thundering all around. I can feel it echoing in my head."

Matt grinned as Ryan rubbed his chin. "Then you're all right. That's just Hooch's tail thumping on the porch."

"Oh my gosh, Ryan!" Sienna cried as she and Sydney weaved their way toward him.

"Did I get hit harder than I thought, or are they falling-down drunk?" Ryan asked as he watched them veer to the right and then to the left.

"There was a pitcher of Rose Sisters' Iced Tea involved. I thought it best if I drove them home. Now, would you care to tell me about this little incident?"

The sound of an ATV started to fill the night and Matt's walkie-talkie went off. Sienna and Sydney stumbled up to Ryan.

"You're hurt!" Sienna cried, touching his bleeding eye. "What happened?"

"Lexington requesting 10-66 for a high priority 10-82." Matt responded with his ETA and tried not to laugh as Sienna and Sydney "helped" Ryan.

"Copy that," dispatch said and then rattled off an address in Lexington.

Sienna could hardly pay attention to Ryan with the sound of Mo's security guards on ATVs racing toward them, mixed with Hooch's tail thumping and Matt's radio. All she knew was the man she loved was injured, and she wanted to take him inside and protect him. But then the dispatch started talking again and a feeling of dread had her falling against Ryan.

"Wait," Sienna shouted and turned to Matt. "What was that address?"

Matt repeated it as three of Mo's guards on the ATVs veered off in the direction the assailant had gone. One ATV started to patrol the fence line and another stopped. She hardly noticed the security guard jumping the fence as she clung to Ryan.

"That's Jaylen Cox's address. Is he all right?"

Matt let out a low whistle of astonishment. "Yes, but he's most likely injured. That's what a 10-82 is. Look, I have to go. They are asking for our assistance."

"Ryan," Sienna cried. "Not Jaylen, too."

"It's okay, sweetheart. I'll go with Matt and see what I can find out. I'm sure Detective Braxton will be there, and I need to tell her what just happened here. Nash will stay with you. Won't you?"

Sienna hadn't even known Nash was standing behind Ryan, but he stepped forward when Ryan said his name.

"She'll be safe."

Ryan leaned down and placed a kiss on the top of her head. "I'll call you with information on Jaylen."

Ryan turned from her arms and Sienna fought back fear that this was the last time she would see him. Another of her players had been attacked at the same time as her boyfriend. Whoever had killed Malik was after all those she loved. She only prayed they would be stopped before they moved onto the next target.

She watched as Matt tossed Ryan a first-aid kit, and they both climbed into the cruiser. "I love you," she whispered as the car drove off.

"So, what's your involvement in this?" Matt asked Ryan as he stopped the cruiser at the yellow crime scene tape.

"I don't know yet. But I'm hoping it's not what I think it is."

"And what are you thinking it is?"

"That we're either looking at two crimes that just coincidentally happened tonight at the same time, or these two crimes are connected under the umbrella of a larger crime ring. I'm hoping they're not, because if it's the ring I think it could be, then there is going to be trouble," Ryan told him, getting out of the cruiser.

Police forensics technicians were snapping pictures of the sidewalk covered in blood. He spotted Detective Braxton interviewing a woman in a skintight white dress. He saw the dress was smeared with blood under the police-issued blanket. The coroner's van was nowhere to be seen, so that bode well for Jaylen.

"You let me know what I can do to help," Matt told him. Ryan gave him a nod, and Matt was whisked up in the duties of gathering evidence and speaking to witnesses.

"Agent Parker. Why am I not surprised to see you here?" Braxton narrowed her eyes as she got closer to him. "What happened to you?"

"I had a visitor tonight."

"I take it that it wasn't a friendly chat?"

"Not exactly. He told me someone wanted a word with me," Ryan told her.

"And where is your visitor now?" Braxton calmly asked.

"He got away. But I have a lead I want to follow."

"Care to share?"

Ryan shook his head. "Not yet. It may be linked to a confidential case. I need to get permission to bring you in on it. Now, what happened here?"

Detective Braxton turned toward the sidewalk and

pointed. "Jaylen and his date were walking from the restaurant a couple blocks away. He reached there," she pointed to the blood on the sidewalk, "and was ambushed by a man in black, driving what we are guessing to be a stolen car. The man shot him in the side and was about to fire again when Jaylen collapsed onto the ground. The woman dove on top of him to protect him. People were pouring out of their houses and that little old man there fired at the car, forcing the shooter to flee."

Ryan looked at the old man with a walker and gave him a nod. "So, there are at least two men carrying out orders for someone. Is there a description of the person in black?"

"Yes. It matched the description of the man seen at Malik's house perfectly."

"Which matched the man I saw at the same time tonight. So, they're a professional group. It's their uniform. They're serious, and you better get Jaylen a protective detail immediately."

"We have officers posted at the hospital, but I think you're right. We need to get him into a secure wing right away." Braxton walked off to issue orders but stopped and turned back to him. "They're going to be out for blood. Stay safe and let me know when you can read me in."

Ryan stepped away from the crowd and dialed the Boise, Idaho, number his handler, Arnie, had given him.

"Agent Shaw, this is Agent Ryan Parker. Arnie Packers is my handler. I need to get a message to him and if my number shows up, it may draw some attention since I've been temporarily transferred."

"Sure thing, Agent Parker. What do you want me to do?"

Five minutes later Ryan hung up. He had conveyed his

worry that The Suit had tracked him to Kentucky and even passed along his belief that Nash was tracking the same person. What he couldn't figure out was The Suit's connection to the Lexington Thoroughbreds and Sienna.

Sienna paced the length of the living room more times than she could count. Nash sat quietly on the couch with Hooch as she vented.

"He shouldn't have just run like off like that. He was injured," Sienna complained for the hundredth time.

"He's a grown man, Sienna. A little scrape isn't going to hurt him," Nash said as he kept glancing at his tablet.

"But what does he think he's doing, running off like that? I mean, I'm so glad to know Jaylen is alive and out of surgery, but Matt could have told me that."

Nash shook his head. "For a shrink, you don't know much about how the male brain works."

Sienna stopped pacing and put her hands on her hips. "What exactly do you mean by that?"

"It means that some of us have dangerous jobs. It's what we do. It's who we are. If you can't accept that, then you shouldn't be with that person. It's obvious Ryan cares for you. He's here protecting you. And when someone comes to your house and makes threats against you, what would you want a man to do? He's going to protect his own or die trying," Nash said, looking back at his tablet.

Sienna started pacing again before coming to a stop in front of Nash. "For your information, I understand his job is dangerous. But Ryan is smart. He always has been. He'll be careful, and he'll figure this out. Did you know both the FBI and DEA wanted him? He's the most capable man I know.

However, when you love someone nothing will prevent you from worrying. Even if that person is a big badass like you, your wife will someday worry about you, too. It has nothing to do with not believing in that person. It has everything to do with loving that person."

"Loving who?"

Sienna spun to the door in surprise. "Ryan!" She hurried across the living room and flung her arms around him.

Nash picked up his tablet and headed for the back door. "I think this is my cue to leave. Call if you need me. I'll be watching."

"Thanks, man. I appreciate it."

"I do too. Goodnight, Nash." Sienna smiled.

Ryan was exhausted. And sore. His jaw was killing him, but the second he opened the front door and heard Sienna's lecture to Nash, he forgot all about it. All he could think about was she had cared enough about him to sing his praises and worry about him. But did she really love him?

He realized he hadn't released his hold on her, and quite frankly he didn't want to. She felt perfect in his arms. The top of her head reached the top of his chest, which made it perfect for kissing exactly as he did now.

"Are you okay? You were bleeding, and I was so worried about you," Sienna said from against his chest.

"I'm fine. Why were you worried about me, Sienna?"

She pulled back, but he didn't let her leave his embrace. When she looked straight into his eyes, he felt as if she were reading his soul, hoping to find an answer.

"Why did you stop wanting me?" she asked quietly.

Ryan ran his hand down her soft cheek and cupped her chin. He tilted it up to his lips and placed a slow kiss on her mouth. "I never stopped wanting you, Sienna. Not for one single day. Why were you worried about me?"

A tear threatened to spill from the forests that were her eyes. "I love you. I've loved you forever, I think. You were right that night eight years ago. I was the one who needed to grow up. I thought it was you; it wasn't. It was me. I opened my eyes and realized the only person I called when I was in trouble was you. The only person I wanted to call with good news was you. You were in my heart long before my mind caught up. I'm sorry it took me so long. Do we still have time?"

"We have the rest of our lives. I love you, too, Sienna. I think I was born just for you." Ryan pulled her in tightly and kissed her. It wasn't the heated kiss from before. It was a slow kiss, allowing him to taste every inch of her. Her tongue caressed his, his hand dropped to her hips, and he pulled her against his arousal.

I'll be watching, Nash had said. Crap, the cameras. He sure would be watching. Ryan moved his hand to her leg and hooked it around his waist. She moaned as the contact brought them closer.

"I want you to make love to me," Sienna said and she plunged her tongue into his mouth, demanding his full attention.

Ryan didn't break the kiss as he lifted her off the ground and wrapped her other leg around his waist. He took a step, and Sienna pulled back gasping for air. "No, here. Now. Against the door, on the floor, over the couch, just here. Now."

"Um," Ryan lost the ability to form words when she started to ride him through their clothes. He stumbled forward, and she ripped his shirt from his body.

"I can't wait to . . ." Sienna leaned forward and

whispered what she wanted to do, and Ryan debated the merits of having a sex tape and a room full of private security watching them.

"Bedroom. We can do that in the bedroom," he panted as he struggled to keep control.

"No, here. Right now!"

Sienna ground against him, and Ryan knew if he didn't get her to the bedroom in the next five seconds, there was not going to be a debate over a sex tape. It would exist and deep down he knew that John Wolfe would find it. With the Rose sisters' elderly act of deception, somehow it would be made public. Then by tomorrow morning his mother would be at the door talking marriage, which didn't sound so bad at the moment, and then the engagement gifts, baby booties, and casseroles would arrive by lunch.

With a herculean effort, Ryan pulled her legs from around his waist and took her in his arms. Running as fast as he could while carrying her, he shoved the bedroom door open and placed her on the bed. The house shook as Hooch lumbered after them, thinking it was a game of chase. Sienna laughed as Ryan slammed the door. But when they looked at each other, the laughter stopped. This had been over twenty years in the making, and he didn't want to wait a second longer.

Sienna kneeled on the bed and slowly pulled her shirt over her head. The emerald green satin bra, covering breasts he was dying to taste, drew his attention as he unbuttoned his jeans. Not saying a word, they slowly undressed for each other. The feminine curve of her hips and the way she wiggled them as she took off her panties had his mouth watering.

"Will you make love to me now?" Sienna asked with a quirk of her lips as she lay back against the bed.

Ryan stepped to the side of the bed and looked down at her. Everything about this was right. Everything in him screamed to be with her. And when he made love to her, he knew he was right—they were meant for each other.

Chapter Eleven

Sienna awoke to the feeling of a warm body next to hers. He was breathing heavily and kissing her face as she opened her eyes. Sienna cracked her eye when it started to feel as if it were raining.

"Hooch," Sienna groaned, and the bed began to shake as he thumped his tail.

The door to her bathroom opened and Ryan walked out with a towel slung low around his waist, his hair still dripping wet.

"Sorry about that. I got up early and took him outside. When I let him in, he ran straight for your bed, put his head on the pillow, and closed his eyes. Since I literally could not get back into bed, I thought I'd take a shower. How about I make you some breakfast while you take yours?" Ryan asked as he pulled the towel from his waist and ran it over his hair.

Sienna was going to answer, but she was too busy staring. She had started with his chest. The small dash of dark hair drew her attention downward where she worked on counting to eight and then, well then, she couldn't count to save her life.

"Sienna?" Ryan asked when he dropped the towel to his side. "Breakfast?"

"In bed?"

"That could be arranged," Ryan's voice purred predatorily as he stalked toward her, leaving the towel to drop on the floor.

Sienna could smell the bacon frying as she ran a brush over her wet hair in her bathroom. That had been the best breakfast in bed she'd ever had. Afterward she'd taken her shower while Ryan had declared he and Hooch would make her a real meal.

Sienna blasted her hair with a dryer before stepping into a pair of peach silk shorts and a flowing, white silk top. She slipped her feet into a pair of wedges and followed the smell of food.

Ryan was setting a plate of bacon, eggs, and toast onto her small table when she entered the kitchen. He looked up and smiled at her as Hooch sat proudly beside him as if he had cooked the meal himself.

"Hope you're hungry," Ryan said with a smile that had her wondering about a second helping of breakfast in bed.

"Starving."

Who was this sultry woman who answered him? "So, what are our plans for the day?" Ryan asked, taking the seat next to her.

"I want to go see Jaylen and see if Detective Braxton has found out anything yet."

"I'm expecting a call—" Ryan was cut off by Hooch leaping up and thundering toward the front door.

Sienna had barely blinked, and Ryan was up between her and the door with a gun in his hand.

"It's okay. That's Hooch's happy bark," Sienna said and placed a gentle hand on Ryan's arm.

There was a quick knock on the door and then the handle turned. Ryan wasn't taking chances and turned the safety off.

"What the hell? Sienna, open the door!"

Ryan put down his gun as they both recognized Sydney's voice.

"Seriously, hurry up and open the door. This is majorly time-sensitive!"

Ryan strode forward and unlocked the door. Sydney burst in in full supermodel mode. Her sandy blond hair was blown out in long soft waves over her shoulders, cascading down her breasts. Her hazel eyes, so much like all the children in the Davies family, were highlighted to perfection in earth tones. Her extremely tailored business suit was the cutting edge of fashion, and the silver Chanel pumps made her the picture of haute couture business.

"This is so much better than when you modeled underwear. Do you have any idea how many of my classmates I had to beat up defending your honor?" Ryan asked as he kissed his cousin on the cheek.

Sydney waved a perfectly manicured hand through the air and laughed. "You Southern gentlemen are all the same. Wyatt said the same thing, but he's my brother. Well, I appreciate the brigade of male cousins defending me, too. It sure makes a girl feel loved."

Sienna stood and walked over to Ryan. "I thought you were on your way to New York City for business meetings."

"I am. I stopped at the café to get one last good meal before my trip, and I had to warn you. You have no more than five minutes before your mother gets here."

"Which one?" Ryan and Sienna asked in a panic.

"Both of them! They know Ryan's been shacking up here, and Aunt Paige is pissed that you haven't been home to see her yet," Syd told Ryan before turning to Sienna.

"And Kenna's pissed that something is going on, and you haven't told her about it. She said Will's been acting funny and talking up Ryan. It's made her really suspicious, especially when she found out my dear cousin here hasn't even seen his own mother yet."

Ryan and Sienna didn't bother thanking Sydney. Ryan lunged to clear the table, tossing all the food into Hooch's dish as Sienna grabbed her purse. In under fifteen seconds, the house was locked, and they were racing down the driveway on their way to Lexington with Sydney standing on the porch screaming, "You owe me!"

Ryan flashed his badge at the officer standing duty outside Jaylen's hospital room and then signed the login form. He and Sienna had laughed all the way to the hospital about their mad getaway. Neither one of them wanted to ruin the magic of last night by talking about what their plans were now. They just wanted to savor the moment a bit longer.

"Right this way, Agent Parker," the officer said and led them down the hall.

"Are you sure you didn't see anything else?" Ryan heard Detective Braxton's voice before he saw her.

"I'm sure, ma'am. I wish I knew what this was about. I haven't done nothing to no one," Jaylen responded as Ryan raised his hand to knock on the partially open door.

"Come in," Braxton ordered.

"Yo, Doc! Man, it's good to see you." Jaylen smiled from the hospital bed. "I'm glad they let you in. No one else from the team is allowed to visit me until I'm released."

"Nothing could keep me away." Sienna smiled, taking a seat on the opposite side of the bed from the detective. Ryan watched her take Jaylen's large hand into hers and give it a squeeze. The big running back grinned and was visibly relaxed. His girl sure had a way about her. *His girl.* Ryan smiled to himself. He was damn proud of Sienna.

Ryan's phone began to vibrate and he almost didn't look at it, thinking it was his mother calling for the tenth time, but when he glanced at the screen he saw that it was a call from Agent Shaw.

Detective Braxton sent him a questioning look over her shoulder, and he held up a finger to tell her to wait before stepping out into the hall.

"Parker," he answered.

"Shaw," was the responding answer. Gotta love FBI agents. They were straight to the point. "I talked to Arnie, and he cleared your local detective. He went to check on Abdul and found him hanging in his cell."

"What? How?" Ryan asked as he began to pace the hallway.

"That's the million-dollar question because he was hanging by a thick piece of rope that could have, in no way, been in his cell. Someone either entered the cell and killed him or had the rope slipped to Abdul, and he followed the unwritten order. Either way, your lead on The Suit in L.A. is dead."

"He's tying up loose ends," Ryan said, shaking his head. "Cleaning house for this big terrorist attack he has planned. The trouble is we don't know which stadium or when, only that *a* stadium was the target. But now that L.A. is too hot, how is he going to finance it?"

"That's what Arnie is wondering. Strange that he sent a crew to Kentucky. Arnie thinks you are considered a loose end. That maybe you picked up something in L.A. that was important and don't realize it yet," Shaw told him.

"I'll go over my notes again today to see if I can find anything I missed before." Ryan stopped pacing. "But what do Malik and Jaylen, two players for the Lexington Thoroughbreds, have to do with The Suit?"

"That's what Arnie wants you and Detective Braxton to work on. He's worried you're not the only target. If The Suit is tying up loose ends, then your doctor friend is a big one, ripe for the picking."

"First my mother and then The Suit. Can my day get any worse?" Ryan asked the universe.

"I don't know about mothers, but The Suit is out there, so be careful. Arnie also said to read your father in on it and see if the Lexington branch can assist in anyway."

"Apparently the answer to today getting any worse is yes. I will now be taking orders from my dad." Ryan let out a suffering sigh as Shaw chuckled.

"Call me if there's anything you need. Talk to you soon, Parker."

Sienna chatted with Jaylen as the detective split her time between listening to every word of their talk and trying to listen to Ryan talking in the hallway. Something was going on, something bigger than just a murder. Even she could tell this was an organized attack.

Jaylen was singing the praises of his date, and Sienna paid attention the best she could. The way Detective Braxton was trying so hard not to jump from her chair and charge into the hallway had Sienna on edge.

"I mean, she leapt on me to protect me. If that isn't true love, I don't know what is. It's just too bad I don't have the money to buy her a nice engagement ring." Jaylen continued talking, but that brought Sienna up short.

"Engagement ring?"

"Yeah, haven't you been listening? That's a special girl right there, and I am locking it down."

"Jaylen, how many dates have you been on with this girl?" Sienna asked.

"Two, why?"

"Don't you think it's a little early to be talking about engagements? After a shock like getting shot, it's not really the best time to be making life decisions," Sienna said in her best doctor voice.

"True love is true love. Why wait?" Jaylen smiled, but as soon as he stopped talking Detective Braxton jumped in, even ignoring that Ryan walked in right then, looking worried.

"Why can't you afford a nice engagement ring? You make millions a year."

"I met with my agent, who had talked with my financial advisor. I overspent like crazy. I have enough for a ring, but not a ring like she deserves for saving my life and certainly not enough for the multimillion-dollar house I wanted to buy. I mean, I can buy it with a mortgage, but my mom taught me never to go into debt. I wanted to walk into the closing and plunk down all this cash. It would have been sweet."

"Did Malik have money problems, too?" Ryan asked, stepping up to the bed.

Jaylen shook his head. "Not that I know of. He saved every penny he made. He lived in a tiny townhouse for the past couple of years and never partied. When he bought a new car it was a Ford Explorer, not a Lambo like some of the guys."

Sienna nodded in agreement. "Before he was killed, he told Seth he was planning on purchasing a big beach house. He was going to be meeting with him to go over all the financial paperwork his advisor had provided. He had his retirement all lined up."

Ryan looked at Detective Braxton and pursed his lips. "I don't know about you, Detective, but I sure wouldn't mind talking to Seth Hayes."

"Me too," Detective Braxton agreed. "Jaylen, who else does Seth represent?"

Jaylen let out a long breath. "Damn, I don't know. About fifty of us in the NFL. A handful of NHL players and about twenty NBA players."

"I'll look to see if any other of his other clients have been roughed up recently while you bring him in for a chat," Braxton said to Ryan.

Sienna didn't like this. Ryan already didn't like Seth and vice versa. Having Ryan bringing Seth in would only hurt matters. "Maybe Detective Braxton should talk to Seth."

Ryan straightened and his cop face fell into place. "And why is that?"

"You're not exactly objective when it comes to Seth," Sienna pointed out. She didn't like the hardness in Ryan's voice when he had asked his question. And right now his eyes were shooting daggers at her.

"Why aren't you objective?" Detective Braxton asked Ryan, even though she was looking at Sienna.

Ryan didn't respond, so Sienna did. "Because I've gone out on a couple of dates with Seth. He wants us to date more and doesn't like Ryan hanging around. Similarly, Ryan doesn't like Seth hanging around either."

"And who do you want *hanging around*?" Detective Braxton asked, making a very small motion with her hand to stop Ryan from saying anything.

"Excuse me? What does that have to do with

anything?" Sienna bristled. The tone of this conversation had gone from conversational to questioning real fast.

"Is that such a hard question to answer? How close are you to Seth Hayes, Dr. Ashton?"

Jaylen looked back and forth between the two women as Sienna ground her teeth together. "Are you trying to imply I had something to do with this? I would never hurt anyone, much less players I care about as if they were my own brothers."

Jaylen nodded his head. "Doc is real good people. She would never—"

Ryan cut him off. "Why can't you just answer the question, Sienna? Who is Seth to you?"

Sienna jumped up from the chair and placed her hands on her hips. "You know exactly who is to me, Ryan Parker."

"So you've dated?" Detective Braxton asked, trying to bring the questioning down a level. "When?"

"The other week. Right before the opening season game," Sienna shot to the detective, who calmly wrote something in a small notepad.

"Are you sleeping with him?" Ryan asked quietly.

Sienna sucked in a breath and Jaylen cursed. "Damn, bro. Don't you know you aren't suppose to ask a woman something like that?"

"Sorry, Sienna, but we need to know," Ryan said in the same quietly forceful voice.

"You do, huh? Give me one reason why you need to know?" Sienna shot back. She felt as if steam were about to come out of her ears.

"Because," Detective Braxton said in the same quiet hard voice, "you had a relationship with someone who keeps popping up in this investigation. And at the same time, *your* name keeps popping up as a common link between crimes. Further, you sure went from Mr. Hayes to Agent Parker pretty quickly. I can't help but wonder if that was to feed inside information to Mr. Hayes."

Sienna pushed back the tears threatening to explode from her eyes and took a breath to hold her broken heart together. "This discussion is over."

Sienna bent to pick up her purse, and Jaylen grabbed her hand. "I know you didn't do it, Doc."

"Thank you, Jaylen," Sienna said as she swiped at her eyes. "I'll check on you again soon. Call me if you need anything."

Sienna lifted her purse over her shoulder and stood up straight. She looked Ryan in the eyes and walked past him out the door.

"Sienna," Ryan called out after her, "why won't you just answer the question so we can move on?"

Sienna spun around as anger and hurt boiled over. "You make love to me, and I tell you how it's always been you I've loved. I tell you that no one matched up to you for years. For someone who claims to have wanted me all that time, who knows everything about me, who is one of the smartest people I know, you sure are stupid to even think we're going to have this discussion. You shouldn't even have to ask if I had something to do with this. You should just know."

"Dr. Ashton," Braxton stepped up to the door and stopped next to Ryan, "we have a job to do, and we need answers. Even if it's to cross your name off the list of suspects. We have to do our jobs."

Sienna made a sound of disbelief. "Please. All you did was make Ryan single again, as if we even had a relationship to begin with! Well, he's all yours, *Andrea*. Did you plan to blame me for a crime I didn't commit the first time you saw him leaning against your cruiser? I remember how you drooled like Hooch over him."

Detective Braxton turned red. "That's ridiculous."

"Now you know how it feels." Sienna spun on her heel and started to walk down the hall.

"I still need your answer," Braxton called out after her.

"Then call my attorney. Agent Parker has her number."

Ryan stared after Sienna as she stomped down the hall. What the hell had he just done?

"Bro, what the hell did you just do?" Jaylen asked from his bed.

"Shit," Ryan cursed, slamming his hand against the door.

"We have to know," Detective Braxton said softly to him. "If we don't ask the hard questions, they will be asked during trial when we do find the person who did it—that is, if it's not her."

"You know damn well it's not her. I got jealous and let it interfere with my work." Ryan clenched his hands into fists over and over again. "Jaylen, I hope you feel better. Call me if you need anything."

Detective Braxton followed him out into the hallway. "Should I call her lawyer and set up a meeting?"

"Oh, I wouldn't advise that," Ryan said, shaking his head.

"Why not?"

"Because her attorney is her mother."

Detective Braxton shrugged. "So? Usually relatives are easier to manipulate. They give too much away since they're so invested in the case."

"You don't know her mother," Ryan shuttered. "Besides, first I need to read you into the case. Let's go to the Lexington FBI office. I need to bring my dad into it as well."

Ryan walked down the hall, assuming Detective Braxton would follow. How had he messed up the best thing in his life in a matter of seconds? Rage and jealousy at the idea of Seth and Sienna having sex made him ill. He'd already seen Seth's hands on her, and the idea of them together had overtaken his mind and his mouth. Now he had ruined something far more important than his job. He pulled out his phone and sent a group text.

Chapter Twelve

Sienna walked up the stone stairs of the old Keeneston courthouse. Keeneston was founded in the late 1700s, and the courthouse had been one of the first buildings the settlers had erected. It had been expanded over the years, but the original courthouse was still the focal point of the building. It was four stories high with beautiful shiny wooden floors. The bustle of the judicial system moved all around her.

She pressed the third-floor button in the old elevator and pulled out a tissue as she rode the rattling ancient cage. She wiped her eyes and when the elevator door opened, hoped she looked somewhat respectable.

Her mother had been in private practice in New York City before she became a witness to a corruption scandal and was forced to flee to Will Ashton for help. Once she arrived in Keeneston, she never left. Even her mom's best friend, Dani, who had been her paralegal in New York, joined her in Keeneston. Kenna married Will, and Dani married a sheik named Mohtadi Ali Rahman. Together, the two best friends started up a private practice firm in town before her mom was voted in as the town's prosecutor.

Sienna walked down the hall to her mother's office. She walked in and found Dani sitting at the front desk. "Hi, Mrs. Ali Rahman."

Dani rolled her eyes. "How many times have I told you to call me Dani? One of your middle names is named after me. The least you can do is call me by my first name. When you call me Mrs., it makes me feel old."

"Sorry, Dani. Is my mom in?" Sienna did her best to smile and act as if everything was all right, but Dani's ice blue eyes zeroed in on her wobbly smile. Dani was up and out of her chair in a heartbeat.

"What is it? What's the matter?" Dani asked as she rounded the desk and pushed open the swinging gate that separated the front of the room from her mom's office. Her long dark hair still managed not to show any gray; whether natural or not, Sienna couldn't say.

"Nothing. I just need to talk to my mom. I'm afraid I might need a lawyer."

Dani wrapped her arms around her and pulled her into a tight hug. "Your mom's in court. Let's go get her. And while we head down there, you can tell me why you think you need a lawyer."

Ryan dropped into the chair in front of his father's desk. This was way too reminiscent of being called into Cole's home office when he was in trouble. Old habits die hard, and Ryan found himself fidgeting with the file in his hands while he waited for his dad to come in.

Detective Andrea Braxton walked in a couple minutes later and sat in the chair next to him. "Okay, we just need to clear the air. Yes, I thought you were hot. As soon as I saw you only had eyes for Sienna, I backed off."

Ryan felt his eyebrows rise. "Sienna was telling the truth about that?"

Andrea blushed again. "I mean, yeah. Look at you. A woman would have to be dead not to notice you."

"So, we've established my son is attractive. Is this what this meeting is about?" Cole asked as he walked into the room.

"No, sir. I was just clearing up something that happened before we got here," Detective Braxton said quickly.

Ryan saw his father shoot him a questioning look that resembled the face he gave Ryan right before he sent him to his grandparents' farm to do manual labor as punishment.

"I wanted to meet with you all to fill you in on my case. Dad knows some, but here's the file. Agent Packers wants you both read in on the terrorist known to us as The Suit. We also have reason to believe he is known as *Rais* overseas."

Ryan filled them in on his undercover work and Abdul's mysterious suicide while in an FBI facility. He further filled his father in on the man who attacked him and then handed it off to Andrea to share what she knew of the murders.

His father nodded as he took down notes. "I'll send a couple of men to help with Jaylen's detail. Detective, you can pull your men from Sienna's detail. I'll feel better if the FBI takes that over. She's like family to me, and family protects their own. Ryan will be with her constantly . . . wait, who is with her now?"

"Nash is."

Detective Braxton turned to face him. "Who is Nash?"

"Nash Dagher is the second-in-command of Prince of Ali Rahman's security detail. He's more than capable of protecting her," Cole answered for Ryan.

"We don't even know if she needs protecting," Detective Braxton mumbled.

Ryan fell back against his chair. His father narrowed his

eyes on her and was in full boss mode as he stared Andrea down. "What exactly does that mean?"

Ryan opened his mouth to try to limit the damage, but his father simply held up a hand. "Not one word, Agent Parker. I was asking Detective Braxton."

Andrea sat up straight and looked his father, the head of the local FBI, in the eyes. "We haven't eliminated her as a possible suspect."

"And what evidence do you have to even consider her a suspect?" Cole asked. His voice was deadly calm, and his eyes never wavered from Detective Braxton's.

Andrea shifted in her chair. "She dated a sports agent named Seth Hayes. He happens to be the agent for both Jaylen King and Malik Coleman. Further, while she won't admit or deny it, Dr. Ashton was seeing both of those players as patients. It's a coincidence and one I want cleared up."

"So, you think Dr. Ashton has terrorist ties with The Suit and is feeding him information about the case?" Cole asked, and Ryan felt like groaning. It was so insane to even think this about Sienna. Jealousy had turned him into someone who acted first and thought second, and that was not him.

"Yes, or what I believe to be more probable is Mr. Hayes is using Dr. Ashton to give him inside information on his players and the investigation."

Cole turned to Ryan, and he had to struggle to remember he was almost thirty, not thirteen. "And, Agent Parker, do you hold those same beliefs?"

Ryan gulped. He hated when his dad and Sienna called him Agent Parker. It was a sure sign they were pissed. "I might have led her to think I believed that. But I don't. It's ridiculous to think Sienna had anything to do with it."

"Either way," Detective Braxton cut in, "we need to question her. I'm going to call her attorney and set up a time to meet at the police station. If Agent Parker is too scared to assist, then I'll do it myself."

Cole gave a cold smile. "Oh, no. I think he should join you. Agent Parker, make the call and set up the appointment."

The way his father was grinning told Ryan all he needed to know. He was a dead man walking.

Sienna entered the lobby of the courthouse and stopped at the line waiting to go through security. Dinky and Noodle, the two senior deputies, were getting ready for a full day of court. Eugene Miller, who liked to noodle catfish — hence, the nickname Noodle — was getting ready to retire. Sienna didn't even know Dinky's real name. He was short and the nickname just stuck.

"Knives, even those used to clean your nails, go in drawers, and you will get them back when court is over," Dinky called out as the people groaned and started pulling out their knives.

"Guns, bats, batons, ninja stars . . . they all go in the drawers. If you can kill a squirrel with it, put it in the basket," Noodle ordered as he looked in purses.

Dinky noticed her first. "Sienna! What brings you by today?" he asked as he signaled for her and Dani to bypass security. He stepped over and gave her a hug. Noodle quickly joined him and wrapped her up in a bear hug as if she were still nine years old.

"It's good to see you. Here to see your mom in action?" Noodle asked.

Dani's hands went to her hips, "You bet. Cole's worthless son is trying to pin a murder on our girl."

Noodle looked confused. "Wait, I thought you, Kenna, and Paige all wanted those two to get together . . ."

Dani nudged him in the stomach to cut him off. "But now he wants to question her about her relationship with a sports agent as if she is colluding with him to murder Malik and Jaylen."

"The Thoroughbreds players?" Dinky asked. He took a bow and arrow from someone attending court.

"That's right," Dani told him.

Sienna just wanted to leave. She should have known better than to involve her family, and Dani was family. The whole town would know about this and a town divided wasn't what she wanted to deal with. The citizens of Keeneston had a tendency to overstep personal space. Although, how they overstepped something they didn't even believe existed was another question for another day.

"Right this way. Court won't start for another couple of minutes so your mom is just working out plea bargains," Noodle told her as he opened the heavy door leading into the mahogany-paneled courtroom.

Sienna saw her mother, McKenna Ashton—or Kenna to her friends—standing at her desk at the front of the room. Sienna walked past the rows of seating and smiled weakly to those she knew while her mother talked with Henry Rooney and Neely Grace Rooney, the husband-wife defense attorney team of Keeneston.

The sight of those she grew up with made her feel safe. Henry was in his shiny silver suit, looking like a mob boss-turned-used car salesman. His wife was in a power suit and repeatedly rolling her eyes at her husband. It brought a smile and a bit of a tear to Sienna's face. Just this morning she had thought she and Ryan would have that. A lifetime together of teasing, laughing, and eye rolling.

As if sensing Sienna, her mother's dark auburn hair turned, finding green eyes similar to her own searching her out. Her mother looked excited, but then, as she took in Sienna, Dani, and Noodle, her smile slipped and she rushed forward.

"What happened? Are you hurt?" her mother demanded and started looking her over for wounds.

"Not on the outside." Sienna took a deep breath. "I need a lawyer."

Her mother's forehead creased. "For what?"

"Did you say you need a lawyer?" Henry Rooney asked as he and Neely Grace joined the group.

See. No personal space. "Yes. Ryan . . . *Agent* Parker that is, and Detective Braxton, the lead detective on the Malik Coleman murder and the Jaylen King attempted murder, think I have something to do with it."

"He what?" Kenna yelled. The courtroom went quiet as everyone in the rows of benches turned to look at them.

"Did she say Ryan is back in town?" someone asked.

"Yeah, and he thinks she's a killer," someone else spoke up.

"Dumbass. I thought he was smarter than that."

"Thank you," Sienna smiled to Mr. Chapman, the town's chronic bumbling public masturbator. It had started when he was in his twenties. He didn't mean to be public about it, he had just been trying to escape his wife's notice. But he wasn't the sharpest tool in the shed and always seemed to be caught in a very public fashion. So now he had a standing court date to keep him in line and he'd turned into something of an eccentric legend.

Kenna grabbed her daughter's hand and dragged her through the open door. "I need your chambers, Your Honor," Kenna said as she dragged Sienna and half the town with her past the judge getting ready to take a seat at the bench.

Sienna, Kenna, Dani, Henry, Neely Grace, and Noodle crammed into the small office. Her mother pushed her down in a chair and turned a serious look on her. "Now, tell me everything."

"Kenna just told Sienna to spill it," Mr. Chapman's muffled voice called out to the spectators in the courtroom.

"Get out of the way!" a woman's voice said from the other side of the door. "Don't make me break this broom over your head. It's my fifth of the year and I'm rather fond of it."

The door to the chambers burst open and Miss Lily, Miss Daisy, Miss Violet, and their husbands poured in.

"We heard. I can't believe Ryan did this. I thought he was such a smart young man," John Wolfe said solemnly.

"And I had twenty bucks riding on an engagement by this weekend," Miss Violet groaned as she sat down.

"Would you like Anton to make you a special dessert to drown your sorrows over the love of your life betraying you? I think something with dark chocolate," Miss Violet's husband, Anton, a French chef, said sweetly.

Sienna nodded. "That sounds lovely, Anton. Thank you."

Miss Daisy handed her a hanky and that was when Sienna realized she was crying.

"Now, dear, tell us everything and we'll find a way to fix it," Miss Lily said softly.

Thirty minutes later, Sienna sat back in the chair. "That's everything."

"That's not everything from what I've heard," Miss Daisy sent her a wink and Kenna shushed her.

"This is my daughter, not some object of gossip. So, this Detective Braxton has the hots for Ryan, huh?"

Sienna shrugged. "I don't know. She was definitely interested when she first saw him, but it was clear he was there to see me. I mean, he has an eight pack. Of course she's going to be . . ." Sienna paused and looked up. All eyes were on her. The Rose sisters and their husbands looked as if they were trying not to burst out laughing.

"Eight, huh?" Kenna said with a quirk to her lips. "Your father only had six."

"Eww, Mom!" Sienna groaned and the others laughed. Sienna had tried not to give away the extent of her and Ryan's relationship, but it was clear they all knew.

Their laughter stopped when Kenna's phone started to vibrate.

"McKenna Ashton," her mother said in that scary professional voice. "Ah, Detective Braxton. I've heard so much about you."

"The detective just called," Mr. Chapman's muffled voice was the only thing that could be heard as Kenna waited while the detective spoke.

"No, that just won't do. If you wish to speak to my client, you can meet at the Rooney and Rooney Law Offices in Keeneston at three today. No other time is available," Kenna said as she looked at her daughter and winked.

"I don't care if that doesn't suit you. It's either three o'clock at Rooney and Rooney or get an arrest warrant." Her mother was quiet for a second as Sienna worried her heart might beat right out of her chest. "Fine. I'll see you then. Oh, and Detective Braxton, tell Agent Parker I look forward to seeing him as well."

Her mother hung up the phone and the entire room let out its collective breath.

"Who knew my mom was a badass?" Sienna chuckled.

"You haven't seen anything yet." Kenna promised. "Henry, do you and Neely mind if I borrow your conference room?"

"About that," Neely started. "You know she's going to play the mother/daughter angle. Let us help."

Kenna nodded and then smiled. "And I think we should give Henry a very long leash."

Henry's lips turned up into a huge grin. "Can I, honey?" he asked his wife. "I've been working on some great material."

"And I would love to hear it," Neely, along with the rest of the room, snickered. Henry was the king of horrible pick-up lines and nothing threw people off their game faster than a well-placed corny line.

A knock sounded at the door and Charlie, Miss Daisy's husband, answered it. The judge poked his head in. "Mind if we start court now? If we need to make it to that three o'clock meeting, we better hurry."

"We?" Sienna asked.

"You didn't think I would miss this, did you? I'll even wear the robe and look intimidating," Judge Cooper, who should have retired a decade ago, said as he wiggled his bushy white brows.

"Judge," Kenna said, shaking her head, "don't you think that would be improper?"

"Hey, I'm retiring at the end of the year. Let an old man have some fun."

Sienna should have felt embarrassed, but instead she felt loved. This town loved her, and this town would stand beside her.

"I'd be honored to have you with me. Thank you, Judge Cooper."

"Can I come, too?" Mr. Chapman asked, and everyone cringed.

"No!" they all responded together.

"I didn't mean it that way," Mr. Chapman mumbled as he walked back into the courtroom, and the room dissolved into laughter.

Chapter Thirteen

R yan didn't want to think about the threat his father left him with. *You better pray your mother hasn't heard of this.* His mother loved Sienna as if she were one of her own and was best friends with Sienna's mother. He know it was possible for someone his size and age to still be afraid of his mother still, but he was terrified, and rightly so. His mother could still shoot a tick off a deer at three hundred yards.

He needed to come up with a plan quickly. Maybe begging from his knees would work? Chocolate, flowers, and him swearing he would never be so stupid again? Something — anything — to get Sienna to talk to him again. But right now he focused all his worry about the future and all the anger he had with himself on one person: Seth Hayes.

Ryan pulled his SUV into the parking space on one side of a flashy Bentley Continental convertible in the Thoroughbreds' parking lot while Detective Braxton pulled into the spot on the other side. Ryan got out and shook his head at the sporty car.

"How much do you think that's worth?" Braxton asked as she stopped to stare at the bright yellow car.

"Probably a little over two hundred thousand dollars," Ryan told her. He was about to walk off when Detective Braxton shook her head.

"Two hundred grand and his driver's side door is banged in."

"Banged in?" Ryan asked as he walked around to the other side of the car. Sure enough, there was a large indentation in the door. "Looks like a basketball thrown with great force, doesn't it?"

"Sure wasn't a post or another car. I guess it's hard to get a Bentley fixed in Lexington," Braxton smiled.

Ryan pulled out his phone and handed it to Braxton. "Take a picture." He stepped forward and, without touching the car, spread his hand out so the picture would show how big an indentation it was.

"Thanks," he said, taking his phone back. "Let's go have a chat with Mr. Hayes."

Ryan found Seth in the conference room with Zack Sanders. Zack was smiling and nodding his head. The large lineman stood up and shook Seth's hand, then grabbed his paperwork and headed out the door.

He gave Ryan and Detective Braxton a quick glance but kept walking. Seth, on the other hand, didn't take his eyes off them as they walked into the room.

"Sanders looked happy."

"Of course he did. He took my advice and the advice of his financial planner and invested correctly. On top of a new endorsement, he also just got a nice fat check for one of those investments paying off." Seth didn't bother to stand or shake their hands. "Now, I have another appointment before I need to meet with Sienna. Would you care to tell me what you want?"

Braxton shot Ryan a look he didn't like. "What are you seeing Dr. Ashton about?"

Seth smiled. "It's personal."

"I bet it is. You two have a romantic relationship, do you not?" Braxton asked while Ryan did his best to stay calm.

"I guess you could say that."

"I *did* say that. I want to know what you have to say," Braxton said calmly.

"I would say yes, we've been dating."

"Were you alone with Dr. Ashton at any time this week?" Ryan asked.

Seth grunted. "You know I wasn't. You were playing lapdog with her this whole week, keeping us apart." He turned to Braxton. "Your boy here thinks he has a shot with her."

Ryan ignored him. "Where were you the night Malik was killed?"

Seth's face lost his smirking smile. "That was horrible. I was out with Sienna the night before, but then I had to go to Indianapolis to meet with my players there. You can call the front office to have that confirmed."

"We will," Detective Braxton told him as she took some notes. "We will need the names of all the players you represent or have represented — dead or alive, retired or playing."

Seth's eyebrow rose and he leaned back in his chair. "Why?"

"Just following a lead. You can have your office send the information to this email address." Braxton handed him her card, and he shrugged.

"I'll clear it with my attorney, and he'll get back to you. Now, if you don't mind, I have another meeting." Seth motioned to another player, waiting at the door.

"Thank you for your cooperation," Ryan said through gritted teeth. "Oh, sorry for that dent in your car. That will cost a fortune to repair."

Seth shrugged. "It's a rental, what do I care?"

"What happened to it?"

"Came out of dinner the other night and it was like that. Someone must have dinged me."

Ryan and Braxton shared a quick look. He was lying, just like he was lying about having a personal dinner with Sienna tonight. There's no way Sienna couldn't see past this scumbag. His buddy-buddy attitude was just a little too fake.

Sienna sat in the leather chair of Rooney and Rooney's law office flanked by half the town. Dani, her mother's paralegal, and Tammy Davies, Henry and Neely Grace's paralegal, claimed they had enough legal training to be included with her mother, Neely Grace, Henry, and Judge Cooper. Sienna didn't know exactly how the Rose sisters talked their way into the front office. Something about someone needed to answer phones.

Sienna took a deep breath when she saw the two cars stop outside. She closed her eyes and waited for the tinkle of the bell over the front door.

"May I help you?" Miss Lily's elderly voice wafted in through the open conference room door.

"Detective Braxton and Agent Parker to see Dr. Ashton."

"What are you doing here, Miss Lily?" Sienna heard Ryan ask. A second later she heard what sounded like wood splintering and a gun being drawn.

"Put it away, Braxton," Ryan said firmly.

"But she just assaulted a federal officer," Braxton

gasped.

"No, I knocked some sense into a boy I've know his whole life . . . a boy who I thought had turned into a man." Miss Lily harrumphed. "A boy who made me break my fifth broom."

"I take it she's in the conference room?" Ryan asked with a little pain to his voice.

"You know she is," Miss Lily hissed. "I had such hopes for you two, and you go and step in it."

Sienna took a deep breath preparing herself to see Ryan after their blowup that morning. Ryan walked in looking devastatingly handsome in his worn jeans over his cowboy boots and a buttoned-up white shirt with the sleeves rolled up. But it was the miserable look on his face that gave Sienna a glimmer of hope. Maybe he was here to apologize? He sure didn't seem surprised to see a roomful of people. On the other hand, Detective Braxton's surprise made up for it.

Ryan saw the red rims of Sienna's eyes from across the room and felt even worse than he had earlier. Miss Lily breaking a broom over his head hadn't helped either. He felt like a scoundrel. As soon as he saw Miss Lily sitting where Aunt Tammy usually sat, he had known he was in trouble. Which was why it was no surprise when he saw Aunt Tammy, Dani, Henry, Neely Grace, and Kenna sitting on one side of the table. Judge Cooper being there was odd, but at this point he wouldn't be surprised if there were a live feed being broadcast at the Blossom Café.

He had tried to warn Braxton about this, but she never saw it coming. She stopped short when she entered the room and took a quick glance at the angry faces on one side of the table. She recovered quickly enough, but by the way

Kenna smiled predatorily, he knew first blood had been spilled already. Poor Braxton just didn't know it was her own.

"Mrs. Ashton," Ryan said as he leaned over the table and placed a kiss on her cheek. "It's nice to see you again."

"I take it you are Dr. Ashton's attorney?" Detective Braxton asked, as she shook Kenna's hand. "I'm Detective Andrea Braxton."

Kenna smiled evilly. "No, I'm not her attorney. They are. I'm just here in the capacity of her mother. I'll just start on this side. These are our paralegals, Tammy Davies and Her Royal Highness Danielle Ali Rahman."

Ryan almost laughed at Braxton's face. "Highness?"

"Yes," Dani said, displaying a rare moment of royal superiority. Ryan had seen Dani's husband, Mo, turn it on before, but had never seen Dani do it. Poor Mo probably had no idea his wife did it better. "But *Your Highness* is the proper way to address a princess such as myself."

Tammy was next to shake hands. "And I'm Ryan's aunt. If you don't think every bit of this conversation won't be reported to your mother, then you are as stupid as Sienna said."

Ryan groaned. His mother was going to shoot him . . . practically. Well, maybe literally.

"It's nice to meet you. You should be proud of Agent Parker. He's very good at what he does," Braxton defended.

Kenna cocked her head. "You seem to think highly of Agent Parker." She let the insinuation hang in the air.

Braxton cleared her throat and turned to Judge Cooper, who sat in his full robe and even brought his gavel with him. "Judge?"

"That's right. Judge Cooper to you, young lady." Judge Cooper rapped his gavel and Braxton jumped.

"And I'm Neely Grace Rooney, Dr. Ashton's attorney. This is my husband, Henry Rooney, my co-counsel."

Henry blatantly let his eyes run slowly over Detective Braxton's body before holding out his hand. Ryan wanted to scream for her not to take it, but it was too late. Henry had a sleazebag grin on his face and now had both hands wrapped around Braxton's.

"If I told you I was packing a deadly weapon, would you strip-search me?"

Braxton's eyes went wide, and she started to sputter. She tried to pull her hand back, but Henry leaned over and placed a kiss on her knuckles before leaping back.

"Ouch, your beauty tased me!"

Ryan had to swallow his laughter. When he caught Sienna's eye, he saw she too was struggling not to laugh.

"Why did you call this meeting?" Kenna asked immediately, and Braxton still sputtered.

Ryan set his face to show no emotion. "Can I have a word with Sienna alone?"

"No," Neely Grace responded at once.

"Fine. Sienna, I know you didn't do anything wrong. I was just so upset that Seth keeps popping up, attached to your name. Not to mention the very clear fact he wants to be more to you than he is. You could do so much better than that douche bag."

"Better as in you? The person who doesn't know me well enough to know I would never commit a crime?"

Kenna placed a hand on her daughter's arm, and Sienna instantly fell silent.

"Ryan, dear, if you want to grovel for my daughter's forgiveness, then you can do that at a later time. It was my understanding that Detective Braxton, however highly she thinks of you, does not think the same of my daughter.

Now, Detective, I'll ask only one more time. What did you need to talk to my daughter about?"

Henry winked at the detective. "Do you have any cuffs on you?"

Braxton went red and fish-mouthed for a second before pulling it together. "I need to know the exact relationship between her and Seth Hayes."

"No," Neely Grace said again.

"No?" Braxton repeated.

"I can think of at least ten things that involve you, that stun gun, and those handcuffs," Henry smiled up at Detective Braxton.

"Stun gun? What would you do with that?" Judge Cooper asked.

"Well, if you set it real low . . ."

"Enough! What is wrong with you all?" Braxton shouted.

Judge Cooper slammed his gavel. "I don't like your tone. State what you want. Hurry up now."

"Where were you the night Jaylen was shot?"

Sienna looked to Neely Grace who gave a quick nod of her head. "I was at the Blossom Café with Sydney Davies and Kentucky State Trooper Matt Walz."

"Here are their phone numbers, addresses, and sworn affidavits backing up Dr. Ashton's alibi. Further, Miss Lily out front was there along with half the town. Feel free to question them," Neely Grace said and slid two copies of the affidavits across the table.

Ryan gave Sienna a pleading look, but she looked away.

"Dr. Ashton, are you currently dating Seth Hayes?" the detective asked.

"No," Sienna whispered before Neely Grace could

answer.

"What is Seth's involvement like with his players?"

Sienna shook her head. "I don't know. I know he's always busy, so business must be good."

"Was Malik Coleman a client of yours?" Braxton questioned.

"Sustained!" Judge Cooper called out, banging his gavel before the entire room objected to the question.

Neely Grace quieted them. "Detective, you know you need a court order for my client to disclose anything about patients or non-patients. Move on to a different topic."

"What does The Suit mean to you?" Braxton asked.

Ryan could have told her it would mean nothing, but the look of confusion was clear as day. She had no part of this. Even Braxton should be able to tell that.

"I don't . . ."

Her mother placed her hand on hers again and quieted her. "Would you care to read us in? This has a lot more to do with the detective being jealous or maybe Ryan being jealous. Either one is an abuse of power when coming to question someone for personal gain. Who is The Suit?"

Ryan put a hand on Braxton's arm to stop her from answering, but she shook him off. "It's confidential. I just need to know if that name means anything."

Kenna gave him a *yeah, right* look. "Look, I'll find out in under a minute, so why don't you just tell us."

Braxton sniffed. "This is an FBI matter, not something civilians can know about."

Kenna sent a text. "Go ahead and answer if it will satisfy Detective Braxton's errant curiosity."

"No, I've never heard the name," Sienna said and glanced at her mom's phone when it pinged. "You think I'm working with a terrorist?" she screamed as she jumped up from her seat.

"What? How . . ." Braxton sputtered as Kenna rose to her feet.

"You have my daughter wrapped up in your undercover work?" Kenna shouted as she pointed at Ryan.

Ryan shook his head. "No, that's the thing. Malik was murdered before I came here."

"How do you know this?" Braxton shouted, and the room erupted in conversation.

Sienna ignored Braxton, as she demanded how they had received confidential information. Her mother had sent a text to Ahmed, Nabi, and Nash. The trio of Rahmi security specialists had more information at the touch of a button than the entire FBI. All three had sent text messages, adding information each time.

"First you accuse me of sleeping with a potential suspect and feeding him inside information, and now you're accusing me of being part of a terrorist organization with a plot on American soil? Are you insane?" Sienna screamed. She had never been so upset.

"Sweetheart, it's not like that," Ryan started as his hands went to his waist in a defensive move.

"Don't sweetheart me, Ryan Parker. You're the one who slept with me while thinking I was a terrorist!"

"I knew it!" Miss Lily tittered from the doorway.

"You slept with my daughter and then did this? Someone give me a gun," Kenna threatened, jumping from her seat. Judge Cooper banged his gavel gleefully.

"Enough!" Ryan yelled. He slammed his hands on the table. "You will listen to me now. Sit!" Sienna had never seen Ryan lose his temper. She immediately sat, as did everyone else, including Detective Braxton.

His hazel eyes flashed gold and green and bore into hers. His square jaw was emphasized as he clenched his teeth together, and his biceps bulged as his hands turned to fists. He had never been sexier, and right now Sienna forgot all about him being an ass.

"One. I never thought you were a terrorist." He held up his fingers and spoke with a barely contained fury. "Two. I came here to protect you from the person who murdered Malik and likely wants to do the same to you."

Sienna heard her mother gasp, but she kept quiet.

"Three. It is natural to hate any man trying to make a move on what is mine, which is you. Four. I was wrong for being jealous, and I'm sorry. Five. I've learned that somehow, the two cases are related. I just don't know how."

Sienna gulped. This was way worse than it had been five minutes ago.

"Now, if you don't mind, I am going to try to stop a terrorist plot, find a murderer, and keep the woman I love safe."

Sienna's eyes grew wide as Ryan stormed from the room with Detective Braxton hurrying speechless after him. He'd given an impassioned speech and then left before they could work things out. Sienna groaned. "That man is infuriating!"

"Eight pack, you say?" her mother asked, sending her a wink. "That can make for a lot of frustration . . . or cause a completely different kind."

"Eww, Mom," Sienna groaned as she sat back in her chair. She didn't hear the conversation about the new terrorist organization striking close to home. She didn't pay attention to Miss Lily rushing as fast as she could to the café to spread the gossip. And she didn't pay attention to the fact that Nash had suddenly appeared by the conference center door, waiting to escort her home. What she did notice was that Ryan was gone. He had told her he loved her, he was going to protect her, and then he left her. The question was, did she wait for him to come back to her or did she track him down to tell him she forgave him?

Chapter Fourteen

Ryan pushed open the door to the café and pretended not to notice the silence that greeted him. *Thwack.* Miss Daisy's wooden spoon cracked over his head. Damn it, that was twice in one day. *Thwack.* Miss Violet followed up with a spatula to the chest.

"That was for acting stupid," Miss Daisy told him.

"Now, what can we do to help put things to right?" Miss Violet asked.

"A pitcher of your tea at our table sounds like a good start," Ryan said with a forced smile. He was exhausted. He'd called in every undercover contact he had to try to find out about The Suit. He'd even asked Uncle Cy, a former spy, to see what he could find out.

A little girl with light brown hair and big round eyes, carrying a baby doll, walked up to him. She couldn't have been more than three or four. She looked him over and her big eyes blinked. Ryan smiled at her to see if he could put a smile on her serious face. She twisted side to side so her skirt swished, and then she pulled back her leg and kicked him in the shin.

"Ow!" Ryan jumped back and glared at the little girl.

"Farrah Butler, where did you learn that?" Ryan's youngest cousin, seventeen-year-old Cassidy Davies, asked as she joined them.

"From you, Miss Cassidy," the little girl said as she continued to swish her skirts. "You told me to kick bad men, and he hurt Miss Sienna."

Ryan let out a breath but then bit back a curse as the little girl kicked the other shin. "Cassidy!"

Cass rolled her eyes. "What do you expect? She's right. You're just lucky it wasn't me kicking you. And you're darn lucky Carter isn't here. You know how protective he is of his older sister."

"Miss Cassidy, can I have dessert now? You said if I ate my dinner I could have dessert," the little girl named Farrah said, reaching up and taking Cassidy's hand.

"Sure, hon." Ryan looked at his younger cousin and smiled. She was the best babysitter in Keeneston—even if she taught little girls to kick men in the shins.

"It was nice to meet you, Miss Farrah," Ryan called out as they walked back to their table. The little girl turned, blinked her big eyes, and stuck out her tongue at him.

This was the story of his life. His head fell back, and he closed his eyes while Zain and Gabe Ali Rahman laughed at him. The twins looked a little different now that they were older. But it was only small things. Zain was half an inch taller than Gabe. Gabe had slightly darker brown eyes. While they both played the field, Gabe seemed to enjoy it while Zain tolerated it.

They got a lot of attention as heirs to the crown of Rahmi. Their uncle was the current King of Rahmi and his son was next in line. But after that it was their father, Mo, and then Zain followed by Gabe. When Zain had turned eighteen, his uncle, having only one child, publically decreed the line of succession in the event his son didn't have a son of his own. As the back-up heir to the Rahmi crown, Zain had been cowed by the duties of an heir while

Gabe had gotten off a little lighter.

"You sure have a way with women. No wonder you need our help," Gabe teased as Ryan took a seat at the table.

"There's only one woman I care about, but I couldn't get near her house tonight. It's full of her friends."

Zain's lips quirked. "Aren't they your cousins?"

"They're traitors," Ryan said, slumping in his chair. "I've screwed up royally."

"If what the Rose sisters say is true, which it usually is, then yeah, you need to crawl on hands and knees," Gabe said, quieting down as Poppy came over to their table with some food and drinks.

"Thanks, Poppy." Ryan smiled and popped a fried pimento cheese ball into his mouth.

"I wouldn't thank me yet. I only did this for these handsome devils. You're a different story." Poppy huffed before spinning and heading back to the kitchen.

Zain leaned forward. "Did you really tell Sienna you loved her? I mean, we all knew it for years, but I thought you'd never have the balls to tell her. Never mind you said it in front of a roomful of people."

Ryan drank the whole glass of special iced tea before answering. It had just popped out, and he had immediately turned and had run. The only person who had seemed truly surprised by his public announcement, other than himself, was Sienna. Sure, he had told her loved her in private, but that was completely different from declaring it in front of her mother and everyone else. Surprisingly, no one else had blinked an eye. Instead they all looked like they were about to say *finally*, as Zain just did.

But now he understood the reason for the deep instincts of protection he felt for Sienna. He loved her. It felt good and right to say it out loud. The trouble was he couldn't say it to her again. She wasn't even talking to him now.

"I love her so much, and I screwed this up. How can I win her back?"

"Right now I think it's more about survival than winning," Gabe teased.

"Well, there's the traditional path," Zain said, taking a bite of food. "Flowers, chocolate, and jewelry."

"I've sent all three. They should be delivered tonight."

"Nah, I think it's got to be more personal than that. Stop thinking so diplomatically," Gabe told his brother. "It needs to be from the heart. You have to do what all men dread more than death."

"What's that?" Ryan asked nervously.

Zain and Gabe looked at each other and some unspoken twin communication went on before they looked back at Ryan. "You need to share your feelings," they said together.

Sienna held up her wine glass for Sophie to fill. Magically, as if knowing she was needed, Sophie had shown up at her house along with her cousins Layne, Piper, Reagan, and Riley. Sydney was still in New York City for meetings, or she would have been at this impromptu pity party as well.

Sophie topped off her glass and passed the bottle to Layne. "I can't believe Ryan would do that," Soph said for the third time in a row.

Sophie and Ryan were just as close as brother and sister. They had been born minutes apart on Christmas. The whole town had been there, and it was quite the story. Sophie was the oldest of Annie and Cade's three kids. She had always been the one Sienna looked up to the most. She had a quiet confidence Sienna envied. But after college, Sophie kind of disappeared. She came back to town sporadically but said she was busy with the biometrics firm she worked for.

"Men," Layne Davies said with an eye roll. "You should see the ones I do physical therapy with. The bigger the man, the bigger the baby. *Oh, that hurts!*" Layne mimicked, and they all laughed.

"Tell me about it." Piper Davies grinned. She was Dylan's older sister, and that alone earned her a medal in Sienna's book. Jace and Cassidy, Piper's other siblings, were too sweet to even count. They never caused problems. Dylan was an entirely different matter. "In the lab I work at, the men think women are the emotional ones. But they're the ones who always throw hissy fits when they don't get the results they think they should be getting."

The twins, Reagan and Riley, rolled their eyes. Their parents, Cy and Gemma, had raised them with the same philosophy the rest of the Davies family believed: girls could do anything they wanted.

"And they can't stand it if they're not the best at everything." Riley pulled her long red hair into a ponytail and took a shot of bourbon.

"It's not our fault we are better riders," Reagan stated, shoving her red hair behind her ear.

"Better shots." Riley ticked off on her finger.

"Better medics." Reagan held up another finger.

The twins both shrugged. "Well, just better," they said together and all the women laughed.

"Cheers to that!" Sienna toasted with her wine glass. "What we need is a male point of view. Nash?" Sienna asked the armed man dressed in jeans and a black T-shirt who was trying to shrink into the darkest corner of the room.

Nash pushed himself off the wall. All six pairs of eyes

swung around to stare at him. Sienna almost felt bad, but if Nash could handle himself with the criminals he ferreted out, then he should be able to handle himself with a roomful of tipsy women.

His eyes found Sophie's, and Sienna noticed her friend's cheeks had turned an interesting color of pink before she turned away to retrieve another bottle of wine.

"I think women are the strongest, most beautiful treasures on the Earth and deserve to be protected — not because they can't protect themselves, but because it is how men show their love. They deserve to be cared for, not because they don't know how to take care of themselves, but because it is how men express their affection. And when most men would give up, women find a way because their hearts won't let them quit.

"I don't know how to tell a woman I love her, but when I protect her, my action tells her that I do, in fact, love her. When I care for her, my action tells her she's the most important person in my life. When you look at a man, don't listen for words. Watch for action, and there you will find what lies in his heart." Nash folded his arms across his chest and leaned back against the wall.

Sienna wiped a tear from her eye as the other girls stared with shocked expressions on their face. "That was beautiful." Sienna smiled.

"Is that why . . .?" Sophie started but then stopped. Sienna could see her friend's mind spinning before Sophie turned her back to the group.

"But what about Ryan questioning Sienna as if she had terrorist ties?" Layne asked Nash.

Nash shrugged. "Smart men can still do very dumb things."

The girls giggled and Piper held up her glass. "Cheers

to that!"

Ryan refilled his glass and stared at his two friends sitting across from him. "My feelings?"

Zain and Gabe nodded again.

"That's right. You have to go deep with that stuff," Zain said with authority Ryan knew he didn't have.

"Wait a second; you've never been in love. Why am I listening to you?"

Zain shrugged. "Just because I haven't been in love before doesn't mean I don't know what women want. They want to feel loved, cherished, and respected. You violated all three of those when you asked her if she was sleeping with that agent and then hinted she could be tied into terrorist activity."

"I told you, I know I was . . ." Ryan started before he realized the brothers weren't paying any attention. Instead they were looking over his shoulder.

"A jackass?"

Ryan winced at his mother's voice coming from behind him. Paige Davies Parker was not someone you wanted on your bad side. Her good side, yes. She was loving, caring, and the perfect mom. But her bad side, not so much. His father still flinches when she asks him to vacuum. He had made the mistake once of getting her an "I love you" appliance as a gift when they were newlyweds.

"No, wait, I know," his mother snapped her fingers. "It's not your fault. It's a disease that you inherited from your father. I knew it would manifest itself at sometime. *Manleus Stupidious* is a very real thing."

"Hi, Mom," Ryan said with a soft smile and turned around. His mother put her hand to his forehead as if feeling for a fever, and then she examined his eyes. Eyes

Ryan was trying not to roll.

"Yep, just as I feared. *Manleus Stupidious*. Now, what are you going to do to fix something I've had planned since you were born?" His mother placed her hands on her hips. Instead of feeling six-foot-two, he felt barely four-feet tall under his mother's gaze.

"I'm going to express my feelings," Ryan mumbled.

"His deep feelings, Mrs. P," Zain added in his defense.

Paige's hands dropped from her hips, and she smiled brilliantly at him, wrapping him up in a hug. "It's good to see you. I'll even forgive you for not coming to see me sooner since you were with Sienna."

Ryan took a gulp and finished the rest of his special tea. "Okay. Feelings. Deep feelings. Got it."

"Good luck!" Zain and Gabe called as Ryan stood and walked determinedly out the door.

"Think it will work?" Gabe asked his older-by-a-minute brother.

Zain shook his head as he tossed some money on the table and stood. "Not a chance. But I'm not going to miss this for the world."

Chapter Fifteen

The doorbell had caught Sienna by surprise. Nash had pulled his gun and Sophie had quietly slipped her hand to the small of her back as she went with Nash to open the door. A deliveryman stood holding a massive bouquet of red roses.

"Sienna Ashton?"

Sienna had stood and signed for the delivery, her friends clustered around while she read the card. *A rose for every year I have loved you.*

"There are twenty-eight roses here." Sophie smiled.

"That's sweet." Riley sighed.

"I want someone to send me flowers," Reagan grumbled as she took another sip of wine.

"Maybe you should stop gloating every time you beat them, and maybe you'll get flowers from a guy once in a while," Piper teased.

Fifteen minutes later Sienna found herself signing for another package. She ripped open the wrapping paper and found a two-pound box of chocolates with a note attached. *To eat while discussing how stupid men are with my cousins, the traitors.*

"Traitors," Layne laughed as each girl grabbed a piece of chocolate.

"When will he ever learn we women have to stick

together? Isn't that right, Nash?" Reagan asked, biting into a creamy melt-in-your-mouth truffle.

Nash just smiled and kept leaning against the wall with his muscled arms crossed over his broad chest.

Sienna sat back and let the conversation surround her. Ryan loved her. He admitted he had been stupid. Should she forgive him? Or the better question was, would he do this again? If he believed in her, it should never have come up. She didn't know what was worse, having love outside her grasp all these years or being loved, but not unconditionally.

The doorbell rang again, and Hooch finally lifted his head. Nash pushed himself from the wall and headed for the door. Sophie stood between Sienna and the door.

"Who are you?" Nash asked in a not-so-friendly tone and the room went quiet.

"I'm Sienna's date, Seth. Who are you?"

Annoyance filled Sienna. But Sophie kept her view of Seth blocked.

"I think you got the wrong night. And I'm pretty sure you're the wrong guy," Sophie said with her arms crossed.

"Who's that?" Piper whispered.

Sienna leaned forward. "I dated him before Ryan got into town. He's a sports agent."

"Do you still want to date him?" Riley asked.

Sienna shook her head in the negative.

"Is this the guy? You know, the one who Ryan went all caveman about?" Reagan whispered.

Sienna nodded her head in the affirmative.

"Look, I'd like to see Sienna. We have a date. I'm her boyfriend, and you still haven't told me who you are." Seth tried to push past Nash, but in a split-second ended up on his butt on the porch.

"Wait here." Nash closed the door and turned to Sienna. "What do you want me to do, Sienna? Is it Ryan or this guy?"

Sienna looked between the cards in her lap and the door. "Ryan. It will always be Ryan."

Nash opened the door. Sienna stood to tell Seth herself, but Nash spoke first. "She doesn't want to see you."

He went to close the door, and Seth shot his hand out. Sienna hurried forward. Nash's whole body had done the opposite of what she had expected. She had expected him to tense, but instead he had relaxed and a slow smile spread over his face. A smile that sent shivers down her back.

"I got this, Nash," Sienna called out and pushed forward with all of her girlfriends standing behind her. She heard Hooch growling from the living room. The thought that her big lump of a dog would move off the couch and do anything was laughable.

Nash didn't budge from his spot at the door.

"Down boy, *woof*," Seth barked with a cocky grin on his face.

Nash just smiled as the group sucked in air. Seth took a step back and his smile faltered. Sienna pushed past Nash onto the porch.

"That's no way to talk to a friend of mine." She was furious. How had she not noticed how arrogant he was?

"Relax. It was a joke. Sienna, what's going on? Some neighbor boy comes home, and suddenly what we had is gone? I can't even come over without being accosted." Seth's eyes darted at Nash.

"My friends are only worried about me because of what happened to Malik and Jaylen. Aren't you worried?" Sienna asked.

Seth put on puppy dog eyes, and Sienna felt as if she

were seeing him clearly for the first time. Everything was an act.

"It's horrible what's happened, but it doesn't affect us."

"You're their agent. It affects you greatly," Sienna pointed out. How could he be so cold about the murder of a longtime client?

"What affects me is the way you're acting. Stop playing hard to get. I know women like to make men jealous, but, babe, in the end I always win. Look at me; this is a five-hundred-dollar shirt. I drive a Bentley. I have a house in the Hamptons, condos in L.A. and New York, and a beach house in Miami. Guys like me always get the girl."

Reagan snorted. "He's a guy with a banged-up Bentley."

Seth stiffened and in his righteous indignation didn't pay attention to the expensive sleek SUV pulling to a stop behind him. The doors opened as Zain, Gabe, and Ryan stepped out. Sienna wanted to scream. Could there be any worse timing?

Seth's nostrils flared. "My car is worth more than that man will make in ten years. I know it's hard for you country girls to understand how much money I'm worth, but trust me, it's enough to keep you very well."

"Keep me?" Sienna's temper flared. "That's all you want, isn't it? Some woman to keep like a pet. Dress her up and parade her around all your friends. Well, I'm not that girl, and I don't give a shit about your car or your money."

"You will care when you're stuck on a government salary because you're unemployable. I'm very powerful, and I'll have you fired from every sports team you can imagine."

"First, she'll have love, and that'll keep her warm at night," Ryan said from behind Seth.

Seth's eyes rolled. "You're like her watchdog. It's pathetic. When she tells you to jump, will you do it?"

"Among other things that I'll be doing for her," Ryan smiled, "and to her."

"T-M-I," Sophie groaned.

Sienna felt the situation deteriorating and stepped forward, getting Seth's attention again. "Seth, you're a fun guy, and someday you'll find someone who is interested in being a trophy for you. But I'm not her."

Seth turned red, and his whole body tensed. "No one says no to me."

"Are you threatening her?" Ryan asked. He came to stand behind Seth, making him choose between looking at him or her.

"I don't have to resort to threats. I'll just have her fired. Her father is only the minority owner after all." Seth shot her a triumphant grin. "I'll talk to the other owners, and you'll be sorry you didn't take what I offered."

"Oh, you want to talk to the majority owner, do you?" Zain asked casually even though his dark brown eyes had turned almost black in controlled anger.

"I'm so tired of all this hired help butting in," Seth complained. "I'm leaving. This is your last chance. Come with me, and I'll forget about this momentary lapse of yours."

Sienna stood with her arms crossed. "I'll never go with you."

"Then don't bother showing up at work tomorrow," Seth spat as he turned away from her.

Ryan stepped in front of him and stopped his descent down the steps. "No one talks with such disrespect to the woman I love."

"Want to hit me? Go ahead. I dare you. Then I can have

you fired, too."

Zain's fist lashed out so fast Seth never saw it coming. Seth spun and lost his balance. Sienna gasped as Seth and his five-hundred-dollar shirt fell down the steps and landed with a thud on the stone pathway. Hooch ambled past Sienna and down the steps. With a groan, he shook his droopy jowls and covered Seth in slobber, sauntering over to the bright yellow sports car and lifting his leg.

"I'm calling the police. I'm having you arrested!" Seth screamed almost joyfully.

"Go ahead. In fact, there's a state trooper right now," Zain said, gesturing to the cruiser flying up the driveway.

Ryan left Seth in Zain, Gabe, and Nash's capable hands and took Sienna's hands in his. Sienna's face alternated between anger and fear, and he wanted—no, he *needed*—to be there next to her to offer any kind of support she might need.

"I'm so sorry," Ryan whispered, wrapping his arms around her. He pulled her close and rested his chin on the top of her head. "I was so jealous. I forgot to be the man I want to always be for you. Instead I acted as if I were an undisciplined child. You're not a toy to be fought over. You're a woman who deserves to be loved unconditionally."

Once Ryan started, he couldn't seem to stop. He saw Matt's cruiser come to a stop and was glad he'd texted him as soon as he saw the neon yellow sports car in Sienna's driveway. He pulled back and looked into Sienna's eyes.

"Let me be that man. I will never have as much money as Seth, but I guarantee I will love you better than any man ever could. Please forgive me, Sienna. Say you'll give me another chance."

Ryan held his breath and waited for Sienna's answer.

He silently pleaded with her to take him back.

"Oh, Ryan. Why have we always been at odds? First it was you chasing me. Then it was me chasing you," Sienna said.

Ryan felt as if a fist has knocked him in the heart. He was losing her, and that terrified him more now than it had when he was a cocky teenager, thinking he could forget her. "I'm done chasing, Sienna. It's you. It's always been you, and I'll be right here waiting for you if you need time."

"Did you really think I was part of some grand terrorist scheme?" Sienna asked. He heard the hurt in her voice and felt it like a stab wound.

He shook his head. "No. I lashed out because I thought I might lose you to Seth. It was a stupid case of *Manleus Stupidious*." When Sienna laughed, his heart soared. "Do you forgive me?"

Sienna nodded, and he crushed her to his chest. "I'm so sorry, sweetheart."

"You're still not forgiven. I believe jewelry is next in the man playbook," she joked before rising up on her toes and tilting her head back to look him in the eyes. "I love you, too."

"And this lowlife punched me! I want him arrested!" Seth's screaming interrupted their moment. Ryan put his arm around Sienna's shoulder and pulled her tight against his side as they enjoyed the show.

Matt held up his hands to calm Seth. "I'm sorry, sir. I can't arrest him."

"You hillbillies are all the same. Everyone's in each other's pocket and related to each other." Seth snorted. "Well, clearly you two aren't related, so arrest him or I'll report you to your superior."

"Go ahead, sir. But I can't arrest someone with

diplomatic immunity, and my boss can't either," Matt said with infinite patience. By the way his eye started ticking, Ryan could tell the patience was wearing thin.

"Diplomatic immunity? Him? He's in jeans and cowboy boots. What kind of immunity does he have?"

"You didn't tell him, Zain?" Matt asked, turning away from a disbelieving Seth.

"Tell me what?" Seth demanded.

"I can't arrest him because he is His Royal Highness Zain Ali Rahman, Prince of Rahmi."

Seth stammered the word *prince* a couple of times before it hit him why the name Ali Rahman sounded familiar. "The majority owner," was all Seth could get out.

Zain grinned in response.

"I'm sorry to have misread the situation," Seth said slowly as he hurried to his car. Ryan watched him give Hooch a wide berth and speed off.

"That was the dick you thought Sienna was sleeping with?" Matt asked into the silence as everyone stood on the porch, watching the bright yellow car race off.

"Matt has a point," Layne said and crossed her arms. Great, now even his cousins were against him. Good thing he snuck in while Seth was distracting them all to get Sienna to forgive him.

Sophie shrugged her shoulders. "I don't know. I might want to be a kept woman."

Nash made a strangled sound from behind Ryan. He didn't want to think about what that meant. Right now he only wanted to think about the woman he loved in his arms and how to get rid of the way-too-many people around them. Where was Hooch and one of his room-clearing farts when he needed him?

"Sophie, when did you get back?" Ryan asked. He

winked at his cousin, hoping she'd get the hint to leave.

"Just a while ago. Imagine me getting home from China to find you home. It's so good to see you, cousin. I feel like we should spend the whole night catching up."

He hated his cousin. Sophie's lips quirked in mock innocence.

It only took a second for the others to catch on. "That sounds divine, Soph. Why didn't I think of that?" Layne asked and came up and laced her arm through Ryan's.

"An all-night slumber party!" Reagan cheered.

"Just like old times when we would all spend the night at Grandma and Grandpa Davies's home." Riley actually clapped like an excited schoolgirl. Oh, he would get them back somehow.

"And we would stay up. All. Night. Long. Together." Piper smirked. "Doesn't that sound fun?"

He felt Sienna's shoulders begin to shake as she buried her head in his chest and laughed. He was going to have to suffer, but Sienna was worth it.

"That sounds great. Sophie, why don't you and Nash share a sleeping bag? And the twins should be with another set of twins. Let's see — I'm with Sienna, so, Matt, I bet you and Piper could fit on the couch together. That just leaves you, Layne. I could call Seth back so you won't be alone, just in case we pair off to play hide and seek."

Ryan was attacked all at once by laughing women, smacking him on his arm.

"Fine. We'll take the hint." Sophie laughed.

Gabe looked around at everyone and frowned. "So, we're not hanging out?"

His brother elbowed him. "Ladies, can we offer you a ride?"

"Yeah, a ride." Gabe smiled.

Nash made another strangled sound behind him.

"Let's go to the water tower. We haven't hung out there in years," Reagan suggested.

"Great idea. Hey, Gabe, does that thing come loaded with a bar?" Riley asked as Gabe and Zain opened the door for the ladies.

"This will make work so much fun tomorrow," Layne said sarcastically and climbed in.

Nash stepped forward after the SUV took off. "Call me if you need me. I'm happy for you both."

Sienna leaned forward and placed a kiss on his cheek. Ryan reined in his jealousy and waited for her to return to his arms.

"Thank you for tonight," Sienna told Nash. "You're a good friend."

Ryan held out his hand. "I couldn't agree more," he said, shaking Nash's hand.

Nash smiled and disappeared into the shadows of the backyard. A minute later the sound of an ATV taking off was their cue they were finally alone.

Sienna kept her head against Ryan's chest as they watched Nash disappear into the moonless night. The wind rustled the leaves and the smell of the approaching fall triggered images of her and Ryan next to a fire. Very quickly, those images turned to something as hot as the fire, and Sienna shifted closer to Ryan.

"Ryan?" she asked quietly.

"Yes, sweetheart?" His warm lips brushed the smooth skin of her forehead in a gentle kiss.

"What's going to happen to us?"

"What do you mean?" Ryan asked softly.

"We love each other, but what's next? What happens

when the case is solved and I'm no longer in danger?"

Sienna felt Ryan hold his breath for just a second. Instead of answering, his fingers ran a tender trail down her spine while his lips kissed her forehead, her eyebrow, the tip of her nose, the path of her jaw, and finally her lips. Her breathing hitched as she melted into him. His hand slid under the waistband of her skirt and squeezed her ass at the same time his tongue grew urgent inside her mouth. Sienna thought he might not have heard her.

Ryan pulled her against him, and she couldn't help pressing herself against his erection. How many years had they wasted when they could have been doing this the whole time? Sienna felt her heart hitch as her movements became urgent. She had to be with him on a completely different level that was far beyond the physical. She gripped the front of his shirt and ripped. Hooch howled, buttons tinkled like raindrops on the porch, and their breath thundered between frantic kisses.

Ryan pulled her back toward the swinging bench as he pushed down her skirt and panties. Sienna stepped out of them and reached for his zipper. Nash's advice to read Ryan's actions fluttered through her mind. And by the desperate way he was preying on her mouth, and the way his hands were memorizing her body, she was afraid she had her answer.

Her heart wept for him, for what might have been, as she pushed him down on the swing and straddled him. And together they cried out into the night. They cried their pleasure, their pain, and their knowledge that this was not meant to be.

Chapter Sixteen

Ryan's phone rang somewhere in the house and woke him from an exhausting night. He and Sienna had not said a word as they made love through the night. They would fall asleep entangled. Then sometime later, he would feel her hand wrapped around him, caressing him from his sleep. He rolled over and took her slowly as their foreheads rested against each other. Their eyes locked, and they came together, then once again drifted off to sleep. He knew the night was over at the sound of the phone. For all their love, they never seemed to be able to find themselves on the same page.

He untangled himself from Sienna's nude body and went to find his phone.

"Parker."

"It's Shaw. Arnie is dead."

Ryan froze. He couldn't have heard that right. "What?"

"They killed him, Ryan. He was found shot in his car outside of his home. Same with Simmons, Landry, and Perret."

That was the entire undercover operation against The Suit with the exception of him! "Do they have any leads?"

"No. I'm sorry, Ryan. Is there anything I can do?"

Ryan shook his head. "No. I have enough backup here, and now I know they are coming. I just wish I knew what this had to do with Sienna."

"I can't figure that out either. The hits against the players are totally out of character. They have to be worried about their identity becoming known to be tying up all these loose ends. The key may be there in Kentucky."

"Ryan? What is it?" Sienna asked from the doorway with nothing but his dress shirt wrapped around her.

"I have to go, Shaw. Thanks for calling." Ryan hung up and looked at the woman he loved. How far would he go to protect her? That was an easy question—he'd protect her with his life.

"We need to move Jaylen, and we can't tell anyone about it. My handler was worried about a leak, and we can't trust the Lexington police, my dad's office, nothing."

"Ryan, you're scaring me. What's happened?"

Ryan stepped into his jeans and then looked at her. Her hair was a beautiful mess and the love she had for him was right there for the world to see in her eyes. "My unit has all been killed. I'll be next. Then it will be you and Jaylen. I need to see you safe before I go after them."

"I'll help you. I'll be by your side the entire time. I may not look like it, but there's a lot of fight in me," Sienna said staunchly.

Ryan didn't answer. He just stepped forward to wrap her in his arms.

"So, our time is up?" she asked.

Ryan couldn't voice his answer, the answer they both already knew.

"Well, I have an idea where to put Jaylen," she said.

"I need all the ideas I can get."

"Keeneston. There is no place safer than Keeneston." Sienna's smile was faint, but she had a point. Keeneston was contained, and they knew every inch of it.

"Now I just need to think of a way to get Jaylen out of the hospital," Ryan said to himself as looked down at the woman he loved—the woman he'd give his life for. And that was exactly what he was prepared to do.

Sienna sat in the booth at the Blossom Café and waited for Katelyn Davies and Emma Miller to show up. Ryan had gone to talk with his father to fill him in on the deaths in L.A. while she set the plan in motion to move Jaylen Cox from the hospital to Keeneston.

Sienna looked at her coffee and stared into its depths. She should have felt paralyzing fear. Instead she felt numb. She knew what she needed to do. She would draw them out. She would offer herself to save the man she loved. She knew Ryan would be furious. But she would do anything to protect him.

"Sienna?" A hand came to rest on her shoulder. She jerked her eyes from her coffee to find Emma standing in front of her. "Sorry to startle you, but I said your name a couple times."

Sienna looked into Emma's concerned eyes and gave a weak smile. Emma was her mother's age, and her brown curly hair was pulled back into a sloppy bun at the top of her head. Sprigs of curls cascaded down the nape of her neck. She had her scrubs on, which reminded Sienna why Dr. Emma Miller was there. She worked at Jaylen's hospital.

"Dreaming of an engagement to my nephew perhaps?" Katelyn Davies smiled as she came up to the table. Sydney's mom had been a model just like Syd. But after her modeling career, she'd returned to Keeneston and opened a veterinarian clinic.

The two women slid into the booth and ordered coffee from Zinnia before Katelyn turned her cornflower blue eyes to Sienna. "What's going on?" She must have sensed it was serious because Katelyn's voice was deadly serious.

"I need your help. Both of you." Sienna sighed. "I don't even know where to start."

"How about at the beginning?" Emma smiled kindly and urged Sienna on.

"I need your help saving the live of a patient of mine," Sienna started and then it flowed out—how her life, Ryan's life, and Jaylen's life were in danger. How the men knew where she lived, had already killed Malik, and had tried to attack Ryan. But she didn't tell them how she planned to sacrifice herself so Ryan could be safe. No one would be suspicious of a woman like her asking for a meeting alone. When they searched her house, they wouldn't find any weapons, but she knew where to get them and how to use them. They would never see her coming.

"You want me to steal a patient from my hospital?" Emma asked slowly.

"And you want me to put him up at my animal hospital?" Katelyn followed up questioningly.

"Yes." Sienna nodded. "And I know that I'm asking a lot, but we have to break some rules to save lives. I'll take full blame if we get caught. I was just hoping you would have an idea how we could get Jaylen out from protective custody."

Emma shook her head and more curls sprang loose. "I have no idea."

"We might be able to help with that, dear."

Sienna looked up at three pairs of matching eyes and permed white hair. "You were eavesdropping?"

Miss Lily just smirked. "Of course."

"But we can help," Miss Violet said encouragingly.

Miss Daisy nodded. "It's been mighty dull around here lately. I have a drawer full of unused wooden spoons I've been itching to use."

Katelyn snorted most shockingly for someone as strikingly beautiful as she, but nodded her head. "I can get us some backup, too."

"You're not going to talk me out of this?" Sienna asked in wonder.

"Oh, honey. You have no idea the things we've done in our lives. This is a piece of cake," Miss Lily said knowingly.

"Zinnia! Poppy!" Miss Violet called out. The two cousins, however many generations apart, came rushing forward. "We're back in action. I need dozens of cookies, pies, brownies, whatever, enough to fill that huge serving cart Mo uses for his fancy receptions."

Emma smirked. "You're going to cram him underneath it, aren't you?"

"Sure am. No one will think twice about three old ladies handing out sweets at the hospital. I even have a candy striper outfit from . . ." Miss Daisy blushed, "never mind from where."

"I'll call Anton. He'll get it for us," Miss Violet said.

"And Charlie and Emma can take shifts checking in on Jaylen at the vet clinic. My Charlie was a great surgeon in his day, and he's been itching to practice medicine again," Miss Daisy said proudly.

"And John will round up the troops. No one will step foot in this town without us knowing about it," Miss Lily said as she patted Sienna's hand reassuringly. "Don't worry, we'll get these guys."

When Miss Lily said it, everyone at the table nodded. The Rose sisters looked practically gleeful. What had happened in Keeneston before she was born? Their parents were definitely not telling them things, especially by the way neither Emma nor Katelyn looked surprised by the idea of terrorists in Keeneston.

Ryan sat in the uncomfortable chair in his dad's office and filled him in on the latest. "Sienna says she has a plan for getting Jaylen out of the hospital. I just feel the less people who know about it the better. I don't want anyone else being considered a loose end or, worse, becoming the next leak."

Cole's phone went off, and he looked down at a text. "Good idea about placing Jaylen at Katelyn's."

"What?"

"Sienna's plan. It's smart," Cole told his son.

"How do you know that's the plan? Sienna didn't even tell me what it was. She said she needed to talk to some people first to see if it was a go." Ryan sat at the edge of his seat and tried to see the text message his dad had just received.

"John. It's on the town text system. So much faster than the old telephone system the Rose sisters could activate when something was going down in the old days."

"Going down? In Keeneston? Dad, nothing ever happens in Keeneston." Ryan let out a frustrated breath. So much for this being a secret.

"You have no idea. Don't worry. This will help you. No one in this text loop will say a word. Think of it as a citizen brigade."

"So, what's the plan then?" Ryan asked grudgingly. At least no one knew of his idea to protect Sienna. He would take down The Suit or die trying.

The next day, Dr. Emma Miller confidently approached the hall, which was guarded by two armed officers, and disappeared into Jaylen's room. Sienna watched from the nurses' station at the end of the hall where she was dressed in scrubs wearing a mask and hair cover. Cole had Dr. Miller put on the approved physician's list, and Emma had gotten Jaylen's regular doctor to take a couple of days off. Something about telling his wife about the affair he was having with the head nurse on this floor. It worked like a charm and now there was no one who was going to stop the Rose sisters as they got off the elevator.

Sure enough, they were in official candy striper outfits as they pushed the biggest serving cart Sienna had ever seen. They stopped in the nurses' station and handed out sweets. Sienna tried to blend in and noticed the guards eyeing the treats and practically drooling.

The Rose sisters pushed the cart away and headed for the officers. They stopped at the only other occupied room, and five minutes later they reappeared in the hallway. Sienna pretended to review the file she held as the sisters stopped in front of the officers. Miss Lily reached up and patted one of them on the cheek before Miss Violet buried the other officer's head in her over-fluffed bosom. Miss Violet looked thrilled; the officer looked like he was having trouble breathing.

The guards took some brownies and cookies, and Sienna saw Miss Daisy signal to go inside Jaylen's room. Dr. Miller made her appearance at the door and smiled at the older women.

"Ladies, did you save me a piece of the peanut butter chocolate brownie I asked for?" Sienna heard Emma ask.

Miss Lily handed her a brownie.

"There is a very hungry man back here, but you better not spoil him. He's still on a restrictive diet. He can only have one. On second thought, I better go with you to make sure he only takes one. He's a charmer," Dr. Miller laughed.

And just like that the officers sat down to eat their treats as the Rose sisters walked into Jaylen's room with Dr. Miller. Less than five minutes later, the cart was wheeled back out by three struggling ninety-five-year-old women.

Sienna saw them trying not to show strain pushing the cart. But with Jaylen lying beneath the white cloth, they were suddenly pushing over two hundred pounds of man along with all their desserts.

"Ladies!" Sienna called out in a full Southern accent. "Can I get one of those brownies Dr. Miller was talking about?"

Sienna held her breath and walked up the hall, taking the brownie Miss Violet held out for her. She took a bite and groaned. They really were delicious. "Have you tried these?" Sienna asked the officers and then proceeded to unload some more of the desserts on them.

"We still need to get the surgical floor; are you heading that way?" Miss Lily asked Sienna who was starting to sweat in her full surgical get-up.

"Sure am, let me help you with this," Sienna said as she tried to effortlessly push the cart to the elevator.

"I gave Mr. Cox a sedative. He was complaining of nightmares. He'll be out for at least six hours," Emma told the guards as she placed Jaylen's chart on the door for the night shift doctor to review.

While the guards were talking to her, Sienna and the Rose sisters pushed the cart as fast as they could to the elevator. Emma smiled at the guards and took off in the other direction from the group pushing Jaylen. "My shift's over. I'll see you men tomorrow," she called out to the guards.

The elevator chimed and Sienna pushed Jaylen inside. She was quiet as the people on the elevator chatted with the Rose sisters and took treats off the service cart. They reached the main floor, and Sienna pushed the cart right out the back door. The Rose sisters kept up their chattering as Charlie and Anton drove up in a big white van to meet them.

Ryan had pointed out the location of the cameras and told Anton exactly where to park so the cameras couldn't pick up the activity going on at the back of the van. Miss Lily opened the back doors while Charlie hopped out to help unload the leftover desserts.

Ryan took the desserts Miss Lily handed to him and stacked them up in the back of the van. He heard Sienna say her goodbyes in a horrible, fake, deep Southern accent and head back inside. Once the top of the service cart was emptied, Ryan and Anton braced themselves against the door. Charlie and Miss Daisy helped Jaylen out from underneath the cart. Miss Lily and Miss Violet took the time to shake off the large tablecloth and slowly fold it, further protecting Jaylen from view.

"Here we go, son," Charlie told Jaylen and helped him stand up.

Ryan and Anton leaned forward and each took a hand. Jaylen grimaced as he moved his leg to climb inside the van. Ryan grunted and pulled while Charlie cursed as he used his shoulder to push Jaylen's butt up and into the van.

Ryan, Anton, and Jaylen collapsed onto the floor of the van. Charlie hurried to load the cart and soon they were all piled in the van and headed toward Georgetown.

Ryan wasn't taking any chances at being followed. His father would pick them up on New Circle Road and watch for tails. If there were none, then they would take the scenic route back to Keeneston.

"Oh, you poor dear. Can we do anything to make you more comfortable?" Miss Violet asked as she pulled a crocheted blanket over Jaylen.

"No thank you, ma'am. I sure do appreciate you busting me out of that place. That detective was starting to get on my nerves. How many times do I have to tell her I don't know anything about Doc Ashton and Seth." Jaylen looked at Ryan and frowned. "I'm kinda surprised to see you still. I thought the doc would have filleted you by now."

"Her, my mother, these ladies, yeah," Ryan said with grin. "Pretty much the whole town let me have it."

"Where is the doc? That other doctor with the curly hair told me what was going on, but she said this was all Dr. Ashton's plan."

"Nash, a security expert, is with her. She'll meet us at your safe place," Ryan told him as he tried to avoid the subject of where this safe place was. He had a feeling Jaylen wasn't going to like it.

The van pulled up to the Keeneston Animal Hospital. The back door was flung open and Katelyn, Marshall, and Cole stood looking inside.

Jaylen winced as he sat up. "Do I hear dogs barking?"

Katelyn smiled. "Hi. I'm Dr. Katelyn Davies and this is my husband, Sheriff Marshall Davies. Over here is Ryan's father, FBI Agent in Charge Cole Parker. Welcome to my place. I have a run all set up for you."

"You mean room," Jaylen said as he shook Katelyn's hand. Katelyn just smiled back, not correcting him. "You look so familiar . . . no way," Jaylen shook his head. "Katelyn Jacks, the supermodel?"

"That's me. But I haven't been a model in decades."

"You're a doctor now, wow. That's impressive. If I weren't in love with the angel who saved me, I would totally want to know if you had a daughter."

Ryan heard Marshall grind his teeth together and place his hand on his gun. "Okay, let's show you where we're going to keep you for the next little bit."

Marshall, Cole, and Ryan helped Jaylen from the van as the Rose sisters and Anton left to return the van. Charlie slowly climbed out and stood behind Ryan.

"Why do I keep hearing barking?" Jaylen asked as they helped walk him through the back door. He looked around at the operating room, and as they passed the storage room, he noticed the bags of pet food. "What kind of hospital is this?"

"It's my animal hospital," Katelyn said as sweetly as she could.

Jaylen stopped walking.

"Your run is right up here." Katelyn opened a chain-link door, and Jaylen peered in.

"No way," was all he said as he started backing up.

"I gave you the double run and even brought in a twin bed, a nightstand, and lamp from home. It's just like a dorm room really," Katelyn pointed out.

"I didn't go to college with a bunch of dogs!" Jaylen yelled.

Katelyn shrugged her shoulder. "I've seen my son's dorm. That's debatable."

Ryan gave Jaylen a little nudge. "You will be totally

safe here. Come on, your bandage is seeping. You need to lie down. Charlie!"

"I'm on it," Charlie opened up an old, well-worn medical bag and snapped on a pair of gloves. "Into bed with you, young man."

"What you are going to do?" Jaylen asked fearfully.

"I need to hook up your IV and probably put another stitch in," Charlie told him, pulling out an IV bag.

"You're like a hundred years old," Jaylen stammered.

"Ninety-five, but who's counting?" Charlie smiled.

Ryan urged Jaylen into bed. "Charlie used to be the head of surgery in Boston. He knows what he's doing."

Jaylen closed his eyes. "This is a weird dream. I'm going to wake up in my own bed in the morning."

Ryan slapped Charlie on the back and grinned. The old man looked elated to stick a needle in someone again. The backdoor opened, and Ryan heard heavy footsteps. His father and uncle were already checking it out. Nash and Sienna came to the run door a few seconds later.

"How are you doing, Jaylen?" Sienna asked calmly and sat on the other side of the bed from the one where Charlie was working.

"This is a dream, right, Doc?"

Sienna pulled out a needle and injected it into the IV. "You'll wake up tomorrow, and we'll tackle it then. Before you fall asleep, Jaylen, what has Detective Braxton been asking about?"

Jaylen yawned. "You mostly. And Seth. I'm sorry, Doc. I don't have the answers. But, I'll give you something she wanted that I wouldn't give her."

Sienna patted his hand. "What's that?"

"The password to my email. She wanted to read it. But I only trust you, Doc."

Ryan watched as Sienna leaned forward, and Jaylen whispered in her ear. She sat back up and Jaylen's eyes were already closed.

"How is he, Charlie?" Ryan asked.

"Good. I just need to replace a single stitch, and then I'll stay here until Dr. Emma relieves me tonight. He'll be just fine." Charlie smiled up at the group.

"I'm staying with you, too," Marshall told him and pulled a chair into the kennel run. "Cole will be checking in as well, and Noodle will stay with his wife for the night shift."

Ryan nodded and slid his arm around Sienna. "Want to have a romantic date reading Jaylen's emails?"

"I'd like nothing better." She smiled up at him.

Chapter Seventeen

Sienna's eyes crossed with exhaustion. She and Ryan had stayed up all night reading Jaylen's emails. Some she could never unread. And she had thought Henry's pick-up lines were bad. The Earth may implode if Jaylen and Henry ever got together. Besides his horrible emails with women, there were the financial reports Seth had finally sent after Jaylen had asked for them at least ten times. Then there were emails with the other players. She'd learned they all liked her, thought the new weight trainer checked himself out in the mirror too much, and they were all scared of Janice.

"Nothing," Sienna complained as she tossed the last paper onto her coffee table. "Please tell me you found something."

"I found out the guys think the weight trainer takes too many selfies."

"Ugh. I found that out, too." Sienna sat up and went to pour a cup of coffee.

Ryan took the cup she offered him and took a sip. "And as much as I wanted to find something horrible about Seth, all Jaylen complained about was him being slow on getting paperwork to him."

"The financials showed that he was making money for a while and then the money was reinvested. During the past year, the investments didn't pan out. I guess that's why it took Jaylen by surprise that he didn't have enough cash to buy a house." Sienna sat down on the couch next to Ryan and laid her head on his chest.

She yawned and wanted to close her eyes, but she needed to get to work. The Thoroughbreds had an away game that week, and she needed to prep some of her players for life on the road. "Do you think you can get Malik's emails? We can compare them to see if there's anything in common."

Ryan put his arm around her, and she struggled to stay awake as he slowly ran his hand over her back. "Yeah, I can do that. I can drop you off at the office and then pay Detective Braxton a visit."

His phone rang. "Speak of the devil."

Sienna shot up. "You can't tell her about Jaylen or the emails. I don't trust her yet."

"This ain't my first rodeo, sweetheart." Ryan grinned before answering the phone.

Sienna smothered a laugh as Ryan acted totally shocked, angered, and desperate, finding out Jaylen was missing. She wanted to give him a high five when he talked Braxton into letting him have copies of Malik's emails to see if there's any hint to a place Jaylen may take himself.

Ryan hung up with a promise to meet the detective within the hour. "It was a good thing you had Jaylen change into his street clothes to leave. They think he left on his own. They can't figure out why they can't find him on the security tape leaving."

Sienna snickered and sipped her coffee. "I have no idea," she said innocently.

Ryan had made sure she was safe behind her office door

and Janice was on full lookout, along with the guards at the stadium, before he left to meet Detective Braxton with Hooch in tow. Sienna was only in her office five minutes before the first knock on the door. Sienna looked up and smiled at Coach Trey Everett.

Trey was in his late forties and still as handsome as when he had played in the NFL. His wife, Taylor, had been America's Sweetheart. She had four Academy Awards on their mantel at home next to Trey's football trophies and their two sons' artwork and trophies. His sons were now sixteen and fourteen years and excelling in high school.

"Morning, Trey." Sienna smiled up at him. She didn't need to pretend with him. He was from Keeneston and had babysat her a couple times when he was home from college.

Trey closed the door and took a seat across her desk. "How's my running back doing?"

Sienna blinked. "I don't know what you're talking about."

"You know, the 215-pound man hiding in a run at the vet clinic."

"John," Sienna grumbled.

"I'm on the text tree. I got the text yesterday and plan to stop by today to check on him. Is there anything I should or shouldn't say?"

Sienna shook her head. "Just make sure he understands the importance of staying put and not contacting anyone."

"Will do. You'll let me know if there's anything I can do for you or Ryan, right?"

"Of course. Thanks, Trey."

Trey stood and opened the door, and Sienna sighed. She already had a line of rookies waiting to talk to her.

Ryan was too tired to pretend to care about Detective Braxton's rant. He thumbed through Malik's emails and made notes about any similarities with Jaylen's. They both had a fear of Janice, and the weight coach was a little more eager to snap a selfie than a grown man should be.

"I know she has something to do with this. I should get a search warrant for her house," Detective Braxton spat as she paced her small office.

That finally drew Ryan's attention from last year's report from Rook Capital Management. He needed a copy of this to compare to Jaylen's. There were emails asking Seth to forward this year's reports to Malik, but he didn't have time to get them before he was murdered.

"Wait, what are you talking about?" Ryan asked. Braxton huffed and then launched on a tirade about how Sienna was harboring Jaylen. Braxton had no evidence of it other than her dislike of Sienna's defensiveness about being tied to terrorism, so Ryan didn't give it much credence.

"She's your girlfriend. Did she tell you where Jaylen is?"

Ryan smirked. "Not at her house, I can tell you that much."

Braxton rolled her eyes at him. "Did you find anything?"

"Not really. It just looks like he was getting all his ducks in a row to retire. Nothing out of the ordinary. No scathing emails against Seth. No *this guy may kill me*. Nothing."

Braxton nodded. "That was my opinion as well. I just have a feeling I'm missing something. I have that creepy, crawling feeling that something is going to happen, and I'm afraid I won't be able to stop it."

Ryan looked down at his arms—his hair was standing

up.

"You don't have to hide your laugh. I know it's silly."

"No," Ryan told her. "It's not silly. It's just strange. I have that same feeling."

Sienna looked at the large lineman crying on her couch and wanted to give him a hug. Zack Sanders may be the biggest man she'd ever known, but he was also the most sensitive.

"I just don't understand why they always boo us. And when we go through the tunnel they yell at us. Don't they know this is just a game? A game we love with all our hearts."

"Zack, fan mentality is something you need to teach yourself to block out. Especially when you're on the road. You have no control over it. It's similar to a mob effect. You don't need to worry about them. You need to worry about yourself," Sienna told him as she handed him a tissue.

"I know. I just want to enjoy the game."

"But once you're out on the field, do you hear them, or are they pushed into the background?"

"I feel the energy. It's awesome. I don't really hear them because I'm so focused on the plays," Zack told her before blowing his nose.

"Have you tried putting in earplugs for away games?" Sienna held up her hand to stop him from talking. "Not for the game, but from the time you leave the locker room until both teams are on the field. That way you can *feel* the energy, the noise, and the excitement, but you won't be worried about running through the tunnel. Keep the earplugs in, your helmet on, and do your pregame concentration warm-up. Focus on you and your love of the game."

Zack nodded. "I can try that, Doc."

"So, now that we have a plan, how is everything else going that we've been working on?" Sienna smiled as she saw Zack brighten up.

"Good. I have a date. With a woman. A real one."

Fifteen minutes later, Zack stood up and wrapped his arms around her. When he hugged her, Sienna's feet came off the ground and air whooshed from her lungs. "If there's ever anything I can do for you, Doc, just let me know. I have to meet with my agent before we leave for the game."

Sienna felt her breathing stop. "Seth's still here?"

Zack nodded. "He had some loose ends to tie up and one more meeting with me. Then he's heading out. See you later, Doc." Sienna gave him a weak smile as he lumbered out the door. He kind of reminded her of a blond Hooch.

A shiver ran down her back; Sienna grew cold. She didn't like that Seth was in the building. He had scared her the other night, and everything inside her was screaming to get as far away from him as possible. She heard his laugh in the hallway and sat rigid in her chair. When the door to the small meeting room down the hall closed, she didn't bother waiting for Ryan to arrive. She needed to get out of there now.

Sienna grabbed her purse and slipped from her office. She walked as quickly and quietly as she could down the hall and sighed in relief when Janice's desk came into view.

"Hello there, sugar. Is that hunk of a man coming up to meet you?" Janice asked and looked Sienna over before frowning. "What's going on?"

Sienna tried to smile, but when the conference room door opened she forgot to pretend that everything was all right. "I was supposed to meet Ryan here, but I don't want to be here anymore. I'm going to the guard's station at the entrance of the parking lot so I can flag Ryan down. If I somehow miss him, will you tell him that's where I am?"

Janice followed Sienna's look to the back of the hallways. "Sure thing, sugar." Janice patted her hand and then shooed her to the elevator.

Sienna didn't think she took a breath until the elevator doors closed. She closed her eyes and collected herself. It wasn't like her to be so scared of one person, but it was as if her body was on high alert. Her heart pounded, her breathing was heavy, and she couldn't stop thinking someone was behind her.

The elevator doors slid open and Sienna peeked out. No one was around. She laughed at herself for being ridiculous. She stepped into the glass lobby and headed for the double doors leading to the parking lot. The security guard was a good distance away, but she needed the walk to calm down. She would see the players' cars and then beyond them the private entrance to the employee lot where Tony would be on duty.

Sienna pushed open the glass door and stepped into the overcast afternoon. Storm clouds were gathering in the sky and the humidity from the summer was starting to fade. A strong wind gusted, and Sienna's hair attacked her face with stinging whips. Sienna pushed her hair from her face and grimaced at Seth's neon yellow car parked in a handicap spot right next to the door.

The wind blew hard and Sienna stopped. She had thought she heard something but the noise had been whisked away on the wind. She took a couple steps forward when she thought she heard it again. Was it thunder?

Sienna's heart dropped to her stomach, and she knew it was an unnatural sound. Slowly she turned toward the noise. Her scream at coming face-to-face with a man dressed in a black ski mask was torn from her by the wind. He stood still, mere inches from her, and slowly his mouth curved out into a smile. The sound of thunder pounded, but this time her ears heard it for what it was. Someone was pounding at the glass doors.

"Dr. Ashton, it's lovely to meet you. I've heard so much about you. If you would be so kind as to come with me." Sienna could barely hear his Middle Eastern accent as the clouds darkened and the wind whipped about them.

From over the man's shoulder, she saw Zack and Janice beating desperately at the door. A door with a crowbar jammed through the handles to prevent it from being opened.

"Come, Doctor. We can do this the easy way or the hard way."

He reached for her, and Sienna reacted. She swung her purse at him, hitting him on his head. He stumbled back, and Sienna raced toward the row of cars. She didn't feel him until it was too late. His hands pressed on her back and pushed. Sienna was suddenly airborne. The scream didn't have time to be released into the storm as the skies opened, and she flew into Seth's car.

Sienna covered her head with her arm as she was flung over the hood. Her body bounced off the sheet metal, and she rolled down the hood and fell in a heap on the wet pavement. Pain shot through her hip as she struggled to stand.

"Let me make myself clear, Doctor. I have no problem with the hard way," the man yelled as rain pounded around them.

Fear shot through her. The man grabbed her hair and pulled her up. "No!" Sienna screamed as she lashed out with her fists. She felt them connect; she felt him loosen his grasp. She tried to dive to the side, but instead of freedom, she felt a fist to the side of the head.

"I like the hard way, Doctor." The voice floated above her as she collapsed to the ground.

Sienna blinked her eyes, but between the rain and the hit on her head the world seemed blurred. A car sped to a stop next to them, and she knew if she was put in it she was dead. Sienna used all her energy and dove under the back end of Seth's car. She tried to tuck herself in a ball under the low car, hoping to gain some time for Zack to reach her, but it wasn't enough. Two strong hands wrapped around her ankles and pulled. Her nails broke as she clawed the concrete and suddenly she was no longer under the car. A foot connected with her stomach and air whooshed from her lungs. Pain unlike anything she had ever experienced hit her as the man kicked her over and over.

Her mind went elsewhere, and she didn't hear the glass breaking or the sound of another car racing toward them. She was just thankful for the beating to have stopped as she was picked up like a wet ragdoll and tossed in the trunk.

Chapter Eighteen

Ryan had sped across town, knowing something was wrong, but what he saw when he turned into the employee lot would haunt him forever. Sienna was lying in a heap on the ground as a man kicked her over and over. Anger, fear, panic, and revenge coursed through him as he floored his SUV. Hooch growled from the back seat, and Ryan saw the glass door to the lobby shatter at the same time the man picked Sienna up and dumped her into the trunk.

The car took off and Ryan sped after them. "I'm coming, sweetheart. Hold on," he murmured and closed the distance between them.

The two cars raced down the row of parked vehicles as lightning struck around them and the earth shook with thunder. Nothing would stop him from getting to her, as they raced around the stadium. He shot around a corner and before he could react, a second car T-boned him. His door crumpled, airbags deployed, and his breath was stolen as the impact sent them skidding into the truck loading dock at the back of the stadium.

Hooch howled in pain, and Ryan fumbled for the gun at his waist. The side curtain airbag prevented him from seeing what the other car was doing, but he heard its doors open and the men yelling to each other as they approached the car. Ryan closed his eyes and rested his head against the front airbag as he put his finger on the trigger of the gun resting in his lap.

"Grab him. Boss will be happy to get them both. Then we'll only have one more loose end to tie up. That one will be simple."

It took the men a minute to pry open Ryan's door and rip down the side curtain airbag. With a lethal calm, Ryan shot the first man to reach for him and had his gun pointed at the head of the second man before the poor bastard even knew what had happened.

"Where did they take Sienna?" Ryan asked the surprised man. It didn't last long as the man reached for his weapon and Ryan shot him in the knee, causing him to drop the gun. The man screamed in pain as a minivan screeched to a halt behind the fallen guy.

Ryan cursed under his breath when Zack and Janice jumped out. With them here he couldn't question the man the way he wanted to. Civilians were too squeamish.

"Did you find her?" Janice yelled through the rain.

Ryan just shook his head and slowly approached the man lying on the ground. He pressed the gun to the man's head, and he saw Zack and Janice freeze in their steps.

"Where did they take her?"

The man just grinned back at Ryan and the temptation to pull the trigger was so great he didn't care that there would be witnesses to him murdering this man.

Janice stepped forward and placed a hand on Ryan as if sensing his urge for revenge.

Zack surprised him by standing over the man and putting a very large foot on the injured knee and pressing down slowly. The man's screams of pain turned Janice's dark skin pale, but she didn't stop Zack.

"He may want to put a bullet in your head, but I want to know what you did with Doc." Zack pressed his foot into the man's knee and ground it against the pavement. The man's screech was so high Hooch howled in return. "I squat over 600 pounds, just imagine what I can do to your knee."

"Go to hell," the man grunted as rain mixed with sweat and ran off his face.

"After you," Ryan held the gun up and shot the man's other knee. He had to give Zack credit; the big man didn't even blink.

Hooch gingerly jumped from the SUV. His tail was at a weird angle and the dog was obviously in pain from it. He needed to get him to the vet's office, and he needed to take this man away before Detective Braxton showed up. Hooch leaned against Ryan's leg and growled at the man on the ground.

Headlights appeared and Ryan held his ground. He didn't know if the car speeding toward them was help or another shooter. The SUV slowed, and Ryan aimed his gun at the driver. Lights from security vehicles flashed in the distance. The police wouldn't be far behind. The door opened, and Trey Everett jumped out into the rain.

"What's happened? The front door to the parking lot is smashed in and security is running all over the place."

"They have Sienna, and this is the only guy left alive to tell us where she is," Ryan shouted.

Trey looked at Zack with his foot on the man's knee, and Janice standing with a hand on an injured Hooch. "What do you need me to do?"

"Can you take this man and Hooch to the vet clinic? Don't tell a soul, though. I'll be there to question him as soon as I wrap things up with the locals." Ryan bent down and checked the man for weapons and took his phone.

Ryan cursed when it was password-protected and slid it into his pocket as he watched the flashing lights growing closer and closer.

"Zack, help me get him in the back of the car," Trey ordered.

Zack and Trey lifted the man up and dropped him in the back before Zack climbed in after him. Janice opened the door and tried to help Hooch up, but the dog refused to budge.

"I'll have to take him when I get done here," Ryan shouted. Before the other cars got close, Trey was flying out of the parking lot.

Janice grabbed his arm as they waited. "You'll find her, won't you?"

"Yes. Nothing will stop me."

The security cars were the first to stop. Detective Braxton was only minutes behind. Janice kept her hand on Ryan's arm the entire time as security looked lost and then relieved when the police took over.

"What the hell happened here?" Detective Braxton hollered through the rain and climbed out of her car.

"They took Sienna. I gave chase and was hit by a second car." Ryan pointed to the second car and the dead guy lying on the ground next to a gun.

"Where's Dr. Ashton now?"

"I don't know," Ryan bit out. "The faster you clear me from the scene, the faster I can find her."

She shook her damp hair and glared at him. "It doesn't work like that, Parker. We don't even know if she was taken or if she went willingly with them."

Ryan felt Janice grow stiff next to him before she erupted forward with a finger wagging in Braxton's face.

"How dare you? I saw the whole thing. They beat her. They *beat* her and tossed her body in a trunk and you're here holding up the one person who can save her."

"Are you the one who broke the window?"

Janice paused. "You bet your scrawny ass I am."

Ryan would have smiled under any other circumstances. Instead, he held out his gun and Braxton took it. "Here. You can match my gun to the deceased. I have another. Excuse me."

Ryan had only made it one step before Braxton was on him. "We'll find her, Parker. You're too involved."

"Detective, you're smart, and you'll go far in your career, but you need to get over this preconceived idea that Sienna is involved. This is now a kidnapping and a federal matter. You no longer have a say in the investigation. I'll take it from here."

Her hand shot out and grabbed his arm. "No, you misunderstood me. I know Sienna isn't involved now. I was wrong, and I could have had people on her if it weren't for me. But I also know how hard it is to solve a case you're too close to. Let me help. I'll assist you, follow your orders, and everything."

Ryan took a deep breath and then gave a nod. "Fine. Let's go up front and see if they dropped anything. Janice, you can walk us through it."

Ryan, Janice, and Hooch climbed into Janice's minivan with Braxton following. They headed for the front of the stadium. Players were standing behind yellow tape and Ryan caught sight of Sienna's father looking on restlessly.

"Ryan!" Will shouted. "Where's Sienna?"

Ryan tried to quiet him down, but several of the players had heard and the word was quickly spreading. Ryan felt as if his feet were made of lead. Having to walk over to

Sienna's father and tell him that they had his daughter was the hardest thing he'd ever do.

"They took her," Ryan said quietly, but it wasn't quiet enough.

"They have Doc!" one of the players shouted and then the whole group surged past the police barricade and surrounded him.

"What you are going to do about it?" Will asked him with worry etched across his face.

"I'm going to find her. Now, if everyone can move back, I need to search this area." Ryan raised his voice and several members grumpily moved back, but Will just fisted Ryan's shirt in his hand.

He yanked Ryan to him and stared at him. "If anything happens to her . . ."

Ryan nodded. "I understand. Please, just let me find her."

Will released his shirt and ushered the players back. They huddled quietly as they watched Braxton and Ryan work. Janice explained what she saw and Ryan combed the ground looking for clues.

Hooch sat next to him, and Ryan was on hands and knees looking under Seth's car. Hooch lowered his nose to the ground and sniffed. He let out a pitiful whine. He missed his owner. So did Ryan. He found parts of Sienna's fingernails broken on the pavement and almost cried as he put them in evidence bags.

Hooch's nose shot up in the air as he dragged in a deep breath. He howled violently and then growled so deeply that Ryan felt it vibrating the earth. He noticed Braxton stop working and looked at Hooch before the dog stood and raced toward the crowd of spectators.

The players were used to Hooch and leaned down to

hug him, but Hooch just bowled them over. He wove his way between legs, around people clustered, and to the back of the crowd. Ryan watched as he froze in place. His crooked, broken tail quivered as he pointed at the man hiding in the last row.

The crowd parted as Ryan made his way to Hooch's hostage. Ryan stopped in front of Seth and in a flash was dragging him toward his bright yellow car. Police officers stopped processing the evidence at the sight of Ryan dragging a man with a dog hot on his heels, huge fangs bared for all to see.

"Parker, I got this," Braxton said quietly, stepping up. The team closed in around them, leaving nowhere for Seth to go.

Ryan tossed him to the ground and stepped back. He leaned against Seth's hood and tried to clear the red from his vision. This prick knew something, and he would enjoy torturing him to get it out of him. But even he knew he needed to take a second to compose himself or he'd be in jail for murder.

Detective Braxton cocked her head and watched quietly as Seth scrambled to his feet.

"What is this about?" Seth demanded, brushing off his slacks.

"It's about your involvement with Sienna Ashton's kidnapping."

Ryan watched him closely. When he saw Seth's eyes look everywhere but at Detective Braxton, he knew Seth was involved. Before he could pummel him, Hooch growled and Seth backed up into a wall of players. They shoved him forward, and he clambered toward Ryan as if he would protect Seth from Hooch. Ryan almost smiled at the thought, but then Hooch charged, and Seth wrenched open the car door and leaped inside. The door slammed and Hooch slid to a stop on the wet ground, his big head stopping just an inch from the driver's side door.

Ryan's eyes narrowed at the dent in Seth's door and then at Hooch's head. "Son of a bitch," Ryan roared before yanking open the door and dragging a stuttering Seth out. "You were the one who broke into Sienna's house. You're the one who gave her information to those men. You better start talking." Ryan accentuated every word with a shake of Seth's body.

"You have no proof," Seth managed to get out before being slammed against his own car.

"No proof? You idiot! The dog left an imprint of his freaking head in your car door!" Ryan shouted as the crowd closed in tightly around them.

"They'll kill me," Seth said quietly.

Ryan's sneer turned Seth white. "You don't need to worry about them. I'll kill you right now, witnesses be damned."

Braxton didn't interrupt him this time. Instead she let out a loud whistle. "Okay, men. Let's go to Dr. Ashton's office to look for evidence." The police quickly filed inside, leaving only the players outside.

"Go," Ryan quietly ordered.

"We got this," a player who towered over Ryan said as he pulled Ryan off Seth.

"Doc helped me with my commitment fears," the giant said.

"And Doc helped me with my fear of being hit after I broke my leg," another giant said as the offensive and defensive lines stepped forward.

"And Doc took my call at two in the morning when I

had a panic attack about the playoffs."

"We owe her."

"She's part of our team."

"And she's my daughter," Will said, pushing through the group of men with murder in their eyes. Seth's knees buckled, and he fell to the wet pavement.

Ryan squatted down in front of him. "I'll give you three seconds to start talking, or I leave you to them. One."

One of the players cracked his knuckles.

"Two."

One of the players cracked his massive neck.

"Okay!" Seth shouted as Ryan went to stand up. "I need witness protection. Then I'll tell you everything."

Sienna passed out. The beating, the car ride—it was all a blur. She vaguely remembered the trunk opening and being tossed over a man's shoulder before things went black with pain. It hurt so badly to breathe. Ribs were broken, an eye was swollen closed, and every organ inside her body throbbed. Ryan. He would come for her. It was only that hope that willed her to go on as her face was slapped and a horrible smell shot her eyes open.

"So we meet, Dr. Ashton. I've heard many things about you, and I have great plans for you."

Chapter Nineteen

Sienna looked at the man sitting in front of her. His legs were crossed as he leaned back comfortably and steepled his fingers. He was no older than fifty. His shoes were Italian leather. His black hair was cut to perfection. His smooth, tanned skin looked as if it were freshly shaven. His expensive cologne danced through the air and teased her senses. And his suit . . . well, his suit was the most impressive work of tailoring she'd ever seen.

Power reeked from every pore of this man's body. It was evident this man cared nothing for her well-being. But she could tell this conversation was something he did care about. She may not be a physical badass like Nash, Ryan, or even Layne, but she could read people, and she knew how to twist people.

"Aren't you curious as to what plans I have for you?" he asked after a bit.

Sienna didn't say anything. Her mind was too busy running through interrogation techniques and the latest studies she had read. While fear and control worked on some, she wasn't in a position to even try. She just had to keep him talking long enough for Ryan to find her.

She saw his fingers press hard against each other as he tried to remain calm. This man was not used to indifference. She needed to go in the other direction.

"I'm sorry," Sienna stuttered shyly. "I'm just in so much pain with my hands tied down like this. I think my ribs are broken. It hurts to breathe."

The man relaxed. "Of course." At a flick of his hand, two guards came and sliced the rope holding her to the chair.

"Thank you. A man of power and mercy." Sienna rubbed her wrists. He could be manipulated. If just one request were complied with, the second would be even easier to get from him. She just had to play this right. She would use respect and deception to gain his trust. Then she would plant the seeds of her survival.

The man bowed his head in acceptance of the compliment. "Dr. Ashton is in no condition to be a threat to my person. You may leave," he commanded.

Sienna took time to notice the luxury she was in. Leather chairs, antique tables, and works of art she'd only seen pictures of filled the room around her. This was certainly not where she thought she'd be when she'd been tossed in the back of the car.

"Like what you see?" the man asked with pride in his voice.

"It's beautiful," Sienna answered honestly.

"What is your favorite?" he asked and gestured to the pictures hanging on the wall.

Sienna sighed longingly. "The Monet. The way the colors mix together in chaos to form a peaceful landscape . . . it's masterful."

The man smiled with pleasure. "I knew we would get along, Dr. Ashton. The Monet is yours . . . that is if we can find a way to work together."

"I'd kill for that Monet. It has to be worth millions." Sienna didn't take her eyes from the painting.

"Excellent. You read my mind."

Ryan slammed the door and started to pace the hallway filled with players. Seth was locked securely inside with officers and Detective Braxton while they waited for the U.S. attorney to get back to them with an immunity offer. No matter how much they threatened Seth, he wouldn't talk. After a couple well-placed punches by some of the Thoroughbreds, he now had trouble talking.

That's when Ryan knew he wasn't helping anymore. He let Detective Braxton take a shot at breaking him and made a call to the nearest U.S. attorney with the authority to handle these kinds of matters.

"How do we know he wasn't the one behind all of this?" one of the players asked the crowd.

Ryan tuned them out. Finding Sienna was the only thing on his mind.

"He was with Zack and then with me. Seth couldn't have done it," one of the players told the group.

Zack! Maybe he was having better luck with the man they captured whom he and Trey had taken away. Ryan reached for his phone but stopped when Wofford continued.

"They were meeting to hand Seth some investment money to deposit with Rook Capital Management."

"Rook?" Ryan asked. "Do all of Seth's clients use Rook?"

Wofford shrugged his thick shoulders. "I think so. Even if Seth's not your agent, he lets us know about good investments. I'm sure he gets a kickback for sending players and coaches to Rook. Why?"

"Because that's the only lead I have right now. Tell the detective to call me if she gets anything."

Ryan rushed down the stairs and into his car as fast as he could. He got to Keeneston in half the usual time it should have taken. Trey's SUV was still in Katelyn's parking lot at the vet clinic when Ryan arrived. He headed straight for the front door, ignoring her secretary as he wound his way to the surgical room.

The sight that greeted him should have made him laugh, but he was too worried about Sienna to care about the six old people surrounding the man tied to the teeth-cleaning station. It was basically a sink the size of a surgical table with a metal grate on top. Miss Lily stood on a stepstool and smacked the man in the face with her broom. Miss Daisy and Miss Violet stood nearby with a wooden spoon and a spatula. Their husbands all stood behind them with tight faces.

"Zack, Trey, has he talked?" Ryan asked the two big men who were leaning against the wall.

"Charlie had to step in after Zack knocked the guy out," Trey told him. "So we handed him over to the Rose sisters. They've irritated the hell out him."

Zack had his arms crossed over his chest, keeping his eye on the man. "I failed. I'm sorry."

"You didn't fail. I did. But I'm going to fix it. I'll find her."

Ryan stepped forward as Miss Lily smacked the man in the face again with the broom. "Thank you for your help."

"Get these old women away from me!" the man yelled as Anton stuffed a noxious-smelling rag into his mouth.

"What is that?" Ryan asked as he recoiled.

"Cheesecloth from Epoisses de Bourgogne. It's a French cheese that is so smelly, it's banned from being allowed on any public transportation in France," Anton said with pride for his native country's cheese.

"We're going to have to burn our clothes, but it will be worth it," John said.

Ryan tried not to breathe in through his nose as he stepped closer to the man. His brown eyes were wild and his complexion slightly green as he gagged on the cloth.

"I'm going to remove this rag and then I want you to tell me everything you know about Rook Capital Management." The man's eyes flashed in recognition of the name, and Ryan felt the first surge of anticipation hit him.

He reached forward and took the cheesecloth from the man's mouth. "Talk."

"I don't know anything about Rook Capital."

"Fine. I was trying to help you out." Ryan shoved the cloth back into his mouth and stepped back. "Miss Violet, you're up."

The man started shouting behind the cloth. Ryan let Miss Violet get one good thwack in before removing the cloth. "Yes?"

"I need a doctor," the man begged.

"You've had a doctor. I see Charlie fixed you up already." Ryan gestured to the man's knees wrapped in bandages. "I know. You need a visitor. Zack, bring the visitor in from the last run."

Zack raised an eyebrow but went in search of the runs without saying anything.

"What's your name? Mine's Ryan."

"I'm not telling you jack," the man spat.

"Fine," Ryan smiled. "I forgot a name of someone else we caught. Who was it? Oh, that's right. Seth Hayes."

The man's eyes betrayed him yet again. He knew the name.

"What does Seth have to do with this?" Jaylen asked from behind Ryan. The man took one look at him and went from green to white.

"Jaylen, meet the man who tried and *failed* to kill you."

"You son of a bitch!" Jaylen tried to charge forward, but Zack held him back.

"You see, this man was just about to tell me what role Seth has in their organization. He's in police custody waiting for an immunity deal. So, I want to offer you a deal all of your own. Are you listening?" Ryan asked the man who nodded in return.

"Either way, you are going to die. You understand that, right? Either we kill you now or The Suit gets to you in prison. Now, Seth is a different story. If he gets an immunity deal, he gets put in witness protection and gets to mooch off the system for the rest of his life. However, if you tell me how Seth is involved, I'll make sure he doesn't get a deal and that you take your chance in prison. I'll share that you didn't cooperate with us, and even under torture, you never turned on your boss. Do you understand?"

"Yes," the man said simply.

"Seth works for your boss, doesn't he?" Ryan asked.

"Yes. He has for three years."

"And your boss is known in the U.S. as The Suit and overseas as *Rais*."

The man nodded and looked to Jaylen.

"And you were supposed to kill Jaylen because of Rook Capital," Ryan stated.

The man let out a long breath and nodded. "Just like Seth had to kill Malik Coleman. They had to keep Malik quiet about Rook Capital. Malik was asking too many questions, and Jaylen was starting to as well." Jaylen fought forward, but Zack and Trey pulled him back again.

"What does Seth do for your boss?" Ryan asked.

"He brings in the high rollers from professional sports. Young kids too stupid to know how to count their millions."

"They help fund his terrorist operations. Operations that include a plan to blow up one of the stadiums during a game, isn't that right?"

"You know more than we thought. It's why a contract is on you. The person who kills you gets a Ferrari." The man grinned at him, but Ryan ignored him.

"And Dr. Ashton?"

"Is alive and with the boss."

"Where?" Ryan held his breath as the whole room waited for the answer.

"I don't know. Boss has a small horse farm outside of Lexington, though."

Ryan didn't take a breath as he asked his last question. "What's your boss's name?"

The man just smirked. "I gave you Seth. That's all your getting."

"Ladies," Ryan said as he shoved the horrendously stinky cloth back in the man's mouth.

"I can't believe Seth is part of this," Jaylen muttered. "I was so stupid. There were never any investments, were there? I gave millions to terrorists." Jaylen seemed on the verge of crying.

"It's a classic Ponzi scheme. It's how the terrorist organization was funded." Ryan shook his head in disbelief as Jaylen, Zack, Trey, and he walked out of the room. He pulled out his phone and sent a text to Detective Braxton.

"But I know the name of the head of Rook Capital Management. I'm supposed to meet with him about my big investment check I promised Seth." Zack smiled.

"Who is he?" Ryan grabbed Zack's arm in surprise.

"Bahir Deron."

Trey nodded. "That's right. I've even met him. I know where his farm is."

"How?" Ryan asked in surprise.

"Seth approached me with an investment opportunity. But with all my money from sports and Taylor's Hollywood money, we are wary of investors we don't know. So Seth set up a dinner at Bahir's farm. We were there with a few other well-off people, including Dani and Mo. From what I gather, everyone invested but the four of us."

"I can't believe it. Rook Capital is among one of the biggest names out there." Ryan shook his head. "But, that's how Ponzi schemes work. They pay off the newest people, like they did for Zack, and get them to put even more money in and then they'll manufacture a loss. Before we all know it, the money is siphoned into foreign accounts and Bahir is out of the country where we can't touch him. Now, where's this farm?"

Five minutes later Ryan headed to his car. "I'm coming, Sienna; hold on."

He picked up his phone and called Nash. "I found him. Meet at my parents' house in ten minutes."

Next he called his brother, Jackson. "Hey, bro." Ryan smiled when his brother answered the phone. He and Jackson had been inseparable growing up.

"Where are you?"

Jackson must have heard the seriousness in Ryan's voice because he didn't bother asking why Ryan was calling. "Ashland. I'm on the interstate heading home for a couple days. What's going on?"

"Sienna's in trouble."

"I'll be there in an hour," Jackson said, and Ryan heard the engine rev over the phone. To get to Keeneston in half the time, Jackson would be flying.

"Meet at Mom and Dad's," Ryan instructed before hanging up.

Chapter Twenty

Sienna let her hand shake as the man handed her a glass of water in the most exquisite crystal she'd ever seen. They had talked about art while drinks were brought in. The storm raged on outside, and Sienna had no idea what time it was or how long she'd been there. She just knew Ryan had to be getting closer with every minute that passed.

She had asked for water and the man had instantly ordered it for her. She was gaining his trust and making him more comfortable with her. As soon as she found out what he wanted, she could start manipulating him further.

"Thank you, sir." Sienna gave him a shy smile as she tried to drink the water. It splashed from the rim and Sienna let the tears fall. "I'm so sorry. I just hurt so much."

The man looked shocked for a second before taking the glass from her and putting it to her lips. Sienna took a greedy sip to wash the taste of dried blood from her mouth.

"No, I am sorry my man got carried away when he brought you to me. I'll have him dealt with," the man told her as he set the glass on the table.

"You're so kind," Sienna said again. "And I don't even know what to call you so I can thank you properly."

The man reached forward and put his hand over hers. "You may call me Bahir."

"Thank you, Bahir."

"Ah, Sienna, we're going to be very rich together."
Bahir let go of her hand and sat back in his chair.

"How so?" Sienna asked.

"Not yet, Doctor. First, I need something from you."

Sienna gave a little nod. "Of course. Anything I can do to repay you for your hospitality."

"You want the Monet." It was a statement, not a question. "Then I need you to kill someone for it."

Sienna didn't try to hide her shock. "But I'm a doctor. I help people, not hurt them."

"But this person is dangerous. I believe you even know him—Seth Hayes." Bahir kept eye contact with her while he talked.

This time Sienna didn't let her emotions show. "I knew he was dangerous. Do you know he tried to attack me at my house the other night?"

That got Bahir's attention. "No. I didn't know that."

"But you'll protect me from him, won't you?" Sienna asked. "Someone as powerful as you would have nothing to fear from a slime like Seth. He's just out for his own gain, and he'll sell out anyone to get it. Good thing you're smart enough to keep him at arm's length. I can see why you would want him gone."

"You can?" Bahir asked, surprised. "So you'll do it? I'll send my men with you, but you have to pull the trigger."

Sienna nodded. "He's the sort that would tattle on you to your teachers in school and blame you for something he did wrong. I thought he was a nice guy, but when I said I didn't want to go out with him, he showed his true colors. He told me he would get me fired by telling the owners of the team all these lies about me. He's definitely not to be trusted. But why should he worry you? You're much too intelligent to let a backstabber like that into your . . . your, I'm sorry, what is it that you do besides collect beautiful art?"

"I'm an investor," Bahir said, standing up. Sienna watched as he clenched and unclenched his fists. He started pacing, and she went in for the kill.

"Oh, that's how you have so much money. I could tell you were business savvy. Not like Seth. He probably couldn't keep a deal to himself to save his life." Sienna laughed, even though it caused pain to shoot through her. "He's the arrogant type that probably hides information on the people he's working with. You know, those corny, *In case I die, here's who's responsible* letters that only narcissistic people would leave."

Sienna held her breath. She celebrated her small victory as she watched Bahir take the time to mull over everything she had said.

He turned to her quickly. "Thank you for such insight. You are the expert. If you feel he would do something like that, then he probably has." Bahir stepped to his desk and picked up his phone. He spoke quietly and quickly into it before slamming it down.

"What's the matter?" Sienna asked, her voice full of concern.

"Nothing you need to worry about. In your studies, where do you find men feel the most secure?"

Sienna shrugged. "That's easy—their home."

"Thank you. Make yourself comfortable. I'll send someone in to keep you company."

Sienna gave him an innocent smile as he wrenched open the door. A minute later, a timid little woman came in with a tray of food. The door stood open, and Sienna looked down the exquisite hallway filled with landscape paintings, dark wood paneling, and deep red carpet lining the hardwood floor. Two armed guards stood on either side of the door, and she could see two more at the end of the hallway. Sienna nibbled on the food and planned her next mental attack. She knew she couldn't take on four armed guards, but she'd already proven she was capable of manipulation. The biggest question: could she make Bahir so paranoid and insecure that he would start to trust her enough she could escape?

Nash and Ryan sat on the couch in his parents' living room as Paige set a plate of cookies in front of them. Her husband, Cole, sat on the chair across from them and shook his head.

"Honey, they're going to invade a farm for a hostage rescue. They don't need cookies."

Paige shrugged. "I have to do something since you told me I wasn't young enough to do this type of thing anymore."

Nash covered his laugh with a cough and Ryan closed his eyes and prayed Jackson would get there soon. His father, bless his heart, was not good with gestures and had a tendency to stick his well-intentioned foot into his mouth. His mother could outshoot the entire family, with the exception of his little sister, Greer, and was beyond miffed to be told she couldn't help out tonight.

The sound of tires locking and sliding on the driveway was the best sound Ryan had heard all night. Jackson was home. The front door was flung open and Ryan's little brother rushed in. *Little* wasn't the best description for a brother who stood just as tall as Ryan and a few pounds of muscle heavier. The main difference between the brothers was their eyes. While Ryan had inherited the Davies hazel eyes, Jackson's were pure silver. When he was happy, they shined. In anger or determination, like they were now, they were cold and hard.

"What's the rundown?" Jackson asked as he hugged his mom and dad.

Ryan started from the beginning and in three minutes gave Jackson a full report of the situation. Then it was Nash's turn to fill Jackson in on some details he had learned about the terrorist organization's headquarters when he had visited the farm as part of Mo and Dani's security team.

"So, there's five of us against possibly twenty or more armed guards on the property," Jackson said, looking at the aerial photo of the farm.

Their mother huffed and stared at their father. "It's just the four of you. Someone thinks I'm too old for this."

Jackson looked up from the map and rolled his eyes at Ryan. "And when did you start listening to Dad? I need you here," Jackson pointed to the top of a hill.

"And Dad can take the high ground here," Ryan pointed.

"Wait a second, I'm not sitting outside while you all go in. I'm the head of the local FBI office, not you."

Ryan grinned at his mom before looking at his dad. "If Mom is too old, and you're older than Mom . . ."

Nash held up his hands. "Mr. Parker, Mrs. Parker, if we can get back to the plan. Sometimes it's easier for a small group to go in undetected."

"Damn right it is, and I should be the one leading this," Ahmed said, walking in with his wife and Nabi.

Ryan heard Nash curse under his breath. Nash didn't have time to put forth an argument when the front door was thrown open. Uncles and aunts poured in, followed by six white-haired seniors, William and Betsy Ashton, and Marcy and Jake Davies.

"We had to find out about this from John?" Aunt Annie accused. "Do you know how long it's been since I broke into a house and shot someone?"

Uncles Cy, Miles, and Marshall shook their head at their sister-in-law. "We actually have experience with terrorists and you didn't call us?" Cade said, pointing to his brothers.

"You all? I jumped out of a plane to save this guy's butt," Bridget said with an eye roll at the guys. "And it's a great butt," Bridget added when Ahmed raised a single eyebrow.

Kenna Ashton clung to her husband's arm. "You love her, don't you, Ryan?" At her question the room went silent.

Ryan took in Kenna's pale, drawn face and the way her fingers dug into Will's arm and knew now wasn't the time to dance around anything. "Yes, ma'am. Very much."

"Then you decide what to do. You won't risk her life with a bad plan," Kenna said with a shaky voice.

The quiet group turned to Ryan. "I can use you all, but I only want the three of us to enter the house," Ryan ordered and motioned for the group to gather around the table with a map on it.

"I want all aunts surrounding the property here. I want all the uncles here. Ahmed, Nabi, and Bridget, I want you close by in case we need you. Do you have Ace with you?" Ryan asked of the current police dog Bridget was training.

Bridget nodded. "When I heard what was going on, I grabbed Ace, Gunner, and Heidi. Ahmed, Nabi, and I can send them in if we need to."

"Sounds good. Dad, do you have enough coms here?" Ryan asked. They had brought enough for five but not the extended family.

"I brought our security team's coms," Nabi told them as he held up a bag. "I had a feeling that we wouldn't be the only people to show up."

"Vests?" Aunt Morgan asked as she grabbed an earpiece from Nabi.

"I have enough of those," Cole told them. He went to the closet to pull them out.

"Annie and I brought rifles for those who don't have their own," Cade said.

"I don't have one," Miss Lily piped up from the back. "And since I've had my cataract surgery, I can see a good deal better."

The room turned and stared at her. Ryan wasn't quite sure what to say. His grandmother, Marcy Davies, stepped forward and put her arm around Miss Lily. "Even if my children don't realize they're getting too old to play hero all the time, we know better and know it's time we take our place on the sidelines. We can run communications, can't we, Cole?"

Cole nodded at his mother-in-law. "Here's the map. You run the show, ladies. Mark where everyone is and make sure they're in position before you give our boys the go signal."

"Perfect, then I don't have to worry about my arthritis accidently setting off the trigger." Miss Violet smiled and took the map.

The next five minutes were spent in silence as bulletproof vests were strapped on, ammunition handed out, and coms tested. "Is everyone ready?" Ryan asked.

Kenna swiped at a tear. "Bring my daughter back to us,

Ryan," she said so softly he almost didn't hear her. She put shaking hands on his shoulders and rose up on her tippy-toes to place a kiss on his cheek.

Will just nodded, unable to speak, and wrapped his wife in his arms once again. They slowly walked from the house with the Rose sisters and his grandparents.

The house cleared in quiet contemplation of what was ahead as they moved to their cars. They would all be meeting a short distance from the farm and would hike into the property.

"Ryan, Jackson, a moment," their mother said once everyone had left. "I may act tough, but I've never been so scared. You are my boys — my children. And I'm letting you put yourself in danger. I can't tell you not to go — it's who you are. But be safe. And if you need me, I will sacrifice it all to save you. Do you understand me? I will bust down that door by myself if I think you're in trouble."

"Yes, ma'am," Ryan and Jackson said together, their voices thick with emotion.

"Good, now go get Sienna. I'm ready for grandchildren."

Ryan stared at his mother as she walked purposefully out the door with a sniper rifle over her shoulder.

"Damn," Jackson cursed and blew out a breath.

"Exactly. I've never seen Mom like that."

"She must really want grandchildren," Jackson smiled then. "Uncle Jackson . . . it has a good ring to it. I bet it would help me pick up chicks. They always go mushy-eyed over men with babies. Hey, I get to be best man, right?"

Ryan shook his head as they walked outside to join Nash. "I haven't even thought about proposing yet, and y'all are already onto babies."

Jackson and Nash snorted.

"What?" Ryan asked, getting into the car.

"Except you've thought about marrying Sienna since you were six," Jackson stated.

"Yeah, even I know you want to marry her. And by the time I showed up in Keeneston, you all had that little love-hate thing going on because she thought you were too young. Then she didn't, and you were too stubborn to let her show you that she wanted you. Does that sum it up?" Nash asked with a slight twitch of his lips.

Ryan crossed his arms over his vest. "Fine, I want to marry her. I love her. But her life is here, and I've made a life for myself in L.A."

Jackson shook his head from the back of the car. "No, you ran away to L.A. Your life is with Sienna, wherever that may be."

Ryan didn't respond. As they traveled down the country roads in the dark rain, all he thought about was getting to Sienna. *I'm coming*, he said in his head over and over again in hopes of the universe passing along his message to Sienna. And as they pulled to a stop some thirty minutes later, his mind was focused and his heart shut down, for what he had to do there was no place for emotion.

He turned to his brother and his best friend and looked at them as they re-checked their weapons. "Thank you for doing this. Thank you for risking your lives for the woman I love."

"I'll always be by your side, brother. Besides, Sienna has some hot friends who will be at the wedding." Jackson slapped him on the back and went to instruct the aunts and uncles to move out.

"I just like shooting bad people," Nash said with a shrug.

Ryan shook his head. "Between you all and my family, not to mention the Rose sisters, I'm starting to think we're not normal."

Nash grinned. "Where's the fun in being normal? Your brother was right about one thing. Sienna has some hot friends, and they always go for us dark, mysterious types. Come on, let's go so I can get some bridesmaid action."

Chapter Twenty-One

"Damn it!" Sienna heard Bahir roar a second before he rounded the corner and stomped down the hall.

She watched with genuine fear as his eyes narrowed on her. "What's the matter?"

"You lying bitch!" Bahir's hand flew back and connected with her cheek before Sienna could block it. The force knocked her from the chair and she fell, stunned, onto the Persian carpet.

Tears she couldn't stop filled her eyes and her face felt as if thousands of needles were sticking it. She gasped in a breath and bit back a sob. Slowly, she raised herself to a sitting position and looked up at the man who had hit her. Gone was the man she had manipulated, and in his place was the powerful terrorist he truly was.

"I don't know what you're talking about?" Sienna stuttered as she scooted back toward his desk, her hands wrapped around her aching midsection.

"Seth, that's what I'm talking about. No wonder you agreed to kill him. You knew the bastard was already in police custody," Bahir accused, reaching to grab her by the hair.

"What?" Sienna shrieked as he pulled her up. She placed her hands on top of his to help minimize the pain. "Bahir, I didn't know that."

Bahir stopped, grabbing her face hard in between his fingers. He put his nose up to hers and stared at her, not saying a word for a full minute. He dropped his hand and took a step back before adjusting his tie. "Please accept my apologies, Sienna. I can see I was wrong. You did not know."

"You're forgiven," Sienna said softly, and she ducked her head, putting a hand to her face. "What happened?"

"Get the doctor some ice," Bahir snapped to a small woman, who went scurrying from the room. He indicated for Sienna to sit on the couch, and he took the chair across from her. "My men went to search Seth's house but found it swarming with FBI. I called my contact and was informed Seth was holding out for the U.S. attorney to arrive and offer him a deal."

"Oh, no. I knew it. He's going to turn on you. Are you safe, Bahir?" Sienna asked, her voice full of concern.

"Not for long. I've called the men in to pack the place up. We'll be leaving in a couple hours."

"What about me? How can I prove myself if Seth is already in custody?" Sienna asked.

"My contact will take care of it. Seth will be dead within the hour. Should be made to look like suicide. Not that I care. But you, my dear, I have plans for," Bahir said before handing her the bag of ice the servant had fetched.

Sienna sucked in air on a hiss and put the ice on her face. "What are they?"

"You are going to take Seth's place. You're going to bring the players' and coaches' money to me to invest," Bahir said with a satisfied smile.

Sienna smiled slowly. "So that's how we are going to make so much money. What kind of cut do I get?"

"Five percent."

Sienna's eyes went wide. "Wow. But why all of this?" Sienna waved to the guards. "You could have just asked me to be a broker for you. You didn't need your men to hurt me."

Bahir frowned. "I'm sorry, my dear Sienna. It's not that simple I'm afraid."

"Why not?"

"Because when we conclude our business deal, you'll need to leave the country with me. You'll be a wanted woman."

Sienna's brow knitted in confusion. "I don't understand."

"Because, my dear," Bahir said, as he leaned forward and took her hand in his, "you're going to help me get enough money to blow up an entire stadium on international television. And when they trace the weapons used, because they always do, they'll trace it to the money you raised for me."

Sienna's vision blurred, and she fell back against the cushions. Bahir held tightly to her hand and squeezed. "And if you don't, I'll kill every single person on your contact list Seth got from your computer. I'll start with your parents. Your father might put up a struggle. But when we slit a man's wife's throat in front of him, it usually takes the fight out of him. And then your little brother." Bahir clucked his tongue.

"Such a shame, too. Carter has such promise in running your family farm. Top of his class in business school . . . all for nothing. And then there's Agent Parker. You really shouldn't keep a journal on your computer. It's too easy to hack. Imagine my surprise when Seth told me you still fantasize about your childhood crush. Maybe you can act those fantasies out with me while he watches before I kill him. And then next will be your best friend. Sydney, isn't it? And then, well, you get the picture, as soon as everyone you care about is gone, I'll put you out of your misery. You will know the full pain of standing against me."

"You bastard," Sienna gasped, silent tears falling from her face.

"I'm glad we understand each other."

Ryan, Jackson, and Nash crept through the shadows of the night. The clouds covered the light of the moon and the downpour hid the sounds of their footsteps as they made their way toward the large Federal-style house. It had two wings going back from the main part of the house. Sienna was in one of those rooms. According to Trey, the main part of the house was for show. A massive dining room, sitting room, and foyer with a grand staircase filled the majority of the space.

"The old horses have been put out to pasture," Miss Daisy's voice said over the coms.

"And the old dogs have learned new tricks," Miss Lily's voice said next.

Ryan, Jackson, and Nash looked at each other and managed a smile. The aunts and uncles were in place along with Ahmed, Bridget, Nabi, and the dogs. Ryan nudged his brother who tapped Nash. The first security detail was approaching. They stepped farther back into the shadows of the garden and waited.

Ryan was in the point and silently drew the knife from his thigh. As the man passed, Ryan stepped from the shadow and drew the knife along the man's neck while Jackson and Nash disarmed him and dragged him into the shadows. In a matter of seconds, it was like he never existed.

Ryan tapped Nash on the back, and Nash broke from the group. Nash would enter through the east wing while Jackson took the back door. Ryan would enter through the west wing. A couple yards later, Jackson grabbed Ryan and halted him. Before Ryan could ask, Jackson's knife was cutting through the neck of another guard. Ryan rushed to help drag the man behind the azaleas before giving Jackson a silent nod of thanks.

Jackson placed his hand on Ryan's shoulder, squeezed, and then was gone. Ryan could barely see his brother heading to the back door. Ryan looked back to check on Nash and found another guard suddenly falling back. A second later, Nash sent him the all-clear signal.

Ryan heard every raindrop as he inched closer to the large window he was going to burst through. His vision was clear, and his breathing was steady. He calmly took out the guard walking around the house. He didn't blink when he wiped the blood on his pant leg, and he didn't make a sound when he looked in the window and saw Sienna holding an icepack to her face as tears streamed down her cheeks. A bruise was already forming near a swollen eye. A man who had to be Bahir stood up and glared down at Sienna before walking from the room. The door was left open and Ryan saw the back of two guards standing on either side.

"Alpha's a go. The package is visible," he barely whispered, not allowing the relief of seeing Sienna alive affect him.

"Beta's a go," he heard Jackson say into his coms.

"Gamma's a go," he heard Nash say tightly.

"Get our girl back. On my three. One. Two. Three." Miss Lily said more seriously than Ryan had ever heard her.

Silently, Ryan slid his knife into the latch of the window and jiggled. Sienna's eyes shot toward him, and he knew the second she recognized him. He barely had to lift his hand to indicate she stay put before she nodded her head.

"I'm in," Nash said. "My tally is four down. Heading your way, Alpha."

"I'm in, too," Jackson said. "Three down. Waiting for Gamma, and we'll clear the way for the package."

Ryan opened the window and climbed in slowly, but it was too late. A small woman he hadn't seen started screaming from the corner.

Sienna had tried to motion with her eyes to the small shell of a woman who was Bahir's servant, but Ryan had looked away to unlock the window and hadn't seen her. The second the window opened and Ryan's foot came into view, the woman opened her mouth. It was like slow motion, and there was nothing Sienna could do to stop the scream from erupting.

She leapt up, and with both hands laced together, swung them like a bat at the first guard who charged into the room. Pain radiated up her arms and through her ribs, but it was enough to send the man stumbling back.

"Get down!" Ryan shouted. She didn't even process the words. She knew by the look in his eyes he was taking these men down. The second she hit the floor, Sienna heard two muffled shots and felt the guards hit the floor.

"Up!" Ryan yelled, and Sienna was on her feet. He reached one hand out to her, and Sienna grabbed it like the lifeline it was. She knew he would come for her.

"I have the package, sending her through the window," Ryan spoke as he pushed her toward the window.

Sienna took the hint and rushed across the room but

slid to a stop as the glass shattered around her. Before she could drop to the ground, Ryan was covering her with his body and dragged her behind Bahir's desk. Sienna could hear the sound of the guards rushing from upstairs and down the hall. They were surrounded.

"Sienna, look at me. We're okay. Put your hand here," Ryan ordered as he placed her hand on the waistband of his black cargo pants. "Just don't let go, and when I tell you to do something, do it."

Ryan peeked out over the desk and fired his gun. Sienna pushed back the panic. She wasn't going to die like this, and she sure as hell wasn't going to let Ryan die trying to save her. She looked where her hand was holding his belt and saw the gun strapped to his shoulder. Pushing up his arm, she grabbed the handgun and cocked it.

Ryan didn't break his concentration on the door to the room where guards were firing into the room. "Do you know how to use that?"

"How hard can it be?" Sienna asked as she pointed it at the back windows and fired at a guard trying to look in. The shot went wide, but it was enough to send the man scurrying back.

Ryan saved his bullets. He didn't have enough to last through a long siege. He counted six men in the hallway, lining up to storm the room. And those were only the ones he could see. "How many are approaching from outside?"

Sienna let go of his waist and from his peripheral vision he saw her crawling toward the window. The old woman covered from head to toe in black material still stood screaming nearby.

"Five!" Sienna called out and scuttled back to his side.

"Does anyone have a clear shot of the west wing?"

Ryan asked into his coms.

"I do," Annie's tight voice came over the coms.

"Take the shot. We're surrounded." Ryan spoke calmly as Sienna shot out the window again.

"Is this the wrong time for me to tell you how much I love you?" Sienna shouted over the gunfire as the two men tried to advance into the room.

"There's never a wrong time!" Ryan yelled back. He fired and took one man down.

"We're pinned down in the front entrance. Hold on, we're coming," his brother yelled into the coms, gunfire erupting in a different part of the mansion.

"Someone's coming in the window!" Sienna screamed, unloading the clip, hitting everything but the man coming in the window.

Ryan cursed. At the same time, three men rushed into the room. Gunfire rang out from all around the property. Ryan had been in shootouts before. But to be in one where every person he loved was at risk was completely different.

Ryan went to reload, but it was too late. The barrier had been broken, and men poured in from outside and the hallway. He pushed Sienna under the heavy wooden desk and felt her grab the gun from his thigh. As if it would do her any good. She was the worst shot he'd ever seen.

"Hands!" The closest guard yelled, holding a gun to Ryan's face. Ryan dropped his gun and raised his hands. He did a quick count—two guards from outside and four from the hallway. Annie and he had done some damage, but not enough.

A man dressed in a suit stepped from the hallway into the room, making sure to stay behind the wall of guards. He didn't look worried as he eyed Ryan.

"So, we finally meet," the man said with confidence.

"Bahir Deron. I would say it's a pleasure, but why start lying to each other at this point?" Ryan asked cockily. He kept his hands up and stepped away from the desk. He had to draw all the attention toward himself and away from Sienna.

"I'm impressed, Agent Parker. You always seem so sure of yourself. Let's see how sure you are when I have the one thing you seem to care about. Grab them and meet me at the other location," Bahir ordered, pushing a panel on the wall. The hidden door swung open and Bahir disappeared behind it.

"Sending in the dogs," Bridget's quiet but steady voice broke through.

The men by the window advanced to the desk at the same time the guards from the hallway went to grab Ryan. Ryan leapt back and was met with a gun pointed to his face. The two men from outside moved to the desk. Ryan was grabbed by one man, as the others kept their guns trained on him. For the first time in his life, Ryan was filled with fear. Not for himself, but for the only woman he'd ever loved.

Sienna held the gun to her chest and leaned as far back in the darkness of the desk as she could. She was surrounded on three sides and overhead by the thick desk, but it didn't make her feel safe. She didn't hear the footsteps of the men sent to get her. All of a sudden, they were just there. First one foot, then two, three, and four appeared as the two men stood in front of the desk.

Sienna's whole body shook with fear and adrenaline, with the feeling she would need to kill or be killed. She braced herself against the back of her cubby and aimed the gun straight ahead. She tried to remember to breathe. She tried to stop the shaking, but when the first guard's face appeared, her mind went blank, she closed her eyes, and pulled the trigger.

Chapter Twenty-Two

T he sound of the gunshot filled the room. Ryan didn't wait. The guards were surprised, and he took full advantage. He reached over his shoulder and grabbed the guard who was fumbling to bind his hands. He fisted the man's shirt at his shoulder and, in one quick motion, leaned over and pulled hard. The man went sailing over Ryan's shoulder into the two guards standing in front of him. He spun with his fist already clenched and hit the fourth guard in the Adam's apple. The guard coughed and fell back.

Sienna fired again, and Ryan took that as a good thing. It meant she was still alive.

"This bitch shot my foot!" the guard behind him screamed.

Ryan dove for the closest guard on the floor. He grabbed the unconscious man's gun from his hand, but he wasn't fast enough to aim it. The other man he'd knocked down was sitting up with his weapon pointed at Ryan.

"I have a gun pointed at your boyfriend's head," the guard yelled. "Come out from under the desk, or I'll kill him right now."

Ryan kept his eyes trained on the guard in front of him as the guard stood. He just had to make one mistake, and Ryan could overpower him. Movement from the hallway caught his eye, and he tried to determine who it was without taking his eyes off the man with the gun.

"Don't move, Sienna!" Ryan yelled back. He waited until the guard looked back at him and then made his move.

"*Stellen!*" Ryan ordered the bite command in Dutch as the small tan female Belgian Malinois sprinted down the hallway. She sailed through the air with teeth bared and slammed into the guard. The guard toppled forward as Ryan lunged at the second guard, who was distracted by the unexpected police dog taking down his coworker.

Ryan grabbed the rifle barrel from the last guard, who was still trying to catch his breath. He yanked it from the guard's hands and instantly slammed the butt into the man's face. The sound of bone and teeth cracking wasn't heard over the fierce growls of Heidi and the screams coming from the guard she had latched onto.

"I wouldn't do that if I were you," Jackson said calmly. Ryan turned and saw the guard who'd had his foot shot, aiming his gun at the desk. "You have two options. One, drop the gun and live. Or two . . ."

Nash fired his gun, and the guard dropped to the ground. "You talk too much."

Sienna scrambled over the dead bodies as she told herself not to freak out. She screamed when hands grabbed her arms and hauled her up. But suddenly she found herself smashed against a warm chest and Kevlar.

"Ryan," she whimpered as she buried her face against the safety of his body. She didn't even know she was crying until she heard him shushing her gently.

"It's okay, sweetheart. You're safe now."

"I, I, I . . . killed him," Sienna stuttered.

Ryan squeezed her tight. "I know. It's okay. You're safe

now."

"We have Sienna; she's safe. The house is clear. You all can move in," Sienna heard Nash say to someone.

"Where's Bahir?" Jackson asked. Sienna felt him behind her.

Ryan kissed her head and pried her from his body. Sienna's teeth chattered as she looked up at the hard set of Ryan's jaw.

"What is it?" she asked. Ryan nodded to Jackson. She felt Jackson's arm come around her shoulder and pull her against his side. She looked into his face and saw a red mark forming on his jaw and blood splattered up his neck. "What are you doing here?"

"It's nice to see you, too. You're going to invite Bethany to the wedding, right?" Jackson grinned down at her. Sienna could only blink.

"What?"

Ryan looked at Nash, and the two nodded. "I have to go now. I can't let Bahir get away. Jackson will take care of you. The others will be here soon. You're safe now, sweetheart. I love you." Ryan bent and placed a whisper-soft kiss on her trembling lips.

Sienna stared in shock as Ryan gave Jackson a hard look and turned to the far wall of the office. He pushed against the panel and the door swung open. Nash disappeared inside and Ryan turned to look at her one last time.

"Wait," Sienna ordered. She swiped the tears from her eyes and pushed away from Jackson. She stepped over the man Heidi had pinned to the ground and stopped in front of Ryan.

"I understand, Ryan," she said and cupped his face gently in her hand. "I knew you would come for me, just as

I know you'll come back to me. I'll be waiting." Sienna rose on her toes and placed a kiss full of promise on his lips and then he was gone.

Jackson came to her side and slung his arm around her once again. "About Bethany . . . she's still single right?"

There was a commotion at the front of the house that prevented her from asking Jackson what the hell he was talking about. "Are those the others?"

"Yep." Jackson smiled.

"Who are the others?"

"The whole freaking town of Keeneston. It's rather embarrassing when your parents, aunts, and uncles demand to come. It's enough to give a man performance anxiety."

Ahmed was the first one through the door. He gave Sienna a wink and called Heidi off the guard she still had a hold on. "Bridget and Nabi are tying up the little presents Ace and Gunner left for us. Good job, Heidi," Ahmed cooed as the little girl of the group of badass police dogs thumped her tail, picked up a lavish silk pillow, and proceeded to wiggle around the room.

"Sienna!" her mother cried, shoving her husband out of the way, leaping over the guard lying bound on the floor, and wrapping her daughter up in a fierce hug.

Her father's arms encircled them both and, for a full minute, Sienna let the tears flow.

"Where is Ryan? I have to thank him," Will asked the room now full of the entire Davies family.

"He and Nash went after Bahir through that escape tunnel."

Sienna looked down the dark passageway. He would be okay. He had to be. Annie gently nudged her aside and ran her hands over the wall. She looked worried as she reached the bookshelf. She picked up an urn and looked inside. She whipped around the room with her brows knitted in concern.

"What is it?" Ahmed asked. The joyous atmosphere shifted suddenly in the room.

"We need to leave, now!" Annie yelled as she flung open the closest windows and started waving for people to climb through, lunging for the desk and yanking the computer from it.

Her husband apparently knew better than to ask why as he simply started shoving his sisters-in-law toward the windows. "If my wife says go, you better haul ass!" Cade yelled. The women dragged their feet, not understanding what was going on.

Jackson shoved Sienna's parents from her side and dragged her to the windows.

"Jackson! Don't push my parents . . ."

Jackson pulled out his gun and emptied it into the large glass windowpane. Glass rained down around them as Sienna stared wide-eyed at the new exit. Jackson didn't give her time to ask questions, he was scooping Sienna up in his arms and leaping through the window before she could blink. "My orders are to see you safe," he grunted and set her down on the grass and dragged her into a run.

Sienna turned and saw her parents and the Davies family sprinting after them. She was about to ask why when the earth rumbled beneath her feet. The force of the explosion sent the group flying forward. Sienna lost her breath as Jackson landed on top of her, using his body to shield her from the falling debris.

Ryan felt the earth rumble as dirt fell from the tunnel he and Nash were following. Ryan and Nash didn't stop when a second explosion rocked the earth and threatened to collapse everything around them.

"Bahir must have had the house rigged to explode to destroy evidence. Way easier and much more secure than walking around with gasoline and a match," Nash said, jogging after Ryan.

"What if they . . ." Ryan didn't want to finish his sentence. The idea was too painful. "I told them it was clear."

Nash didn't respond; they simply picked up their pace and hoped their loved ones were safe.

It felt as if they had been running forever, but then Ryan heard something—a crackle in his ear. "Ryan. Nash. Are you there?"

"Miss Lily!" Ryan shouted into his coms.

"Ryan? He's here."

"Speak up, I can barely make out what you're saying." Ryan pressed the coms tighter against his ear.

"A man popped out of an old, dilapidated barn. He's here now. He's opening the doors to the barn," Miss Lily whispered.

"Get down, he's dangerous!" Ryan ordered. He and Nash sprinted forward.

"He hasn't seen us yet. Wait, he's going back inside the barn." Miss Lily paused. "A car! He's leaving. Should we follow?"

"No!" he and Nash screamed at the same time.

"Just see which direction he goes," Ryan commanded.

"Look," Nash called out, and Ryan squinted into the dim corridor.

Ryan saw the outline of a door against the darkness and raised his flashlight to find a wooden door. Ryan pushed, but it didn't open. Nash motioned for him to move and fired off a couple rounds into the hinges. The door teetered and then fell down.

Ryan stepped over the fallen door and out into an old barn. A tan canvas tarp lay on the ground where a car had probably been moments before. He and Nash ran from the barn with guns drawn hoping to catch Bahir.

Off in the distance, the van that held their coms was hidden behind a line of trees. The group from the van was already outside waving them down.

"The house exploded," Ryan called out to them. He didn't breathe as he waited to hear if everyone he loved was safe.

"They're okay, Ryan," his grandmother called. She had a death grip on Betsy Ashton, her best friend and Sienna's grandmother.

"Annie got them out. It's always handy to have a former DEA agent in the family," his grandfather said with a shaky voice.

"Thank goodness," Ryan let out the breath he was holding, and they cut through the tree line, stopping in front of the group of seniors.

"He went that way in a bronze SUV. I couldn't see the brand," Sienna's grandfather said, pointing toward Lexington.

Ryan and Nash surveyed the vehicles around them. A large van full of communications equipment and people over eighty years old, two pickup trucks, three SUVs, a minivan with dog crates in the back, and a black McLaren 570 Sports Series that looked like the devil coming for you from the shadows with its low nose and sleek two-door design.

"We'll take Ahmed's car," Ryan said with a grin.

"You will do no such thing," a cold and deadly voice said over the coms.

"Hotwiring is no different on a $200,000 sports car, right?"

"The keys are under the back driver's side tire," Bridget's voice said over the coms.

"Honey, I am not letting someone drive my baby," Ahmed said with authority.

"You've gotten uptight with your old age," Bridget lectured her husband.

Ryan and Nash weren't asking in the first place. They pulled the coms from their ears and opened the butterfly doors upward to the sports car. Ryan slid into the low car and turned it on. The engine purred, and when he slammed the gas down the car ate up the road.

Having grown up on the gently curving country roads that ran through and all around Keeneston, Ryan was completely comfortable behind the wheel. He gently pressed the pedal and the car responded immediately as he sailed down the road over 100 miles per hour.

Nash and Ryan didn't speak as he drove. Instead, Ryan kept a lookout for the bronze SUV. The rain had stopped, and the full moon was shining on the countryside flying by. Horses, cows, soybeans, corn, and houses were a blur as Ryan focused on what was ahead, not daring to take his eyes off the road. Nash reloaded his guns and then turned in his seat. A moment later he turned back with two rifles.

"I'm sure there's a rocket launching system in here, but I'm not about to try to figure it out," Nash deadpanned. This was Ahmed's car and that may or may not have been hyperbole.

"There!" Ryan called as the taillights of a dark-colored SUV came into view.

The SUV ahead of them raced onto the onramp for New Circle Road, a road aptly named as it made a circle around Lexington. Traffic was light at midnight, allowing both cars to race freely on the open road. The SUV passed one of the only cars on the road, and Ryan floored the McLaren. The sports car raced easily over 120 miles per hour, and Ryan guided it around the car on the road.

Nash cocked the rifle and lowered the window. "No pressure, but you do realize Ahmed will kill you slowly if you get so much as a scrape on his car, right?"

Ryan just smiled and came side by side with the SUV. "Is it Bahir?"

Nash responded by firing off a round into the SUV's tire. Bahir overcorrected and the SUV lunged at them. Ryan pulled the steering wheel sharply, and the sports car eagerly responded, flying past the SUV. It narrowly missed crashing into Nash's door. The side mirror, on the other hand, went flying off and landed somewhere in the grassy median.

The SUV swerved and the tire broke apart, sending the vehicle tumbling over and sliding down the road on its side before coming to a stop.

Nash fell back into his seat. "We're dead."

Ryan nodded as he slammed on the brake pedal and pulled the emergency brake. He turned the wheel hard and pushed the car into a controlled spin, stopping 180 degrees later with his headlights facing the crumpled SUV and oncoming traffic. The other car had stopped on New Circle behind the wreckage of Bahir's SUV, and people were climbing out of the car with their phones to their ears. One seemed to be calling in the accident and the high-speed chase, while another was videoing the wreck.

Ryan and Nash pushed up the butterfly doors and

stepped onto the road. Nash tossed him a rifle over the top of the sports car. People screamed and dove behind their cars at the sight of the two of them stalking forward. The sounds of sirens sounded in the distance; emergency vehicles were being deployed.

Ryan pulled his badge from behind his bulletproof vest and let it hang like a necklace against his chest. He turned to Nash. "Let's finish this."

Ryan saw the shattered windshield of the SUV being kicked out. Bahir crawled through with guns drawn.

"Put them down, Bahir. It's over."

Bahir didn't listen; instead he stood shakily on his legs and pointed the guns at Ryan and Nash. Ryan fired a shot that pinged off the concrete right in front of Bahir's feet.

"I'll die a martyr. I'll become even more famous in death than I did in life," Bahir shouted over the sounds of the sirens for all to hear.

Police cars, ambulances, and fire trucks slid to a stop all around them, lighting the night with blue and red lights.

"I'm getting real sick of hearing that," Ryan yelled back, ignoring the officers with their weapons trained on them. "I'll tell you what I told Abdul. You won't matter. See, tonight the news is going to report that David Kirkpatrick died in a single-car accident in Lexington. This accident is nowhere near your compound. My buddy, Nash, will be confiscating all phones and videos, so no one will ever know you were captured . . . or killed. Your choice."

"It won't matter. I will become a legend that lives forever," Bahir challenged as he rose to stand in front of Ryan.

"Maybe, maybe not. We have a couple of your men, and we'll see how much information we can get from them first," Ryan shrugged, seeing Detective Braxton step forward with her gun trained on the back of Bahir's head.

"We'll create a story that you had decided to run off with the money Seth got for you. We'll float rumors of you buying outrageously expensive things, living the life of luxury, and laughing at those who seek to continue this terrorist cell. That is, the lucky ones who somehow escaped us. Your followers will be too busy chasing a ghost to blow up a stadium — and they certainly won't have the funds for it."

Bahir smiled coldly at Ryan and stepped forward, dropping his arms to his side. "Let's be men and settle this right now."

Ryan lowered his gun and met him halfway with Nash a few steps back. Detective Braxton stood behind the overturned SUV, her arms resting on the side of the hood and her gun aimed on an unsuspecting Bahir. But here, in the middle of the street, in the middle of the night, it was really just the two of them.

Ryan came face to face with the man he had chased for so long — the man who wanted to kill tens of thousands of innocent people — the bastard that dared lay a hand on the woman who held his heart. For this one moment, the lights flashed, the sirens wailed, and the two men smiled at each other as if they were each the devil's own.

"Now that it's just the two of us, Bahir. Tell me why," Ryan asked quietly. "Why plan a terrorist attack at all?"

Bahir just shook his head and smirked. "It was never about the attack. It was always about the money. I have more money than I can ever spend on attacks. It would take nothing to blow up this or that. All those young stupid kids were eager for fame and fortune. They did whatever I told them. All the while, it was the investments I wanted. And here's a secret for you, Agent Parker . . . I do have the ability to disappear with all this money. And I will."

From above, the sound of helicopter blades slicing through the air could be heard over the sirens. "And when are you going to do that?" Ryan asked as he waved to the police and Nash all with their guns trained on him.

"Right after I kill you," Bahir growled and swung his arm up to shoot.

Ryan didn't have time to raise his gun. Instead, all of his anger shot through his body. He used his forearm to block Bahir's gun hand and then was on him. Ryan tackled him, and the two went down hard on the pavement. Ryan scrambled to gain the upper hand as he straddled Bahir and landed a punch to the man's face.

"I can't get a clear shot. Move!" Nash yelled.

Ryan didn't want it to be that easy. He didn't want death to come quickly. He wanted Bahir to sit isolated in a cell for the rest of his life as he watched his life's work come crumbling down. He would die an old man, knowing he hadn't made an ounce of difference in this world.

Ryan brought his hands up to cover the side of his head as Bahir tried to box his ears. The butt of the gun stung as it connected with the back of his head, and Ryan fell on his side to the pavement. Bahir struggled to his knees and tried to aim his gun again, but Ryan wasn't done yet. He slammed his fist into Bahir's stomach. When Bahir doubled over, gasping for breath, Ryan jumped to his feet and stood in front of evil.

Looking at the top of Bahir's dark hair, Ryan was done. As he fought for his life, he knew he was done with taking unnecessary risks. He was done with running, and he was done with hiding to avoid love. All he wanted was to get back to Sienna in one piece. And to do that he was going to finish this—his way.

"Bahir Deron, you have the right to remain silent," Ryan said, reaching behind his back for his cuffs.

Bahir roared, shots were fired, and Ryan slammed his knee into the man's face. In a second, it was over. Bahir lay on the pavement unconscious. He looked down at Bahir and the bullet hole in his gun hand and smiled at Detective Braxton, who was walking forward with her gun still drawn.

"Braxton," Ryan smiled, "I hope you didn't give Seth a deal."

"Parker," she smiled back, "I got your text first and pulled the U.S. attorney from the room. Sorry I didn't believe you about Sienna. I should have trusted you. I was just trying to prove myself. It's hard being a woman in a man's world. Knowing how it is, I shouldn't have accused Sienna of what people accuse me of daily without evidence. I'm sorry."

BANG!

Ryan and Detective Braxton spun with drawn guns and saw Nash with his rifle pointed toward the sky. The helicopter Ryan had assumed belonged to the police went into a tailspin.

"Shit!" Ryan yelled as the black helicopter sent to rescue Bahir careened toward them.

Ryan and Nash grabbed Bahir by the arms and dragged him as they ran. The sound of the blades grew louder as the helicopter plummeted from the sky.

"Ahmed's car!" Nash screamed as he dropped Bahir's unconscious body to the ground.

Braxton, Nash, and Ryan watched from behind the safety of the overturned SUV in horror as the helicopter plunged from the sky and crashed onto the road right behind Ahmed's car. The blades were still spinning, sending sparks flying as they tore apart the road. The helicopter slid forward, and Ryan stared open-mouthed as a blade ripped off the taillight of Ahmed's car and finally came to a stop.

"That can be fixed," Nash said as he exhaled.

Ryan sniffed the air, and he and Nash registered the smell at the same time the spark caught life and the helicopter shot up in the air by a giant explosion. Ryan watched in shock as the fully ignited helicopter fell as a fireball from the sky and landed right on Ahmed's car. The gas tank caught fire and a second explosion rocked them all.

"I don't think that can be fixed," Braxton said in awe, staring at Bahir's rescue helicopter melting onto what had been a McLaren.

Chapter Twenty-Three

Sienna was surrounded by the entire town of Keeneston, yet she felt all alone. After the explosion, the entire group had moved to the Blossom Café. Poppy and Zinnia had been called in and were making pots of strong coffee for everyone who had gathered in the restaurant.

Annie, Cade, and Nabi had taken the computer from Bahir's office to see what was on it. But when they left, more people came. Dani, Mo, Zain, and Gabe showed up first. Then Jackson had texted something to one of his cousins, and the next thing Sienna knew, most of the older Davies cousins were sitting around her as she alternately drank coffee and held an icepack to her face.

Sienna pretended not to notice when Miss Daisy waved Poppy over to the table next to them. "Dear, I'm having trouble keeping up with all the bets," Miss Daisy so-did-not manage to whisper.

"What do you want me to do, Cousin Daisy?" Poppy whispered, but then had to repeat louder.

Sienna rolled her eyes and put the icepack back on her face.

"You're family, so I trust you. I need you to take the bets for me. Just mark down the bet at the top and then you write their name, amount they gave you, and if they are for or against said bet. Then for the final column, if there's a number involved, like Lily just bet Ryan would propose by tomorrow, put tomorrow's date there," Daisy again failed to whisper as she showed Poppy the betting book.

"No problem, Cousin Daisy." Poppy smiled fondly at her elderly cousin before being whisked away by all of Sienna's supposed friends.

Sienna didn't listen to her friends gushing over Ryan, Jackson, and Nash's heroism. She didn't even listen when they talked about how Ryan loved her so much. She didn't care what they thought. She only cared about Ryan coming back to her.

The door opened and Sienna's head shot up hoping to see Ryan. Instead, she smiled at Katelyn walking in with Jaylen.

"I've been sprung, Doc!" Jaylen said happily, bounding over to her. "Doc Charlie and Doc Emma gave me the all-clear. I can't do much, but at least I can go home and see my girl."

"And eat!" Zinnia exclaimed. "You've lost weight. Come here and let me feed you. Do you like hot browns? You need to keep your strength up to get back on the field. I have you on my fantasy team."

Sienna smiled as Jaylen followed Zinnia to the small table near the kitchen and sat him down with plate after plate of food.

Jackson slid into the chair next to her. The table had cleared out to not-so-subtly place bets with Poppy.

"He'll be okay," Jackson said quietly, and he put an arm around her shoulder. He had taken off his vest and looked relaxed in black cargo pants and a tight black T-shirt stretched over his chest and biceps.

"You're lying," Sienna said with a surprising lack of emotion. "Your eyes are more pewter-colored. It's a dead giveaway."

Jackson smiled at her, and she heard Zinnia let out a sigh. Sure, Jackson was handsome, dangerously so. But Sienna had never thought of him like that. He was always Ryan's little brother. After tonight, she realized he was a grown-up. He'd protected her, taken care of her, and did it all because his brother loved her.

"Thank you for everything you did tonight. I don't know how I can ever repay you for putting your life on the line to rescue me."

Jackson just smiled at her and wiped a tear from her face. "Hey, it's my job. And you're family — or at least I hope you soon will be."

"Thank you, Jackson, but . . ." Sienna couldn't finish her sentence. The door to the café opened, and Ryan and Nash stepped inside. His eyes immediately searched her out, and by the time his eyes reached hers, she was already running toward him.

She had never felt such relief and happiness in her life. His arms wrapped around her, and his lips crushed hers as her hands ran down his arms.

"You're safe," Sienna cried, finally pulling back from his kiss. She had to see him, all of him, to make sure he was really here.

Ryan chuckled when she continued to run her hands over his body. He gently grabbed her upper arms and straightened her up. He leaned forward, and Sienna felt his hot breath tickle her ear. "If I get out of here alive, you can do that when we're both naked. Deal?"

Sienna felt her face flush, but then she nodded. She couldn't ask what he meant about getting out of the café alive before friends and family surrounded Ryan and Nash. Her parents hugged him, her mother cried, and her father thumped him on the back so many times Sienna was worried Ryan would be bruised tomorrow. And that was all before his parents got to him.

But the whole time he never let go of her hand. His fingers were laced with hers, his thumb absently rubbing circles over her skin. It seemed like forever for the crowd to calm. All she wanted was to be home with Ryan. She didn't know when she had started to think of her place as their place, but it was their home. Or at least she wished it would be.

"So, what happened?" Bridget asked finally.

Ryan told of the car chase and how Nash had shot out his tire. "Braxton shot the gun out of his hand a second before I knocked him unconscious," Ryan told the group as they hung on every word.

"We didn't want him anywhere in the system, so we took him to Mo's farm. We met Nabi, Annie, and Cade and set guards on him in the secure room that's there. When I left, Nabi was on the phone with the president and the FBI director to decide where to send Bahir for the rest of his life."

"That's not the only interesting part of the conversation." Nash smiled. "Tell them."

Ryan looked away from Sienna, and she knew it was bad before he said it.

"Since my boss was killed by Bahir, the FBI director wants me to take over the L.A. office."

The café was silent. As one, they all turned to look at Sienna. What could she do? They knew before they had even had sex it wasn't meant to be. Timing was just never their thing. "That's wonderful news. Congratulations." She smiled up at him.

Ryan looked at her finally, but he wasn't smiling.

Instead he just frowned. "Thank you," he said seriously.

"How did you fit Bahir into the McLaren?" Ahmed asked as he stepped forward.

Ryan's hand tightened on Sienna's, and he and Nash went pale.

"We used Detective Braxton's cruiser," Ryan said stiffly.

"Then where's my car?" Ahmed asked with a deadly tone to his voice, causing Sienna to shiver. He'd always been "Uncle" Ahmed, but when he looked the way he looked now, she could only picture him as the terrifying soldier he had been in his early years.

"Um," Nash started, taking a big breath and bringing his hand that had been behind his back forward. He extended it to Ahmed and with a steady voice said, "Here you go."

Sienna cocked her head and looked at the object in Nash's hand. She bit her lip trying hard not to laugh at the fear in Nash and Ryan's face and the absolute devastation in Ahmed's.

"Is that my side mirror?" Ahmed asked and took the mirror from Nash. "You broke my mirror?"

"Honey, it's just a car," Bridget said softly. "We can put a mirror back on, right? Is the car outside? I'm sure it won't look nearly as bad as you think, Ahmed."

Nash cleared his throat. "Um, the car isn't outside right now."

"Where is my car?" Ahmed demanded.

Ryan dropped Sienna's hand and took a half step forward. "It's my fault, sir. The car is on New Circle Road."

"You left a McLaren on the side of the road?" Ahmed's asked with a rare moment of emotion.

"Not exactly. It's more *on* the road. As in melted . . ."

"What?" Ahmed yelled. He actually yelled this time as the people in the café started looking nervous.

"Twenty bucks Ahmed kills Ryan by strangulation," Miss Lily whispered. "Write it down, Poppy."

"I'll take that. He'll skin him alive," Zain said.

"Waterboard first, then beat him," Gabe proclaimed and handed his money to Poppy.

Ahmed and Ryan ignored them. "What happened to my baby?" Ahmed asked finally as if he was working really hard not to explode.

"Well, Bahir had this chopper that was coming to pick him up and, well, we couldn't let the pilot get away and tell everyone we had captured Bahir. So Nash shot him. Great shot, by the way," Ryan said to Nash who just nodded with fear in his eyes.

"Okay, that's what I would have done," Ahmed agreed as he tried to remain calm. "This still doesn't answer my question."

"It kinda does. See without a pilot, the chopper went into a tailspin and fell onto New Circle Road. It slid into your car and ignited, which shot it into the air as a fireball, what fifteen feet?" Ryan asked Nash.

"At least twenty," Nash said before slamming his mouth shut at the look of horror on Ahmed's face.

"And what goes up must come down . . . onto your car. A car full of gas." Ryan didn't finish. Ahmed had turned red — bright red.

"Honey, breathe. It's just a car. They caught the bad guy and saved Sienna. All worth more than a car."

And then it happened. What no one thought they would ever see. A gasp filled the room and then it was so quiet you could literally hear the tear fall from Ahmed's cheek and hit the floor.

Chapter Twenty-Four

Sienna unlocked the door to her house in silence. She felt Ryan standing close behind her as they stepped into the darkened living room. The sun would be coming up soon, but Sienna didn't think sleep would come. She placed the keys on the side table and dropped her purse to the floor.

"Where's Hooch?" she asked quietly and turned to where Ryan was watching her.

"With your parents. I'll pick him up tomorrow," Ryan told her. He reached out for her. His warm hands closed around her upper arms, and he pulled her forward.

"Are you leaving tomorrow? For your new job?" Sienna asked against the tight muscles of his chest.

"I have to go to D.C. first," Ryan answered quietly.

"So, tonight is our last night before you take over the FBI office? You'll be a wonderful boss, Ryan." Sienna fought the tears in her eyes and hated the way her throat felt as if it were swelling shut with emotion.

Ryan didn't answer. Instead he bent his head and captured her lips in his. His hands came to cup her face, and Sienna rested her head in his hands. She'd place her whole heart in his hands if he'd let her. If tonight was the last night, then it was going to be one to remember.

She ran her hands down his T-shirt and pulled it from his pants. She bunched it up in her hands and at the last second pulled it from his body, breaking their kiss. Sienna moved her lips to trace the line of Ryan's jaw and pushed him back against the door. She ran her hands over the ridges of his abdomen and let her lips follow before falling to her knees in front of him.

"Sienna," Ryan groaned as she pushed down his pants and bent forward. Her named sounded pained, revered, mourned, and loved all at the same time.

Ryan closed his eyes and let the pleasure heal him as his fingers tangled with Sienna's hair. He needed her love. And tonight he was going to show her that. He didn't have fancy words to tell her, sonnets to recite, or feelings to share. He wasn't that kind of guy, but he knew how to show her he loved her. He was going to show her she had his whole heart and always would.

With all the strength he had, he pulled away from Sienna and swept her into his arms. The bedroom had never seemed so far away as he carried her in his arms. Setting her onto her feet he kissed her eyelids, the tip of her nose, and down her neck, while slowly unzipping her dress. He kissed her shoulder, her collarbone, and then slowly went down to his knees in front of her, kissing her along the way. It was his time to worship her. He guided her to sit on the edge of the bed before lifting her leg and kissing the back of her knee. In slow, savoring kisses, he worked his way up her leg to her center. After tonight, Sienna should never doubt what she meant to him.

Sienna grasped the sheets as the world exploded around her. And when Ryan moved up her body, she wrapped her legs tightly around his waist and gasped as he filled her.

She was complete. But it was only for tonight. Tonight she would be his and he would be hers. Then it would be gone. As he moved inside her, she forgot to mourn what might have been. Instead, she lost herself in the now — in Ryan and in their love.

The sun was high in the sky by the time Ryan quietly shut the door to Sienna's house. She was still sleeping, and he knew he was taking the coward's way out by leaving without saying goodbye. He just didn't have the answers to the questions she would ask. The problem was, it wasn't just one night he had to think about. It was a lifetime of bad timing, friendship, and wanting.

"You ready for this?" Nash asked from the other side of the fence where he sat atop a large chestnut horse.

Ryan climbed the four boards of the black fence and dropped onto Dani and Mo's property. Nash handed him the reins to the big black horse with a white diamond on its nose.

"As ready as I'll ever be. It's not everyday we get debriefed by the FBI director," Ryan said as he mounted his horse. "Thanks for meeting me here."

"I thought you all would be tired this morning. I didn't want the ATV to wake up Sienna," Nash explained. "And I wanted to give you this."

Nash held out a flash drive and Ryan took it. "What is it?"

Nash just smiled. "You forgot about the camera in the living room."

Ryan shot a murderous glance to Nash. "Did you watch this?"

Nash shook his head. "Nah! I saw you two enter the house and kiss. That's when I turned off my tablet. This is the only copy of the surveillance from Sienna's house. I thought you might want it."

"Thank you," Ryan said as he pocketed the flash drive and pushed his horse into a gallop. "What's going on at the main house?"

"Ahmed had to fly Kale in overnight," Nash said of Ahmed's son who was away at MIT.

"Cade couldn't hack Bahir's system?" Ryan asked, astounded.

"It's a young person's game now. The best hackers all over the world are teenagers. Bahir had a system on his computer that Cade had never seen before. Kale broke it in twenty-four minutes. Annie laughed, Cade shook his head, and Ahmed beamed with pride. It let him forget about the car . . . for a moment."

"What did they find out?"

"They forwarded it all to the director. We'll talk about it in D.C. I also had them print it out so we could look it over on the plane. But the short version is, we found the target and the area is being swept for explosives as we speak. The information on the computer, along with the information we got from Bahir and his cohorts, has led to the FBI rounding up twenty-seven people so far. That includes eight FBI agents all across the country who were on Bahir's payroll. We also found the money. All of it. It should be able to be returned to the investors eventually. We're thinking Bahir should announce his retirement in an email to investors and have someone undercover from the government step in as the new head of the company and funnel it back. We'll then have him close the doors to the company. That way, no one will connect Bahir's investments to terrorism and it ties in the story of Bahir retiring to the lap of luxury."

"Good plan," Ryan told Nash. They slowed the horses to a walk. Two farm workers ran forward to take the horses from them, and they met the rest of the group.

Bridget stood next to Ahmed and their son. Kale already towered over his parents and was still growing. Annie and Cade stood next to them with the computer and multiple large files in their hands. Behind them stood Ryan's father, Cole. Bridget elbowed Ahmed, who looked pained.

"I'm really sorry about the car, Ahmed," Ryan said for the hundredth time.

Ahmed's lips pursed, but then he took a deep breath. "I'll let you live this time. Bridget said I could get the new 650." He smiled then and Ryan felt the first tinge of relief. Now he just had to have a little chat with the FBI director.

"The plane is ready for you. First stop D.C. After your debriefing, Kale will snag a flight back to MIT while you all come home . . . or some of you will. The director said you could take their plane back to L.A.," Ahmed explained to Ryan.

"Let's not keep the director waiting," Ryan said with a sense of foreboding. The sooner he could close the book on this chapter of his life, the better.

Sienna waved at Sydney and walked into the Blossom Café that evening. Her best friend had been out of town during this mess. As soon as she had landed in Lexington, she had called Sienna to set up dinner. It had been her phone call that had woken Sienna to find Ryan gone. A note on his pillow that read *Don't forget that I love you* was all he left behind.

He hadn't even picked up Hooch for her like he'd promised. Sienna hadn't wanted to face her parents yet, so she told them that she'd pick the slobbery beast up tomorrow. As if by tomorrow she would forget what she had lost.

"I go out of town for a few days and miss the most exciting thing to ever have happened in Keeneston!" Sydney gasped as she wrapped Sienna up in a tight hug. "What is it? What's the matter?"

Sienna sat in the booth and looked at the ceiling for a moment to gain her composure. "He's gone."

"I know. Mom and Dad told me all about it. Someone gave my mom a gun? What is that about?" Sydney joked.

Sienna shook her head. "No, not Bahir. Ryan. He left this morning for L.A. The FBI director personally asked him to become the Special Agent in Charge of the L.A. office. It's a huge promotion; it's one of the biggest offices in the United States and a clear chance to become the FBI director later."

Sydney sat stunned as Sienna took a big gulp. She was not going to cry.

"Hey, girls. What I can get you tonight?" Zinnia asked, stopping next to the booth with her pad in hand.

"Better make it a Rose Sisters Special Iced Tea," Sydney told her. "And chocolate. Whatever you have that's mostly chocolate."

"You got it. I heard about Ryan leaving this morning. John told us all about the job offer in L.A. and how he's meeting with the director today. I'm sorry. I really thought you two were the perfect couple. I even placed $20 on it with Poppy." Zinnia gave her a sad smile and hurried off to make their order and, Sienna was sure, to spread the word that she was broken-hearted.

"Now, tell me everything. And I mean everything. Like why you were still asleep when I called you this afternoon." Sydney winked and Sienna laughed. She was strong. She didn't need a man to fulfill her life, but it would have been nice to have Ryan to share it with her.

Ryan sat back on the plane and closed his eyes. The president and the director had grilled him and Nash for hours. Every bit of evidence was combed over and scrutinized. Kale presented his findings. For a moment, Ryan thought he'd end up in jail for laughing at the FBI director's initial lack of faith in Kale's ability, but Kale was now on his way back to college with a job offer in hand.

There was one thing Ryan needed to do before he could move on and start over. And it would be something that made facing the president seem easy. But he could do it, he told himself. He had taken down a major player in the international terrorism scene. He shouldn't be nervous about the future.

Ryan let out a deep breath. He just needed to accept it. It had to be done.

"We're preparing to land," the captain said over the intercom as the plane descended.

In short order, Ryan was off the plane and in a borrowed vehicle. It had been a long day and an even longer night. The moon was high and cast a yellow glow on the road as he drove. He practiced the speech he was going to have to make.

By the time he arrived, the sun was just starting to crack over the horizon. He felt the new warmth on his face as he jumped out of his car and looked at the place that would be the first step to the rest of his life. Ryan took a deep breath. Here went nothing.

Ryan knocked on the door and waited. He looked into the security camera mounted overhead and gave it a nod. He heard movement inside and then the door opened.

"What are you doing here so early?"

"I've come to ask permission to marry your daughter, Mr. Ashton."

Chapter Twenty-Five

Sienna didn't want to get up. The sun was bright and shining a new day upon her face as she pulled the pillow over her head. She didn't want to face her parents. She didn't want to face a day that didn't include Ryan in it. And she certainly didn't want to face the pitying look of the patrons of the Blossom Café when she went to get her morning muffin. They had all seen her break down the night before and stuff her face with chocolate.

No. Sydney had made her swear that last night was her time to pity herself. Today was the first day of the rest of her life, and she wasn't going to spend it hiding in bed. She was going to get her dog and give him all the love she had in her heart for Ryan. She'd start with a trip around her parents' farm while she rode one of their horses. Then they would both have hamburgers for lunch and cuddle on the couch with a movie for the night.

Sienna groaned and smothered the pillow over her face. She was treating her dog like the man she loved. How pathetic was that? Okay, one more day of pity and maybe doing these things with Hooch would encourage her to get out in public tomorrow. Yes, that was the plan. Tomorrow was Monday, a perfectly good day to start the rest of her life. Today was all about survival.

The white house Sienna had grown up in had changed very little over the years. The trees had gotten bigger and the bushes fuller, but the feel of the house had never changed. Even when her mother completely renovated the house three years ago, it still gave the feel of home. Then why was she dreading going inside? Her father opened the door, and Sienna finally had the motivation to open her car door as Hooch ran out to greet her.

"Hey, boy. Did Grandma and Grandpa take good care of their granddog?"

"You know we did. Your mother spoils him rotten. Goodness knows what she'll do with a grandchild." Her father wrapped her up in a hug, and Sienna tried not to cry. There would be no grandchild for a very long time at the rate she was going. Good thing her younger brother, Carter, was so handsome. He'd have no problem finding a wife who couldn't wait to supply baby after baby to feed their mother's grandmother demands.

"That's why she shouldn't retire. Can you imagine what kind of trouble she'd get in with all that free time on her hands?" Sienna shuddered. She loved her mother, but she might have to move to Montana to hide from her meddling. She could move to L.A. That was even farther, but Ryan hadn't even asked her to join him out there. He didn't ask because he knew her life was here. Sienna sighed and wiped Hooch's drool onto her jeans.

"True enough. What are your plans for the day?" her father asked, leading her to her mother, who was working on the caseload for court on Monday.

"I thought I would take Keeper for a ride and let Hooch run for a bit."

Her mother looked up and smiled at her. "That sounds lovely. Have a good time. Maybe when you're done you can stop by for a minute. I should be done with all this work by then."

"Sure, Mom." Sienna gave her mom a quick kiss on the cheek and headed out the back door. She gave a quick whistle, and Hooch thundered after her. His big body bounced with the excitement of going for a run.

Sienna headed for her favorite part of the farm. The stallion was six years old now and had just retired from racing. Quarterback Keeper had done his father, Naked Boot Leg, proud and won his fair share of stakes races. He's been a nice addition to the stud program, too.

For some reason, the big stallion had fallen in love with Hooch when Sienna first brought him by years ago. Hooch had killed a mouse in Keeper's pasture and the two had been inseparable ever since. The big horse looked at Hooch as some kind of protector and would follow him all around the farm if he could.

Sienna leaned over and gave Keeper's neck a pat as they headed toward the beginning of the wooded area at the back of the farm. There was a trail there that followed the gently rolling brook that cut through their property.

Hooch paused and stuck his nose up in the air and sniffed. He let loose a howl and tore happily off into the woods, his tongue hanging out the side of his mouth flapping in the wind. Sienna smiled even though she knew she'd have to wash a mud-covered dog when she got back to her parents.

Sienna was almost to the tree line when Hooch came bounding back with something in his mouth. Oh, gross, he'd killed another mouse. Sienna stopped Keeper and hopped down, tying the stallion loosely to a tree to prevent him from wandering off.

"Come here, Hooch," Sienna cooed. "Give it to Mommy."

Sienna tried to catch him, but Hooch growled playfully and evaded her grasping hands.

"Hooch! Drop it!" Sienna commanded, only to have Hooch go down on his haunches and growl playfully again as his big tail wagged.

"Fine, I don't want it. But don't you dare think of licking me after you eat that mouse." Sienna turned away and ignored him as she walked back to Keeper.

Hooch followed after her with his head hung low. He didn't like to be ignored so he rammed his big head against her hip. When Sienna ignored him, he did it again. Sienna smiled at using reverse psychology on a dog and looked down at her droopy-faced pal with his jowls covering the prize.

"Are you going to drop it now?" Sienna asked as she placed her hands on her hips and looked down at her dog as if he were a toddler.

Hooch rolled his eyes and then opened his mouth. A square black box inside a plastic baggie dropped to the ground. Sienna stared at it before bending to pick it up.

"What did you find now?" Sienna asked as she opened the plastic baggy and pulled out the black box. She opened the lid and gasped. A perfect single solitaire diamond was looking back at her. She gulped as she pulled the ring out to get a closer look. She turned the heavy band and saw something written inside. All around the inside of the band were initials. The last ones were CP+PD.

Sienna felt her mouth drop open. This wasn't just a ring. This was Ryan's mother's engagement ring. And Hooch had somehow found it. Oh, please let it be found and not stolen, Sienna prayed and put the ring back in the box.

"Where did you get this?" Sienna asked Hooch.

Hooch howled and took off into the woods with Sienna hot on his trail. She followed him through the trees, past the berry bushes, and to the small clearing by the brook. Hooch stopped and leaned against the man standing there, watching the water bubble over the stones in the creek bed.

Sienna must have gasped when he turned around. He looked at her hand and smiled. Her heart stopped as he stepped toward her looking devastating in worn jeans and a tight gray FBI T-shirt.

"You found it," Ryan said with a smile that made her forget what he was talking about.

"I found, what? Oh, your mother's ring." Sienna handed the bag to him and shook her head, reminding herself to breathe. How was she going to move on when just the sight of him caused her heart to soar?

"I was afraid Hooch stole it," Sienna said as Ryan took the bag from her hand and pulled out the box.

Ryan shook his head and gave her a crooked smile. "No, he didn't steal it. He did exactly what he was supposed to do."

"Do? What was Hooch supposed to do?" Sienna asked in confusion while Ryan gave the dog a pat on the head.

He bent down on one knee and turned the open box to face her. He took her hand in his and his eyes looked straight into her soul. "Bring you to me."

Sienna opened her mouth but nothing came out. Instead, she stared at the man on one knee in front of her, her eyes darting between his gentle but nervous smile and the ring he was now holding up to her.

"Sienna Danielle Paige Ashton, I love your fierce independence, your ability to throw a football, your sharp mind, and the way you so nicely put me off until I was older. I didn't want to admit it when I was younger, but it was for the best. We had to grow and come into our own before coming together. What we have is something so strong we could have lost ourselves in it when we were teenagers. But not anymore. We know how to be ourselves and how to be together. We don't need each other to survive. But we are strong and better when we are together.

"I want to be there for you every day. I want to wake with you in my arms and come home to you every night. I want to find you at the café, complaining about me to your friends. I want to make love to you like every time is the first time. When I was five years old, you were the first girl I kissed, and I lost my heart. It's always been you, and it always will be. Sienna, will you marry me?"

Sienna's heart had stopped beating the second he said her full name. Tears slid down her cheeks as she saw the love he had for her in his eyes—the love she knew was reflected in her own eyes.

"Yes! Yes, I'll marry you. Nothing would make me happier," Sienna said as joy filled her. Ryan let out a whoop and wrapped his arms around her waist. He stood, picking her up with him and twirling her around. She looked into his face and lost herself in their future. She moved her hands from his shoulders to cup his face and bent her lips to his. He stopped spinning and kissed her. The slow kiss told her all the things she already knew—they were madly in love and this was just the beginning.

Hooch howled, and Ryan smiled against her lips. He loosened his grip so she slowly slid down his body. "It would make me so proud to give this to you." He held up the ring and slid it onto her finger. She stared at the ring that had been given to generations of Parker brides and would one day be given to their son's fiancée.

Ryan didn't want to let her go. He knew he had a goofy grin on his face, but when he slid that ring onto Sienna's finger he had never known such pride or pleasure before. Still, deep down, he couldn't believe someone as amazing as Sienna had said yes to marrying him. He would make sure every day he showed her how thankful he was that she was part of his life.

"How did you know where I was?" Sienna asked. She finally took her eyes from the ring on her left hand and looked up at him.

"Your mom," Ryan smiled. "She's a great co-conspirator."

"My mom knew? And she was so normal when I saw her. Did my dad know, too?" Sienna asked with surprise.

Ryan nodded and kept his hands hanging loosely around her waist. "Sweetheart, by now the whole town knows. I went to your parents and asked your father's permission. Then I headed over to my parents to get the ring from Mom. Then I went to Dani and Mo's farm where Nash sped me to the back fence on the ATV after your mom sent me a text as to where you were going to be. I can guarantee my mom and your mom called Dani, and Dani told Bridget, who told Annie, and well, you see where this is going."

Sienna tilted her head back and laughed up into the trees. How blessed she was to have so many people who cared for her. "Wait," Sienna said quickly, the smile falling from her lips. "You said you started your new job tomorrow. You have to leave so soon? I can't possibly get out to L.A. tomorrow."

Ryan pulled her back into the tight circle of his arms. "I

am starting my new job tomorrow. My new job as appointed by the FBI director himself as Special Agent in Charge of the FBI's Lexington Office."

"What?" Sienna practically yelled as Ryan laughed.

"I turned down the L.A. job. I've missed you, and I've missed Keeneston. It was time for me to come home. Dad went with me to Washington since he was technically my supervisor during this takedown. When I turned down the job, the FBI director asked my dad if a new agent had been appointed to his position yet. When Dad said no, the director offered it to me, and I gladly accepted."

"But, the L.A. job was going to lead to a job in Washington. You shouldn't give that up for me," Sienna protested.

Ryan couldn't help but kiss her. This was why he loved her and why they would do remarkable things with their lives, because they supported each other. "Sienna, I don't want a job in Washington. At least, not yet. Let's see how I do as the head of the FBI office here in town first. I may not be cut out for the political role. But, if I am, then we'll discuss it as a family."

Ryan stopped further questions with a kiss. But a kiss wasn't enough, and Ryan wondered if it would ever be as he pulled her tight against him. He ran his fingers down her spine and smiled against her lips as she shivered with anticipation. This was the woman he loved. He pulled her shirt over her head and filled his hands with her breasts. This was the woman he wanted to spend the rest of his life protecting, loving, and cherishing. Ryan pushed her jeans down as she frantically kicked them off while reaching for his zipper. And this was the woman he was going to show how much he needed her every day.

Sienna wrapped her legs around his waist, and he

placed his hands on her ass, holding her to him. And today was just the beginning. He smiled against her neck as he went about showing her just what a great couple they made in more ways than one.

Chapter Twenty-Six

Ryan swung his leg over the saddle and reached down for Sienna's arm. She placed her foot in the stirrup, and with his help was quickly seated on his thighs. Ryan wrapped his arms around her and took hold of the reins. Using his knees to apply pressure to Keeper's sides, the horse responded and took off at a canter across the field.

Ryan felt Sienna lean back against him, and he had never felt such contentment, such happiness, and such excitement for the future. "I love you," he whispered into her ear as they headed for her parents' house.

Sienna tilted her head back and smiled at him. Her eyes, the color of the grass in the pastures, shone with love. "I love you, too."

They rode, holding tightly onto each other, as they shared their love in whispered words.

"Oh no," Ryan groaned.

"Oh no? I'm sorry, I thought it was a good thing we love each other." Sienna smirked.

"Not that. That's wonderful, and I'll never get tired of hearing you say those words. It's that." Ryan nodded his chin forward.

"Oh no." Sienna cursed as they crested a small hill and came into view of her parents' house. Or what she could see of the house through the dozens of parked cars in front of it.

"Looks like we'll have to wait to celebrate privately again," Ryan whispered near her ear, placing a kiss on her neck. Shivers ran through her body in anticipation. But knowing they had the rest of their lives together stopped her from turning Keeper in the opposite direction.

"I can't wait. But first, wave at our parents," Sienna whispered back and wiggled her bottom just to hear him groan. She had a little payback to dish out for running away from his feelings for so long.

"I can't believe it!" her mother called out as she and Paige clung together with smiles across their faces.

"Finally." Sienna could have sworn she heard her mother then whisper to Paige, whose grin only grew larger in response.

"Let me help the old married woman down," Sienna heard from the other side of Keeper. She turned her head and squealed.

"Carter! What are you doing here?" Her brother held up his hands and grabbed her around the waist. In a quick move, he had her on the ground and was smiling down at her.

At twenty-six, Carter was so much like their father with a sprinkle of their mother thrown in. Sienna was the complete opposite of that. Carter was just a half-inch shorter than Ryan, with dark brown hair that showed auburn highlights if the sun hit it right. And his strong square jaw and dimples had a bevy of girls swarming him throughout high school and college where he played wide receiver. But underneath the muscles and dimpled smile was the kindest man she knew. And she didn't think that just because he was her brother. He was quiet, observant, and sweet. Someday he would make an excellent husband

and father.

"Mom called and told me what was happening. I didn't want to be the only person not here. Congratulations. I know it took you two a while to come together. It's just like wine. Drink it too soon and it's sour. Give it time and it's perfection. And you two are perfection." Carter bent over and placed a kiss on her cheek, then he was pushed aside and enveloped in hugs from her mom and Paige.

"Oh, look at the ring on her finger." Paige sniffed as she held Sienna's hand in hers and smiled. "A perfect fit."

"I'm so sorry, Mrs. Parker. This is your ring; you should be wearing it," Sienna said a little worriedly, but her future mother-in-law just laughed.

"Honey, it's also tradition when you give the ring to your son that your husband gets you a new one. A much bigger one for putting up with them for so long." Paige flashed her finger and now it was time for Sienna and her mom to drool over the large emerald-cut diamond now gracing Paige's finger.

"And for heaven's sake, you're a grown woman and about to be my daughter. I think you can call me Paige at the very least."

"And you can finally be an official part of my family!" Sydney squealed as she ran over to Sienna and wrapped her in a hug.

Ryan thumped his father's back and hugged him. Will was still looking questionable about this arrangement, though. When his father finally let go, Will stepped forward and held out his hand. Ryan's smile dropped from his face as he seriously shook his future father-in-law's hand.

"I still don't know how I feel about this. It's hard to let your daughter go, but I guess I feel the most comfortable knowing it's you. You always did love her. Promise me you'll take good care of her. She's my little girl."

Ryan tightened his grip on Will's hand. "I promise on my life I will make her happy."

"You better or I'll kill you," a low menacing voice said from behind him. "Brother."

Ryan turned around and saw Carter standing there with a serious look to match his father's. But then he smiled and thumped him on the back. "Welcome to the family."

A gentle hand touched him on the elbow, and he turned to find his grandparents standing with Sienna's grandparents. They were in their late eighties now, but still very much in love. That's what he wanted with Sienna, and the two examples of how to live were right there in front of them.

Ryan leaned down so his grandmother could kiss his cheek. "I'm so happy for you both. I didn't think I'd live long enough to see one of my grandbabies marry."

"Grandma," Ryan smiled, not wanting to think about them not being around in the future.

"You think you can finally die happy now, my dear?" his grandfather asked with a quirk of his lips. The Ashtons laughed and Ryan suddenly felt as if he were on the outside of a joke.

His grandmother patted her husband's wrinkled hand and smiled at him. "Not yet. I think I need a great-grandbaby first."

Then it was a blur of cousins, aunts, uncles, friends, and somewhere a bottle of bourbon appeared and quickly disappeared. The whole time he kept Sienna in sight, if not by his side. The sun set over the black four-board fences, and all the people they loved celebrated his and Sienna's engagement. It almost made him feel bad he was going to sneak away with Sienna for their own celebration. Almost.

Sienna laughed at Ryan's dramatic groan as Sydney told him they both had to let her design their wedding attire. Sydney punched her cousin in the arm, and Sienna just laughed harder.

"Can we elope?" Ryan asked before being whacked on the back of the head by too many women to count.

"Not a chance. I can't wait to see what Sydney designs for us," Sienna said excitedly.

"Me too," Layne jumped in. "I look very nice in blue or green."

Sienna, Sydney, and Layne broke out in laughter as Ryan rolled his eyes and latched onto the only other man brave enough to enter wedding talk.

"Which color would you prefer, Jackson?" Ryan asked his quieter, younger brother.

"I don't care as long as Bethany is in a dress with easy access."

Sienna smacked his arm. "You're lucky Greer is at school and didn't hear you say that."

Jackson gave a mock shudder of the youngest Parker. Their little sister was a crack shot and very much believed women could do anything men could do and most of it better. So far, she'd proved her two older brothers she was right.

"Don't worry, I'm texting her now," Abigail, Ahmed and Bridget's daughter, joked as Jackson lunged at her phone.

"Then I'll text Dylan what you told me over Christmas," Jackson threatened.

Zain and Gabe joined them as the two of them went shrieking off.

"We'll plan the bachelor party," Gabe grinned.

Sienna just shook her head. "I don't even want to know."

"It's okay, we're going to plan the bachelorette party." Reagan and Riley grinned and a silent challenge was issued. Layne and Piper held up their hands and took a step back. It was going to be twins versus twins on who could throw the best party.

Kenna Ashton raised her glass of champagne and clinked it against Paige and Dani's. From their seat on the outdoor couch, they watched their children lost in each other's eyes.

"It took longer than we thought, but not bad for our first try," Kenna toasted.

"I'll drink to that." Paige smiled.

"So will I," Dani said, clinking glasses with her two best friends.

"Did you write it down?" Kenna asked.

"Sure did," Dani told them and held up the spiral notebook.

Paige shook her head. "I can't believe Miss Lily handed over her matchmaking books for safekeeping until we pass it down to Zinnia. There are generations of matches in here. I saw ours. The Rose sisters had us all picked out before we even knew it."

"How many does this make?" Kenna asked.

"I have twenty-four notebooks at home. Dani just started number twenty-five," Paige said in amazement.

"One hundred forty-nine marriages," Dani said, looking up at Sienna and Ryan. "Well, we'll just count this as one hundred fifty."

"And they had no idea we planned it all along." Paige raised her glass and the three best friends cheered again.

"But who's next?" Kenna asked as she looked at the

men and women celebrating around them.

"Zain?" Paige wondered.

Dani shook her head. Her oldest wasn't ready yet. "He's getting there, but not yet."

"What about Sophie?" Kenna asked the group, and they swung their gaze to where Cade and Annie's oldest stood talking with Miles and Morgan's only child, Layne.

"Look," Dani pointed to the shadows. "I'd know that look anywhere."

"You think?" Paige asked.

"Yeah, I'm not so sure about that. But what about Sydney? She's almost twenty-eight. She's seen the world with her modeling career, established a major business, and even appeared on the Forbes list right under the designer Allegra Simpson for most powerful influences in the fashion industry. All she's missing is someone to come home to at night." Kenna smiled.

"Perfect," Paige agreed.

"I've got her name written on this page, but who do we write on the other page?" Dani asked.

"Oh." Kenna slumped back in her chair. This wasn't as easy as she thought.

"We might need some help with this one. Luckily, I know just the person to ask," Paige said conspiratorially.

"Then a toast to number one hundred fifty-one," Dani said, closing the notebook and holding up her glass.

"Cheers!" the women said, dissolving into giggles.

"Amateurs," Marcy Davies whispered to Betsy Ashton as they clinked their own glasses in celebration of their grandchildren's engagement while they watched the three best friends across the room.

"Do you miss it?" Miss Lily asked her two sisters as they

watched Sienna and Ryan quietly sneaking out of the party.

Miss Violet shook her head. "No, look how happy those three are."

Miss Daisy and her sisters looked to where Kenna, Dani, and Paige were laughing. "They didn't even have a clue we were helping them on their first match."

"Bless their hearts," the sisters said all together.

Ryan didn't let go of Sienna's hand while he drove her car home. They didn't need to say anything either. Their feelings were plain as day on their faces. He parked the car and went to open the door for his fiancée. He liked the sound of that, although he liked the sound of wife better.

Hand in hand, they walked up the steps onto the porch. Ryan dropped her hand while Sienna unlocked the door, and then he scooped her up into his arms. Sienna squealed merrily, and Hooch howled his delight as Ryan carried her over the threshold.

"I think you're supposed to wait to carry me over the threshold until we're married," Sienna giggled.

"Who said I was carrying you over the threshold?" Ryan asked, the corner of his lips quirking up.

"Um, you just did it," Sienna said, breaking out into laughter.

Ryan shook his head. "No, sweetheart, I'm carrying you to bed." Ryan used the bottom of his foot to close the door.

"One of these times, I'm going to walk to our bedroom."

"But not tonight."

Ryan carried his future wife to their room and celebrated the night and all the nights yet to come.

Epilogue

Keeneston, eight months later . . .

"Damn. That's enough to bring a man to his knees," Jackson whispered in Ryan's ear. They stood in the front of the whole town and the entire Thoroughbreds franchise and watched Sienna on her father's arm walk toward them.

Ryan couldn't form words to agree. He simply gave a single nod and watched his soon-to-be wife walk toward him. Her long auburn hair was gently swept up with pearl combs. The ivory lace dress fit tightly against her breasts, her trim waist highlighted by a satin ribbon, and her deliciously curved hips caressed by the column of the dress before it fell straight to the floor. Behind her, the dress flared, and pools of delicate lace seemed to float as she walked.

And then she was there, standing in front of him. If you paid him a million dollars, Ryan wouldn't be able to tell you what happened next. All he knew was he'd never experienced such happiness in his life. And when Judge Cooper pronounced them man and wife, a sudden shift occurred deep in Ryan's heart.

Nothing had really changed, but everything had with that simple proclamation. He had a wife. A wife to share his life. A wife to raise a family. A wife to love and protect.

And in that one moment, their whole life flashed before him: kissing her when they were children, seeing her standing up to the boys who didn't want a girl on their flag football team, seeing her after their first real kiss as they spied on Nabi and Grace, seeing her in Bahir's office sending him off with the order to come back to her, seeing her naked in bed in the early morning light, and now seeing his *wife*. He smiled and stopped them both in the middle of the aisle to kiss her.

The guests cheered and Sienna heard the noise drift away as her husband stopped their exit down the aisle, placed one hand around the top of her neck, one arm around her waist, bent her over, and kissed her. He must have been thinking all the things she had, for his kiss was full of loving promise. It had taken Sienna's breath away when her father offered her his arm and escorted her to the front of the aisle. She had seen Ryan, devastating in his tuxedo, and had almost run up the aisle toward him.

Ryan pulled his head back and ran his thumb over her cheek. "I love you, Dr. Parker. Now, let's go party and get everyone drunk so they won't notice when we disappear early."

Sienna laughed but didn't disagree, especially after getting through the receiving line. But soon enough she was in his arms as they slowly danced their first dance as husband and wife. Their mothers cried. Their fathers pretended not to. And Hooch's tail happily wagged, nearly knocking over the table holding the wedding cake.

"I have a confession," Ryan whispered in her ear as they swayed to the music.

"What's that?" Sienna asked, smelling a trace of his cologne and feeling the urge to sink farther into his embrace.

"I can't wait to see what happens next." Ryan smiled at her as her head fell back and she laughed. Hooch howled, and Sienna had never been happier.

Jackson twirled Sydney around the dance floor as her cousin and his new wife laughed and stood outrageously close to each other. She let out a sigh. Not for the first time, she wished she could find that. But who had time? She certainly didn't.

"They look sickeningly in love," Jackson said to her, spinning her.

"I wonder how long until we hear the pitter-patter of little feet running around," Sydney smiled.

"Odds are 5-2 within one year," Poppy whispered from where she was dancing nearby with Gabe.

Jackson shook his head. "Nah, I think they'll be married two years before they have a baby. You got my bet, Poppy?"

"Sure do!" Poppy called out gaily as Gabe spun her away.

"May I cut in?"

Jackson stopped dancing and smiled as Sydney's younger brother, Wyatt, took his place. At twenty-six, Wyatt already acted like he was forty. He'd always been the quiet, serious type who had impeccable manners and a Southern drawl that made the girls melt before him. While he was more uptight than Sydney, Wyatt was the best brother a girl could ask for.

"How's your evening going so far, Wyatt?" Sydney asked as her brother pulled her into a perfect dance.

"It's a nice break from being on call," Wyatt said, a little tired. After graduating from veterinary school, their mother, the local small-animal vet, brought Wyatt on board to take care for the large animals of Keeneston. He'd been elbow-deep in half the cows in the county ever since.

"It's called paying your dues. I had to do it, too, as a model."

"I know. Have you seen Great-Grandma Wyatt recently?" Wyatt asked.

"A couple days ago. I went out to read to her and show her some of my new designs. We talked fashion and business for about an hour before she got too tired and fell asleep."

"Good. I haven't had the time to see her recently. I'm going over tomorrow to tell her about the wedding. I'm sure she'd love it if you joined me."

Sydney smiled as she thought about their great-grandma. She'd raised their mother and had been a staple in their lives as well. She favored flowing gowns, huge hats, and bright red lipstick. The preference for bright red lipstick and big hats had rubbed off on Sydney as well, especially with Aunt Paige designing said hats.

"I would like that. How's ten o'clock?"

Wyatt slowed as the music drew to a close. "Great. I'll meet you there. Now, I need to find out if Bethany prefers a Southern gentleman or the dark, mysterious type."

With a wink, her brother sauntered over to one of the other bridesmaids. He lifted her hand and placed a kiss on her knuckles. Smooth, very smooth. Sydney stepped off the dance floor and watched as Ryan and Sienna not so subtly tried to leave, only to be thwarted by the Rose sisters and their husbands.

"You look beautiful tonight. Would you care to dance?"

Sydney turned and smiled at a tuxedo-clad Nash. He looked so good in that tux that the sight had her contemplating what he might look like out of it. And when he pulled her near, she gasped.

"Don't worry, it's just my gun," Nash said with a little gravel to his voice.

"Merciful heavens," Zinnia gasped as she danced by.

Nash's lips quirked slightly. "Trust me, you'd know if it was *that* gun."

Sydney felt her face flush. She might die on the spot if he stripped naked. Definitely too dark, too mysterious, and well, was there really such a thing as too handsome? But that didn't mean she couldn't have a little fun.

"Lead on, my dark knight, and then shots all around!" Sydney laughed as her cousins cheered.

"Are they looking?" Ryan asked Sienna.

"No, Dylan just unbuttoned the top half of his shirt to show a tattoo over his heart. Trust me, no one is looking at us right now," Sienna said with excitement.

"Excellent!" Ryan scooped her into his arms and dashed out of the tent in her parents' backyard.

Sienna giggled with glee as he ran to the limousine. "I can walk, you know."

"Not tonight, wife."

Ryan slid into the backseat and kissed her senseless. It was then Sienna came to the conclusion that walking was overrated when you had a strong, handsome husband intent on carrying you to bed.

The End

New Release Notifications for Kathleen Brooks,
Sign Up Here:
www.kathleen-brooks.com/new-release-notifications
Subscribers will be the first to learn about the new Forever
Bluegrass series coming soon.

Please visit the retailer's product page if you have enjoyed
this story to leave a review. It helps me to know which
characters and story lines the readers enjoy so I can make
future books even better. Thank you!

Other Books by Kathleen Brooks

The return to Keeneston is almost complete! The Rose Sisters will be getting a book in August/September of 2015. And then the Bluegrass Legacy series will begin very soon after the Rose Sisters' book. If you haven't signed up for new release notification, then now is the time to do it. More detail on upcoming books will be included as the email goes out for new releases.

www.kathleen-brooks.com/new-release-notifications

If you are new to the writings of Kathleen Brooks, then you will want to try her Bluegrass Series set in the wonderful fictitious town of Keeneston, KY. Here is a list of links to the Bluegrass and Bluegrass Brothers books in order, as well as the separate New York Times Bestselling Women of Power series:

Bluegrass Series
Bluegrass State of Mind
Risky Shot
Dead Heat

Bluegrass Brothers Series
Bluegrass Undercover
Rising Storm
Secret Santa, A Bluegrass Novella
Acquiring Trouble
Relentless Pursuit
Secrets Collide
Final Vow

Bluegrass Singles
All Hung Up
Bluegrass Dawn
The Perfect Gift
The Keeneston Roses

Forever Bluegrass Series
Forever Entangled
Forever Hidden – coming January 2016
Forever Betrayed – coming mid-2016

Women of Power Series
Chosen for Power
Built for Power
Fashioned for Power
Destined for Power

About the Author

Kathleen Brooks is a New York Times, Wall Street Journal, and USA Today bestselling author. Kathleen's stories are romantic suspense featuring strong female heroines, humor, and happily-ever-afters. Her Bluegrass Series and follow-up Bluegrass Brothers Series feature small town charm with quirky characters that have captured the hearts of readers around the world.

Kathleen is an animal lover who supports rescue organizations and other non-profit organizations such as Friends and Vets Helping Pets whose goals are to protect and save our four-legged family members.

Email Notice of New Releases:
www.kathleen-brooks.com/new-release-notifications

Kathleen's Website:
www.kathleen-brooks.com

Facebook Page:
facebook.com/KathleenBrooksAuthor

Twitter:
twitter.com/BluegrassBrooks

Goodreads:
goodreads.com/author/show/5101707.Kathleen_Brooks

www.ingramcontent.com/pod-product-compliance
Lightning Source LLC
Chambersburg PA
CBHW021220250626
47155CB00008B/2884